The *Second* Verse

Janet Lee

ISBN-13: 978-1516990245
ISBN-10: 1516990242

This is a work of fiction. Names, characters, businesses, places, events and incidents are either the products of the author's imagination or used in a fictitious manner. Any resemblance to actual persons, living or dead, or actual events is purely coincidental.

Cover created by Red Ribbon Editing
Cover art by www.SplitShire.com

Available from Amazon.com, CreateSpace.com, and other retail outlets

To my daughters – May the path beneath your feet take you where you want to go.

Chapter 1
Miranda

Buzz. Buzz. Buzz.

Dear Lord, please make my phone stop ringing. I really, really need it to stop. Today is the one day I do not need any issues. In fact, today is the probably one of the most important days of my lackluster career. The small advertising agency I work for is about to pitch a campaign to our largest potential client to date. Countless hours I did not have were poured into every detail of today's presentation. Even though my supervisor, the owner's son, Jonathan, will be the one pitching my ideas as his own to our soon-to-be client, I'm still very excited to see it all come together.

Working as an administrative assistant at the very successful advertising agency of Miller & Sons is definitely not my dream job. Not by a long shot. Sitting behind a desk all day, tapping and clicking away, was never part of my plan. But at thirty –two, I can no longer cling to my childish dreams. All of that needs to be put aside and bills need to be paid. I'm just relieved to still have a decent paying job that offers benefits.

As if my prayer was heard, miraculously, my phone stops vibrating. *Thank God*, I think all too soon, because seconds later it begins again. I shift in my chair trying to look casual as I frantically try to press ignore on the cell phone wedged in my pocket. Damn these too tight slacks. Damn my too fat thighs squeezed in to these too small slacks. Damn not having enough time in the morning causing me to woof down a bagel with cream cheese contributing to my too fat thighs wedged into my too small slacks. Just as my index finger grazes the screen the phone stops vibrating, but a moment later starts again. The persistence of the caller means only one thing. Well, more like one of two things, but regardless this is the worst possible time.

My eyes touch each person seated around the table, searching for signs they notice the incisive buzzing. Luckily, it appears no one does. I breathe a sigh of relief, but it's caught in my throat when I feel Jonathan's sticky, hot breath on my neck.

"Is there a problem?" he whispers harshly, the spicy scent of his cinnamon gum stinging my nose and eyes.

"No," I answer, seemingly leaning forward to straighten a stack of papers, but really to put some space between us.

Both Jonathan and Gerald Miller, Jr., work in the office in some capacity. Gerald Miller, Sr., is the founder and president of the agency. Gerald Jr. is the older of the two and is the spitting image of his father, with matching light blue eyes and graying brown hair. Even their personalities are similar. Their easy going temperaments are soothing and calming. On several occasions I have seen them show genuine interest in the opinions and ideas offered from members of the team. Always quick to offer a compliment and acknowledge the achievements of others, they are part of the reason I've continued to work here for the last eight years.

Jonathan, on the other hand, makes my skin crawl. He's the younger of the two and is a complete asshole. I fight the urge to punch him in the throat on an almost daily basis. If there was ever a man who encompassed the adjective 'douche bag,' it's Jonathan. He was a year ahead of my brother, Sam, in high school and was a tool back then, too. Never having to work for anything and rarely hearing the word 'no' has inflated his ego to supernatural proportions. Well, rarely hearing 'no' until he met me. Now, he hears it almost daily.

For as long as I've worked here, Jonathan has flirted with the line of professionalism and sexual harassment. I put up with it for one reason: I need this job. Of course I need the salary, but also the health insurance it offers.

A heartbeat later the phone begins to ring again.

"Either take the call or shut it off, Miranda," Jonathan snarls.

Nodding my head, I avoid eye contact with the half dozen questioning eyes now focusing on our exchange. Quietly, I push my chair away from the table and tiptoe from the conference room with my chin tucked into my chest, my thick black hair shielding my face. I hate that I put up with that asshole. Lord knows, if I wasn't so stubborn, I would have listened to my brother's nagging and quit a long time ago. My brother constantly asks me to work for him as his office manager, but each time he asks I decline. It's not that I don't think I can do the job. I have no doubt I could do it with my eyes closed; I'm just not sure if working with family is a good idea.

Silently closing the door behind me, I glare at the offensive screen in my hand. Perfect, the elementary school has called five times. That's never a good sign. My stomach ties into knots as I rush back to my desk, listening to the voicemail left by the school nurse asking me to return her call immediately. Slumping into my chair I hit redial. After two rings a whiny voice answers.

"Good afternoon, Belham Elementary. This is Nurse Susan."

"Hi, Susan, it's Miranda Cross. I received your message," I say, trying to mask the concern in my voice.

"Ah yes, Mrs. Cross. I have Paige here in the office with me. She fell off the top of the slide during recess and cut her arm."

"Oh my god, is she all right?" I ask in a panic, grabbing my bag from the bottom drawer of my desk.

"Yes, she's fine. I've cleaned the cut, but I'm afraid it might need stitches. When I couldn't reach you I tried to reach the other emergency contact listed, Paige's uncle, Sam. He informed me he is currently out of town," she explains.

"Yes, he's in New Hampshire for the week," I explain rummaging to find my keys and punch a few buttons to power down my computer. "I'm leaving work now. I'll be there in twenty minutes," I say before ending the call.

I'm not the least bit surprised Paige has injured herself. She's not the most graceful child in the world. I love her to death, but she has more bumps and bruises than any child I've met.

Before I can step out of my cubicle, I see Jonathan coming down the hall. He prowls toward me like a lion stalking a gazelle.

"Miranda, beautiful, where do you think you are going?"

I roll my eyes. Not only do his words make my skin crawl, but I know he is exaggerating. My straight black hair has become flatter and flatter as the day has progressed. My black slacks are a tad too tight and are pinching into my sides, which is not only slightly uncomfortable, but is also causing a roll at the top of the waist band. A muffin top as my oldest daughter, Katelyn, would call it. I call it disgusting, but I swore I wouldn't buy new clothes in a larger size. Not only is that promise meant to motivate me to lose some weight, but I also don't have the spare money. I try to hide my excess by slightly tucking in my royal blue button up blouse. I love this shirt. I love how the shade of blue enhances my eyes.

Feeling Jonathan's eyes rake over my body causes bile to burn my throat. I force it down, slinging my oversized bag over my shoulder before turning to meet his gaze.

"Jonathan, I'm sorry, but Paige had an accident at school and I have to take her to the hospital," I explain.

"You can't leave," he says, matter of fact. "Find someone else to take her." He rolls his shoulders back and crosses his arms in front of his chest.

"What?" I ask in total disbelief.

"You heard me. We're just about to begin the presentation and you can't leave," he insists, narrowing is eyes, challenging me to say something. He lowers himself to sit on the corner of my desk, extending his long legs out in front of him, blocking my only route of escape with a smug look on his face.

Jonathan looks nothing like Gerald Sr. or Jr. His blonde hair has been lightened by hours in the sun, which has darkened his skin. Shallow brown eyes are highlighted by well manscaped eyebrows.

Sneaking a glance at my watch, I calculate I have to be out of the building within the next five minutes if I'm to have any chance of not hitting traffic on my way across town.

Sighing heavily, I square my shoulders. "Jonathan, I have somewhere I need to be," I say forcefully.

A vile smile curls the corner of his mouth. Leaning closer he says, "The only place you need to be is beneath me, sweetheart."

His breathe reeks of cinnamon and his words drip with sex, but they don't turn me on. Instead they make me want to vomit.

I cock my head to one side, trying to think of a way out of this situation. I don't want to cause a scene, and I definitely don't want to cross a line which I can't cross back over. I need this job desperately, but I'll be damned if I let him know it.

Out of the corner of my eye, I see an office door at the end of the hall cracked open just an inch. My mouth pulls up on one side. This time I lean forward, closing the space between us just a few inches. Misinterpreting my intentions, Jonathan slowly licks his lips and moves to close the remaining space. I twist my fingers in the soft fabric of his expensive designer suit. It feels sinful and screams money. I'm sure it costs more than my monthly car payment. My arm stiffens, holding him in place, keeping a couple inches between our faces.

"Jonathan," I purr.

"Yes sweetheart?" he moans. His eyes are fixed on my mouth. Sucking in my bottom lip, I let my teeth scrape across it as I slowly release it. A dark cloud shadows his eyes and his pupils dilate.

"Jonathan," I whisper, batting my eyelashes. "If you don't get out of my way, I swear to God I will scream so loud the people in the lobby five floors below will hear me, never mind your father who's a mere twenty feet away in his office. Now move," I say through clenched teeth, shoving him back.

His eyes widen with surprise before his mask of confidence slips back into place. An evil chuckle vibrates from his chest as he slowly stands, creating only a few inches of space for me to pass by. Sweeping one arm to the side, he silently dares me to move.

I draw in a deep breath and attempt to squeeze past him, but there isn't enough space for all of me and my breasts rub against his chest as I pass. A low growl escapes his throat. My hand twitches with the desire to punch him in the face, but I fight the urge. He may be a complete asshole, but it would be frowned upon to punch the boss in the face, sexual harassment and all.

As I walk away, I feel his eyes on my ass until I round the corner near the elevators. Pressing the call button, I lean my back against the brick wall and release a heavy breath.

"What an asshole," I mutter. Checking the time once again, I cringe. Shit, there is no way I am going to miss mid-day traffic now.

After hitting the call button repeatedly, I tap my foot and anxiously wait for the car to arrive. "C'mon. C'mon. C'mon," I chant aloud before hearing someone call my name from behind.

"Miranda, oh, Miranda," Jonathan sings, stalking toward me.

I straighten again and stare at him, mouth wide, in shock. This asshole doesn't give up. The elevator finally arrives, its doors sliding open with a ding. I look back toward the empty car and then to Jonathan. Deep in my gut I know this is one of those moments. The kind of moment when you know there is really only one choice to make, but you know once you make it, there's no going back. Beyond a shadow of a doubt, you know that moment will change everything. I know all about no-going-back moments.

I've been working here, in the same position, for so long that the years have begun to blend together. I have spent countless hours pouring myself into my work. School performances missed. Sporting events overlooked. Instant breakfasts and pre-made dinners, served haphazardly on paper plates and plastic utensils, day after day. Days of tiptoeing around mounds of laundry that never seem to get folded and piles of dishes that never seem to be washed, despite my best efforts.

Just then, my phone vibrates in my hand once more. It's a text from Sam. He's worried and asks if I need him to end his trip early to take care of Paige.

Anger and guilt assault me. What is wrong with me? My brother is willing to put his life on hold to help me and my girls, yet here I am debating whether or not I should leave work to pick up my injured daughter from school and take her to the hospital. Have I lost my damn mind?

I turn my back on Jonathan and step into the elevator. Pressing the button for the ground floor, the doors begin to slide shut. Jonathan's hand flies up and grips the door, forcing it open.

"If you leave you are fired," he threatens, his jaw clenched tight.

My internal debate is over. A decision has been made and it's one I should've made a long time ago. I feel a mixture of adrenaline and rage in my chest, every cell in my body humming with energy. A buzzer somewhere in the elevator car begins to ring, caused by the doors being held open for too long.

My lips curl in to a sinister smile. "I have waited eight very long years to tell you this. Go fuck yourself. I quit."

A look of complete shock crosses his face. Jonathan takes a step back, as if my words have struck him. His mouth slacks open and his eyes go wide. The doors begin to slide shut once more, and this time he doesn't try to stop them. Through the remaining few inches of empty space I flip him off and finally release a deep breath. It's not until the elevator opens to the lobby does the haze lift and the reality of what I've done slam into my chest. I slump against the back wall.

"Shit, now what am I going to do?"

THE SECOND VERSE

Chapter 2
Miranda

Several hours later, I sit at the kitchen table sipping a cup of hazelnut coffee, enjoying a very rare moment of peace and quiet. Paige needed five stitches. Of course she loved going to the hospital. As for me, it made me sick to my stomach. She loved watching them sew up her cut. Her tan eyes sparkled with intrigue. The sight of the needle made me nauseous. She wanted to chat to every nurse who walked by. Even at seven years old, her bubbly personality and bright smile drew in complete strangers. I only answered when necessary and then counted the seconds until we could leave.

By the time we got home with her favorite pizza in hand, it was almost six o'clock. Katelyn was sitting in her favorite spot near the back window playing her guitar, completely oblivious that we were there. Judging by the dazed look on her face, I suspect she had been sitting there for hours. While Paige is my little sports all-star, bruises and all, Katelyn is my rock star. Since she was a toddler she has been strumming that same guitar, a guitar that was a gift and is now one of her most prized possessions. It's amazing how different two siblings can be.

The three of us ate together while they took turns telling me about their day. I've always been big on family dinners and sharing what happens in our lives apart from each other. Even when they were very young I would ask them mundane questions, questions I already knew the answers to, just to engage with them. Now the conversation flows freely, and I love every second of it.

Tonight, when it was my turn to share the details of my day, I skipped the part about quitting my job. Of course they knew about the presentation; I had

7

been slaving over the details for the last several weeks. So when Katelyn asked how it went, I simply told her I left before the meeting to be with Paige. I wasn't exactly lying, but I didn't go into further detail. Neither of them should worry about my current unemployment. With any luck I'll find something else before they find out.

Now, with both of them upstairs in their rooms, Paige asleep and Katelyn finishing her homework, I finally let my emotions wash over me. The panic and fear of hearing the nurse explain Paige's injury. The rage and anger I felt toward Jonathan. The overwhelming anxiety I feel and the need to take care of my family, coupled with the irrational guilt that I am failing.

All the emotions and lack of sleep finally catch up to me. My limbs feel weak and my head heavy. Large pools of tears build behind my lids and finally spill over. I let them fall freely for a minute or two before sucking in a deep, shaky breath. Swiping the moisture from my cheeks, I swallow the remaining trepidation.

After placing my mug in the sink, I lock up and turn off the lights before heading upstairs. With each step my exhaustion grows, as does the dull throbbing behind my eyes and a sharp pain between my shoulders. Curling up in bed has never sounded so good, but when I pass Katelyn's room and hear her humming and lightly strumming her guitar, my fatigue is forgotten. I stop and lightly knock on her door, but she doesn't answer. I knock once again before gently pushing it open.

"Katelyn," I call out, seeing her sitting on her bed.

Her head snaps up from her lap and she nervously bites on her lip. "Hey, Mom," she answers her voice laced with embarrassment.

"Sweetheart, I thought you were reading," I say before sitting on the corner of her bed.

"I was, but I had this tune stuck in my head. It just kept playing over and over again, and I couldn't concentrate on what I was reading. I must've read the same paragraph six times," she says tucking her hair behind her ear. "I thought if I could just get the song out of my head and down on paper it would stop singing to me. The problem is, once I start writing, I can't stop. Seconds, minutes, hours go by, and I don't even notice. I'm lost in a sea of lyrics and melodies," she rambles, her cheeks blushing when she finishes.

I can't help but smile. Once upon I time, I was her. I know exactly how she feels. Looking into her royal blue eyes paired with her long black hair is like looking into the mirror at my own fourteen -year -old reflection. The resemblance is startling at times.

"Mom," she begins her voice quiet and shaking slightly, "there's a talent show at school two weeks from Thursday." She pauses and I wait for her to find the words to continue. "I entered."

"Oh Katelyn, that's great," I say pulling her into a hug.

"You think so?" she asks nervously against my chest.

"Absolutely," I assure her, placing my hands on her shoulders and pushing her back to look at her. Peering into her eyes, a mirror image of my own, I see how nervous and unsure she is. "You're talented Katelyn. Don't ever doubt that."

"Will you come to the show?"

"Do you even need to ask? Of course I will. I wouldn't miss it for anything," I promise her. "But it's time to take a break for the night. Let what you have so far rest. This way you can look at it with fresh eyes in the morning." I pull the guitar from her lap.

"Mom," Katelyn says.

"Hmm," I answer, resting the instrument against the wall by the door.

"Do you think one day I'll be as good as you?" She nonchalantly pulls her hair into a ponytail.

Her question stops me dead in my tracks. My throat swells with emotion, making it hard to speak. "What?"

"Oh c'mon Mom, we both know you're amazing. You missed your calling. You should've been a singer. Traveling from place to place, performing every night on stage, not sitting at that stupid office all day," Katelyn says climbing into bed and resting back against the headboard.

This child is wise beyond her years. I swear she is a forty -year -old trapped in a teenager's body.

"I didn't miss my calling, sweetheart. I heard it loud and clear, but sometimes when we take the path we're called to follow we wind up in the most unexpected places," I say crossing the room and placing a kiss on her forehead. "Sometimes those places are better than our wildest dreams."

A childish smile spreads across her face. Her cheeks tinge pink.

"I love you, Mom."

"To the moon and back, my love," I say before quietly slipping through the door.

After changing into a pair of shorts and an oversized t-shirt, I slip between the sheets of my side of the bed and snuggle under the comforter. I'm beyond tired, but my mind won't rest. Needing something to drown out my thoughts, I scroll through my phone until I find the playlist I'm looking for.

9

Soon, the sticky, sweet lyrics of "Amazed" by Lonestar, fills the room. Staring up at the swirling design of the plaster, I follow the pattern with my eyes, telling myself that everything will be all right until sleep finally claims me.

Chapter 3
Jace
Then

How much stuff can a seventy -year -old woman own? This is a question I've been asking myself for the last four days, since arriving in No-Where, Massachusetts from sunny South Carolina with my mother to help clear out my grandmother's house. From floor to ceiling, wall to wall, there's nothing but junk and that's putting it kindly. Don't get me wrong; I loved my grandmother. Well, as much as you can love a woman who lived nine hundred miles away my entire life, but this is ridiculous.

My mother often told me the only way the two of them could have a relationship with one another was if they didn't see each other too often. A Sunday morning phone call was enough to keep their relationship going for over eighteen years. That's why, when my mother sat at the kitchen table two Sundays ago trying to reach my beloved grandmother for more than two hours with no luck, we knew something was wrong. Sure enough, when the police arrived to check on her, they found my grandmother dead in her bed. The coroner assured us her death was peaceful and from natural causes.

Since my mother and I were her only living relatives, we didn't have a service. Instead, we quietly spread her ashes in the few places she mentioned years ago and that was all. Now we are left with trying to clear out her two story, Cape -style house, so it can be placed on the market. For a half second, my mother debated on whether or not she should keep the place, but her life is down south and as for me, well, soon my life will no longer be my own.

"Jace," my mother calls up the stairs.

"Yeah," I call back, tossing a bunch of old newspapers into a large, black, heavy duty trash bag. Dragging it across the hardwood floor out into the hall, I look over the banister down to my mother. My mother and I share the same brown eyes, but that's where the similarities end. I can thank a man I've never met for the rest of my good looks.

"I have to run into town to meet the realtor. Do you think you'll have that room finished soon? Susan is going to want to take pictures to put in the ad and Lord knows no one will buy this place if they take a look around with the way it is now," she says, brushing a few strands of short blonde hair from her eyes.

"I think so. I already have one of the bedrooms empty. I'm working on the other now," I say.

"Great. I won't be too long," she promises. "I'll grab a pizza while I'm out. Okay?"

"Sure." I shrug.

"Oh, and don't forget to take Boomer out. He needs to burn off some energy," she calls back, as I watch her disappear around the corner.

Wiping the sweat from my eyes with the back of my hand, I look down at my nine year old Jack Russell terrier. He looks up at me expectantly. His head tilts to the side causing his tongue to fall out of his mouth.

"C'mon, boy. Let's fill one more bag and then I'll take you out." Hearing the work 'out' makes him jump a few feet off the floor.

Shaking my head, I climb back into the room and begin breaking apart empty cardboard boxes. This old house doesn't have air conditioning and, though it's not as humid as it is in South Carolina, the air is still stifling. Needing some relief, I pull off my sweat drenched tee-shirt and toss it into the corner. Maneuvering through the maze of empty boxes, stacks of newspaper, and old magazines, I make my way toward the only window in the room. Down below I see my mother's gray Ford Explorer backing down the short driveway, but I don't watch her pull out on to the street. Something - no someone - catches and holds my attention instead.

A girl around my age sits bent over a guitar on the front porch of the house next door. From this angle I can't see her face; her dark as the midnight sky, pin straight hair falls below her shoulders and shields her face. Despite the fact her thin frame is concealed by a large tee-shirt, I can still make out the curve of her waist and the small swell of her breasts. Even at this distance, and even though I can only see pieces of her, I can tell she is beautiful.

I watch like a creep as she casually strums the guitar in her lap. Curious, I gently pry the window open and squat down, resting my forearms on the sill and my chin upon my arms. A light breeze hits my face and carries the music she is playing. Instantly, I recognize the song. It's one of my favorites right now – "Bent" by Matchbox Twenty. I listened to the CD a dozen times during the thirteen hour ride north, but never has it sounded like this. Her voice weaves in and out of the chorus, harmonizing with the chords she effortlessly creates with the strings.

I know the song's lyrics by heart, but hearing them fall from her lips it's as if I am hearing them for the first time. I never put too much thought into the meaning behind these words, but even from a hundred yards away the emotion in her voice makes me listen more closely. Hidden beneath the catchy beat is a sad and angry song.

When the last few notes linger in the air she wipes what I assume are tears from her face. Tucking her chin to her chest she continues to play a sad melody, but this time it's a song I don't recognize. She tests out a few chords before starting again. I know I should get back to cleaning this room; we will only be here are few more days and there is so much more to do, but I can't look away.

Lost in the sound of her voice, the world and everything in it fades, including Boomer, who apparently isn't happy about being forgotten. He chooses this moment to dig into the bottom of a pile of newspaper. I hear rustling only seconds before the entire stack comes tumbling down with a loud bang. With wide eyes I stare, frozen in place.

The girl's shoulders tense and, before I have time to react, her head snaps up and her eyes meet mine. I know it's going to sound corny, and dammit if my friends back home hear this they'll beat the shit out of me, but I swear the Earth stopped spinning. Everything fades to blue. The clearest, most vibrant shade of blue I've ever seen.

Shaking my head a few times, I try to coax my blood to return north to my brain before quickly ducking out of sight. Damn I am such an idiot. I wait a few seconds before slowly rising to peer over the window sill in time to see a sad smile curve the corner of her perfect lips. I watch her push herself up from the wooden porch and wonder for a split second if she is going to come over, but the thought vanishes as she opens the screen porch and slips inside.

Staring at the empty spot where she just sat, I find myself thinking the most unusual thoughts. I wonder what her favorite color is or if she has a favorite movie. I wonder how long she has been playing the guitar and who taught her. Most of all, I wonder what it would feel like to hold her hand in mine or to hear her laugh. Where did that come from? Now is not the time to wonder any of these things. Soon I will be leaving and the last thing I need to worry about is a girl, even if she is the most beautiful girl I have ever seen.

Readjusting the raging boner I'm sporting, I glare at my trouble making best friend.

"Smooth," I say talking to both my dog and myself.

Looking around the cluttered room, I decide I have had enough cleaning for one day. Patting my thigh for Boomer to follow I call out, "C'mon, troublemaker. Let's go outside."

Later that night, hours after my mother returned from meeting with the realtor and I ate an entire large pizza by myself, I sit on the lumpy couch in the dusty living room staring at the peeling wallpaper.

"I can't keep my eyes open a minute longer," my mother announces with a yawn. "Between rummaging through all this clutter and dealing with that dreaded woman all afternoon, I'm beat."

She takes the cardboard box into the kitchen and returns, leaning against the door jamb. "I'm going to bed."

"Yeah, I probably should too," I say, not because I want to, but because there's nothing else to do around here. My grandmother didn't have cable and there's no way in hell I'm going to read a book.

The sound of heavy bass and laughter leaks through the single pane windows and rattles the picture frames still hanging on the walls. The music began shortly after cars started arriving next door a few hours ago. I peek out the window and see cars now lining both sides of the street. I'm surprised the other neighbors haven't complained, but my bet is this is a common occurrence.

"It sounds like they're having a party next door," my mother says, moving the blinds to the side to peer out. "You should go check it out."

"Yeah sure, I'll just stop in and say 'hi'," I scoff, rolling my eyes and expecting her to laugh. When I look up however, I find her staring at me with one brow raised. "You can't be serious? I don't even know those people. I can't just show up."

"Of course you can. Haven't you ever crashed a party before?" she asks causally, but a glimmer of humor in her eyes.

I stare at her like she has seven heads. What mother encourages her son to crash a party? I ask just that, causing her to laugh.

"Seriously Jace, you are eighteen years old, not eighty. Geesh, the things I was doing at eighteen ..." she muses.

"Ew, enough," I groan, covering my ears with my hands.

"Did I ever tell you about the time you grandmother found me and a group of friends skinny dipping out back? God, I thought she was going to have a heart attack," she reminisces.

"*Mom*, stop, that's gross. This whole conversation is wrong on so many levels," I beg, which causes her to laugh more.

"I'm serious, honey. Go over there. I bet they don't even question who you are." She pushes herself away from the wall and comes closer. Leaning down, she kisses me softly on the forehead. "Go. You only get to be a teenager for a little while longer. Have some fun," her voice cracks gently.

I turn and look out the window toward the house next door again. I know for certain if I go there I'll run into the girl from earlier today, but I wonder if that's a bad thing.

"Don't be out all night," my mother calls from the end of the narrow hall before shutting the door to the first floor bedroom where she has been sleeping.

Since she already assumes I'm going over I guess I might as well, right? I mean, what's the worst that could happen? If I bump into that girl and she asks me to leave then I will. No harm done. But, if I run into her and I can get a chance to talk to her for a few minutes, then it was all worth it.

I only agonize over my decision for a few short seconds before I find myself standing in the center of the neighboring backyard. A stone patio the length of the house meets the short, well maintained lawn which leads all the way down to the edge of a small lake. In the center of the backyard is a large, roaring fire. Several lawn chairs are set up around the blaze, some filled with people laughing and talking, the rest empty. There's a small crowd nestled around a table on the patio where a game of beer pong is set up. Drunken slurs mixed with rowdy cheers ring above the music playing in the background.

My eyes scan the party. Searching for what I'm not sure. Shit, who am I kidding? I know exactly what I'm looking for, or rather who, but I don't see her. Instead of standing there, looking like a complete idiot, I decide to grab a drink. I've only been drunk once, when I was fourteen, and that was more than enough. Since then, I've learned that holding a red Solo cup filled with Coke and claiming it's spiked with rum is better than listening to the constant badgering to drink with everyone else. Plus, the ability to blend in helps relax me.

After filling my cup I begin to mingle. Just as my mother predicted, no one questions who I am or what I am doing here. Most assume I am a friend of a friend, someone who was brought to the party and hasn't just wandered over from next door. A few girls throw their arms around my shoulders and rub their tits on my arm, but their glazed eyes and garbled words don't do it for me. Call me crazy, but I would like a girl to remember having sex with me the next morning, not black the whole thing out.

"C'mon. I can be *shhh* quiet," the latest stage five clinger says, her thin finger pressed against her lips.

"Not interested," I say, trying to pry her hand from my bicep.

"But, why?" she begins to whine, but then suddenly breaks into a squeal. Bouncing on the balls of her feet, she claps her hands, like a child who just spotted their favorite candy.

"Yay, I was wondering when she was going to sing," she cheers, turning and stumbling toward the fire. After two steps she sways to the left, and I catch her before she completely loses her balance.

"Who?" I ask, righting her on her feet.

"You know she's going to be famous one day," Drunk Girl says.

"Who?" I ask a second time.

"Then I can say I saw her perform before she made it big," she continues.

"Who?" I ask once more, beginning to feel like a damn owl.

"Miranda," Drunk Girl says rolling her eyes, pointing an unsteady hand toward the fire.

I follow her finger and suddenly feel like I've been punched in the gut. There she is, the girl from this morning. Her raven hair is now pulled up in that high messy bun -thing girls wear, giving me a clear view of her face. Her skin looks so smooth and soft. My fingers itch to touch it. The warmth of the flames kisses her cheeks, leaving them flush and pink. Her lips pull into a tight line as she nods to the girl sitting beside her and messes with the stings of her guitar.

Once she seems satisfied everything is ready, she plays a couple chords. Silence blankets the small crowd and is replaced with the melancholy sound of "Best I Ever Had" by Vertical Horizon. I've only heard this song once before and on the radio it sounded nothing like this. A voice like I've never heard comes pouring out of her with the opening lyrics. Her eyes drift closed, blocking out the rest of the world as she seemingly loses herself in the music. She begins to sway side to side, her voice flirts with the melody. The two mingle effortlessly through verse and chorus, until finally the guitar fades and only the crackling of the fire joins her for the falsetto.

One thing is for sure. Drunk Girl was right. With a voice like that, this girl is going to be famous one day.

Just as soon as it began, the song comes to an end and silence surrounds us once more. It only lasts a heartbeat before dissolving into applause and whistling. Drunk Girl rushes forward and slings her arm around the girl's – Miranda's – shoulders, pulling her into an awkward side hug. Several feet away, on the other side of the fire, I notice a guy with sandy brown hair eyeing Miranda like she just tore his heart out and stomped on it. I can't help but wonder who he is. I think I hear him call her name, but if she hears him she doesn't look in his direction. Instead, she wiggles out of Drunk Girl's hold, turns on her heels, and stalks down to the water's edge. The guy moves to follow her, but is stopped by a group of people who block his path.

I turn my attention back to Miranda, who's now only a small figure seated at the end of the wooden dock that juts out from the shore. From this distance she seems so small and fragile, the confidence and power I just witnessed during her performance evaporating into the darkness of the night.

I don't know anything about this girl. I don't know who that guy is to her. I don't know what's going on between them. Hell, I don't even know if I'll see her again after tonight. But the one thing I do know is if I only get tonight, I'm going to make the most of it. Tossing my cup into a nearby trash bag, I tuck my hands in my pockets and make my way down to the lake.

Chapter 4
Miranda
Then

A light breeze causes goose bumps on my skin and strands of my hair to fall free from its tie and dance into my eyes. Tucking the wayward locks behind my ear, I step from the rocky shore on to the boat dock that extends out into the lake I grew up on. Adam, Sam, and I used to jump off this dock for hours when we were kids. From late morning until early evening we would spend our days in this lake; swimming, fishing, boating, you name it, we did it.

I lower myself to sit on the splintered wood and dangle my bare feet over the edge, just inches above the smooth surface of the water. I pull the hood of my favorite UMass sweatshirt over my head and shove my hands in the front pocket attempting to ward off the shiver running up and down my spine.

Music and laughter make up the soundtrack to the party Adam and Sam decided to throw to celebrate the beginning of summer. I knew I should've stayed inside the house. I hadn't planned on singing tonight. I knew most people expected me to and I suspect some of them came only for that reason. I know it sounds so self-centered, but it's true. Some people are good at sports. Others are good at drawing or painting. I just happen to be pretty good at playing music. I never put much thought into it. It has always been my way of escaping.

I thought I'd come out say hello to everyone and then disappear inside. Most of the people scattered around the back yard are Adam and Sam's friends, some from high school and others from college. No one was here to see me except Adam, but I didn't even know he had returned after leaving so abruptly earlier this afternoon. Deciding I should make an appearance, I pulled a comfortable hooded sweatshirt over my head and made my way outside, only to be stopped dead in my tracks.

It only took me a second to spot Adam across the yard. My eyes always seem to find him in a crowd. But seeing him tonight wasn't what made me pause; it was who was pressed up against his side, hanging on to his every word as hard as she was hanging on to his bicep – Bethany Miller.

Bethany was the captain of the cheer squad and graduated the same year as Adam and Sam. She's the reason cheerleaders are stereotyped the way they are. She is bubbly, blonde, and dumb as a stump. I always thought it was part of the act. You know, playing a role. But the curtain closed on her high school cheering days several years ago and she is still as annoying as ever.

Seeing the two of them together fueled something inside of me. After my conversation with Adam today, it only took a second for the sight to ignite an inferno. Pushing the sliding glass door open, I stomped my way back into the house, yanked my favorite guitar from its stand, and marched out to the fire. I knew it would only take a moment for people to notice. Normally I would get a small knot of anxiety in my stomach before performing, but tonight if I did, I didn't notice.

I strummed the first few chords, sliding my fingers across the strings. The emotion I felt brewing inside came pouring out with every word. I could feel Adam's eyes on me, but I could also feel a weird flip in my stomach. The two mixed together was confusing and in that moment I tried to push them aside.

When I was finished, a hush settled across the yard before being broken by applause. I lifted my eyes and found Adam staring at me through the flames. I think I heard him call my name, but I didn't wait to see for sure. I needed to get away. If he was finally ready to talk, this was not the place to do it. We needed privacy for this conversation. I set my guitar against the side of the Adirondack chair, evaded everyone who crowded around, and quickly walked toward the water, not even looking back to see if he had followed me.

These last few weeks have been brutal. Knowing Adam would be coming home from college for the summer should make me happy. It's always hard when he comes and goes throughout the school year. We have been together for, well, forever, really. Adam and I grew up together. He was my brother's best friend before he was ever my boyfriend. Thinking back, I can't even tell you when or how it happened. It was like one day I was following him and Sam around, annoying the hell out of them, and the next we walked down the sidewalk holding hands.

Adam is three years older than me, and he was a senior in high school when I was a freshman. The age difference never seemed like an issue until it was time for him to go away to college. Living in a small town in western Massachusetts, the drive to UMass - Amherst is not too long, but with a soccer scholarship and the need to be at the field or in the gym all the time during the season, he opted to live on campus. The days and weeks he was away were difficult. Like any teenage girl, I had my doubts in both myself and him. I often lied awake at night, wondering what he was doing or who he was with. Adam called me as much as he could and drove home on Sundays after home games. Somehow we always made it work. After the season ended he would come home more often and we always fell back into an easy rhythm.

That was until a few weeks ago. Adam's junior year ended in May. His finals were grueling this semester, so we hadn't had much of an opportunity to talk. It's my fault really. Well, it's my fault we hadn't talked, but it isn't my fault why we needed to talk. I was so stupid for putting it off – so, so, stupid. When he finally came home there was so much excitement around me graduating high school and getting ready to head off to college in the fall, the moment never seemed right. But when he came over this afternoon, I knew I had to tell him. It couldn't wait any longer. *I* couldn't wait any longer.

I'm not sure how I thought he would take the news. I guess I had envisioned it going one of two ways. He would either be very happy, sweeping me off my feet, or he would be angry and maybe even a little sad. But in every scenario I had played out in my head, I never thought he would be as mean and spiteful as he was. The way he reacted was nothing I could have ever imagined and not something I ever want to see again. It was like for the first time in seventeen years, I was seeing someone completely different. He yelled. He screamed. He said a lot of mean words. All things I can overlook. All things I can forgive. But when he turned and walked out the door after telling me I'd ruined his life, I was crushed. I've never felt more sad or lonely in my entire life.

After I watched him peel out of the driveway, I did the only thing I knew would bring me back to center. I grabbed my guitar, collapsed to the floor, and sang. I poured my sobbing heart into that song until I was left feeling dizzy and drained. Lyrics of being bent and broken, begging for the other person to pick you up and not turn their back swirled around me until the last note broke from my chest.

Drawing in ragged breaths, I tried to pull myself together. When my world shifted back to into focus and I opened my eyes, I knew I was being watched. I could feel someone staring at me and the feeling was coming from old Mrs. Harper's house. Mrs. Harper passed away a few weeks ago, and I

THE SECOND VERSE

knew someone had been there the last few days trying to clear the place out, but I had yet to see who it was. Looking at the house, I was able to pinpoint where the person was watching from- a second floor window. I couldn't make out anything about them, but whoever it was, the weight of their stare made my stomach clench and roll – and not in a bad way.

This evening by the fire I felt the same flip in my stomach.

A bright full moon fills the sky, blocking out the twinkle of most of the stars. The only sound I can hear is the hum of music in the background and the racing of my own mind, until the thump of heavy footsteps approach and stop just inches behind me.

Not bothering to turn around I simply say, "Hi."

"Hi," he says after a short pause, only 'he' isn't who I thought he would be. This 'he' has a deep rich voice with a slight southern twang. My head snaps around, making me slightly dizzy, and my eyes widen with surprise. Standing only a few feet away is one of the most handsome boys I've ever seen. I scan him from top to bottom taking in his details. His short, buzz cut hair is barely visible in the darkness but offers a hint of its natural dark brown color. A strong jaw frames full lips set beneath warm, milk chocolate eyes. His shoulders are broad and his waist narrow, but his frame is not overly large. He is built like a wide receiver, strong but lean.

With his hands tucked into the pockets of perfectly fitted jeans and an easy, crooked smile brightening his face, he nods his head toward the empty space beside me.

"Mind if I join you?" he asks smoothly.

I blink a few times, letting his words jingle inside my head before moving over a few inches, making room for him to sit.

"Sure."

He lowers himself and sits beside me. The space I created for him is not nearly enough and I can feel his heat through my jeans. Both of us stare straight ahead into the shimmering moonlight on the calm, clear surface of the lake. Internally, I scream at myself to say something, anything, but nothing comes to mind for several minutes and the silence stretches between us. I sneak a peek at him out of the corner of my eye. If he's fighting the same inner battle, it doesn't show on his face. He seems as cool as a cucumber.

"I'm Jace, by the way," he finally says after an eternity, cutting through the night.

"Miranda," I squeak. Clearing my throat I try to speak again. "Are you a friend of Sam and Adam's?"

21

A sheepish smile curls his lips. "Neither. I actually wandered over from next door," he says, a hint of embarrassment flash in his eyes. "I'm actually up here for a few days with my mother clearing out my grandmother's house." He points over his shoulder. "I heard the music and came over."

"Mrs. Harper's house? She is ... was your grandmother?" He nods solemnly. "I'm sorry," I say softly.

"No worries. We didn't get to see each other all that much. My mother could never afford too many trips up here and after a while it was too difficult to Gram to come down to see us."

"She was a great woman. She used to watch my brother and me when we were younger and my dad had to work. She made the most amazing chocolate chip cookies. Every Christmas she would visit with a giant tin of them." I stare across the lake. "I'm going to miss her," I add sadly.

Jace doesn't respond. Instead, his eyes return to the water. The silence creeps back in, but I refuse to let it swallow us. Now that we have broken the ice, I want to keep going.

"Down where?" I ask.

"Huh?"

"Before. You said your grandmother used to come down to visit you. Down where?" I ask using air quotes around the word down.

"Oh," he chuckles, deep and rich. "South Carolina. My mother and I live in a small town on the coast."

"Wow. That sounds amazing. I'd love to wake up every day and see the ocean outside my doorstep and only be a few feet from the soft sand." I know I shouldn't complain. It's only a two hour ride from here to the ocean. I know some people go their whole lives never seeing it in person, but it would be amazing to see it every day.

"I guess. I never really thought about it all that much. It's simply home." He shrugs.

I can't help but smile at the sound of his voice when he says the word 'home', like it's one of the most precious things in the world.

"So are you going to school?" I ask vaguely. He looks to be close to my own age, but looks can be deceiving.

"I just graduated a few weeks ago."

"Me too. Which college will you be going to in the fall?" My question causes him to laugh loudly. His smile is infectious and soon I find I am grinning as well.

"Ah no, college and I would never get along. Hell, I was lucky enough to graduate on time." He rubs a hand over the back of his head. "Nah, I enlisted in the Army. I leave for basic training in a couple of weeks."

I can't explain why, but hearing that causes my muscles to tense and a wave of unease to swirl in my stomach. I've only just met Jace, but the thought of him being in danger sets off something inside of me. I blink my eyes, feeling the prickle of forming tears.

Sensing the shift in my body, Jace turns slightly. His warm eyes search my face, narrowing before widening when he finds the answer to a silent question.

"Don't worry about me, Blue. My recruiter told me that unless World War III breaks out, I'll probably never see any real combat. I'll most likely be stationed at a domestic base, or there's a small possibility I could go overseas, but I won't be in any real danger."

A breath I didn't realize I was holding rushes from my lungs. My tension easing just a bit. I'm only slightly relieved hearing this, but worry still hides beneath the surface. I just can't wrap my brain around the idea of an eighteen - year -old making such a serious decision that will affect the rest of his life. Well, on second thought, I guess I don't really need to imagine it.

I sit here for a few moments losing myself in his beautiful warm brown eyes. Being this close, and under the light of the moon, I notice there are the tiniest flecks of hazel swimming in those pools of brown. A mischievous glimmer and a sly crooked smile tell me he knows he's affecting me.

This entire situation is wrong. I just met him. We've only been talking for a few minutes. I know nothing about him, but in the oddest way I feel comfortable sitting next to him. Glancing down, I notice that the sliver of space that separated us has almost vanished. We now sit shoulder to shoulder, thigh to thigh. Deep in the back of my mind a part of me is screaming to get up and walk away, but I don't listen.

"Did you just call me Blue?" I finally ask.

The corner of his mouth curls just a fraction. "I did."

"Why?"

Jace lifts his right hand and slowly drags his knuckle from my temple down along my cheek to my chin. Goose bumps rise across my skin. Holding my chin between his index finger and thumb, he gently raises my head so we are eye to eye.

"Because you have the most beautiful blue eyes I've ever seen," he says quietly. The space between us closes, until his lips are a breath away from mine. "So beautiful," he whispers.

23

Just as his lips brush against mine I blurt, "Ihaveaboyfriend."

Jace stops and pulls back an inch. His brown eyes meet my blue. With the small space between us, I repeat with a heavy breath, "I have a boyfriend." My eyes drift shut, not wanting to see the look on his face. Whether it's one of hurt, sadness, or anger, I can't bear to see.

The warmth of his breath leaves my lips and his hand falls from my face. Even tucked in my sweatshirt, a cold shiver runs up my spine. After a few long tense seconds, I finally peel my eyes open.

Jace begins to push himself up from the dock. "I'm sorry. I didn't know. If I had I wouldn't have ... Shit, who am I kidding. I probably still would have," he rambles, rubbing his hand over his short hair. "Anyways, I'm sorry."

Stuffing his hands back into his pockets, he turns on his heel and begins to walk away. He makes it a single step before my hand involuntarily snaps up and grabs his wrist. I have no idea why I am stopping him. I should just let him walk away. God knows I have enough problems without complicating it with one reckless night, but knowing he is leaving soon and that our lives will never collide again makes me reluctant to say goodbye. *It's only one night*, I tell myself.

"Wait. Please, don't go," I beg. "I'm sorry, too. I should have, I don't know, mentioned him somehow. Stay. Please."

Jace stays frozen, his stare fixed on my hand on his arm.

"Why?" he asks, lifting his eyes to mine.

I shrug. "I'm not ready to go back up there, but I don't want to be alone either. Plus, it was warmer with you sitting beside me." I raise a brow. "Sit with me a little longer. Please."

Slowly he nods and returns to sit beside me again, this time not leaving a fraction of space between us. To be any closer would be to sit on his lap, with his arms around me. A giddy thrill runs through my veins at the thought, but I stamp it back. I can't let my mind go there. It's not fair to him, and it will only make it worse on me when this night is over. I afford myself only the small contact of the sides of our thighs and the weight of his hand. I'm not sure how it happened, but my fingers went from gripping his wrist to sliding into his hand and intertwining with his. Our joined hands rest in his lap and we fall into comfortable conversation.

For the next couple of hours we sit on the cold wood talking. The noise of the party fades to nothing. The night is dark, except for the shining moon and shimmering stars. The breeze eases and dies.

There's lightness to the way Jace talks. His smile comes easy and there's a glimmer in his eyes. It's odd how easy our conversation flows. Jace tells me about his mother, who happens to be a high school math teacher in the same school he attended. When he was younger, he liked that his mother was a teacher. She was always able to help him with his homework and he always turned in the best project or reports. But once he entered high school, all that changed. Apparently Jace found himself in trouble a lot, and his mother, naturally, would always find out. I'd assume knowing his mother worked at the same school would make him try to be on his best behavior, but that wasn't the case. It felt good to laugh as he told me of the pranks he pulled, even if they weren't the brightest ideas. One prank almost got him expelled.

Jace tells me about his dad, or his "sperm donor" as he put it. Jace doesn't know a lot about his father. His mother and father met in college and fell madly in love, until one day his father fell madly in love with someone else. Jace was a few months old when his father left and never looked back. Asshole. How do you willingly leave your child? I'll never understand that.

I tell him about my father who works as a lineman for the state's largest electric provider. It's a dangerous job, but I couldn't imagine him doing anything else. My dad could never sit behind a desk all day, wearing a suit and tie, pushing papers around. His job requires him to work random shifts with no rhyme or reason. Those ever -changing shifts are the reason Sam and I often found ourselves next door at Mrs. Harper's or, as we got older, why parties are often thrown here. My dad is not a dumb man. He knows what happens when he's away, but we've always been responsible and have never gotten into any trouble.

Soon the conversation turns to my mother, who is not someone I normally bring up willingly. Sure, naturally people ask, but this is the first time I can remember in a very long time that I bring her up. Even though my heart hurts, I tell him about her battle against an illness with no cure. Explaining schizophrenia to people is never easy. It's such a misunderstood disorder that affects different people in different ways. People have preconceived ideas about what people who suffer from the disease are like, and it's so difficult to change their opinions that after awhile I stopped trying. But for some reason I want Jace to know. I tell him about her current treatment plan and the halfway house she lives in. Never once did I see pity in his eyes. He simply listened while I talked.

Every so often my plans for the fall come up, but I always change the subject or deflect back to Jace. I've barely come to terms with the truth, but discussing them with someone I just met, no matter how comfortable he makes

25

me feel, isn't something I can do. It's best to stay away from the topic entirely, but somehow he manages to sneak it in every so often.

"I heard you sing earlier. You're really good."

"Thanks." I feel my cheeks blush.

"Really, you're talented," he continues. "Damn, I wish I was good at something like that. You should be a performer. You know, singing in places big and small all around the country. That would be cool."

"Someday."

It's one simple word, a word that holds so much promise. Anything can happen on someday. The most impossible can become possible. Yes, someday holds hopes and dreams, but the tricky thing about someday is it's always just out of reach.

I could tell him about my scholarship to Berklee and my plans to move to Boston in September, but I don't. I don't mention Adam's plans to finish college next spring and then follow me to the city. Topics dealing with what's next are avoided, because while I'm certain I'm about to start a brand new chapter, I'm not sure which book I'm reading from anymore.

Eventually our conversation slows and the distant background noise from the party seeps back in. The yard is quieter than before, so all that can be heard is the music playing from the CD player Sam had set up on the patio. I strain my ears to hear what is playing and immediately recognize it.

"I love this song."

Jace's eyes squint and he tilts his head to the side. "I don't think I have heard this one before."

"Really? It's one of my favorites." I peer back towards the house and notice almost everyone has left. There are only a few people seated near the almost extinguished fire.

"I should probably go help Sam clean up," I say with regret.

Jace nods, pushing himself up and then reaching down for my hands. Pulling me close, I stand in front of him and peer up. Pins and needles prick the back of my legs and calves from sitting for so long. Standing near him I notice, for the first time, truly how tall he is. He is close to six feet tall, towering over me by about six inches. Holding both my hands in his, he runs the pads of his thumbs over my knuckles. Warmth from the friction and the contact spreads across my skin. After a moment, he lifts my hands and places light kisses along the same path.

"Thank you," he says lowering my hands, but not releasing them.

"For what?"

26

"For the best night of my life," he says, finally dropping my hands. Without pause he turns and walks back to shore, the moonlight lighting his path. The ache in my chest grows with each stride he takes. The greater the distance between us, the stronger it becomes. *This is silly*, I think to myself. I barely know this boy. It's completely irrational to feel heartbroken over his leaving, but I do. For some crazy reason I do.

Once he steps down from the dock and begins to climb the cement stairs I can no longer take this feeling.

"Jace," I call out, racing toward him, my bare feet slapping against the cool wood.

He stops, turns, and waits. When I'm finally a few feet away I launch myself into the air, crashing against his chest with a thud. I wrap my arms around his middle, tuck my chin and rest my head against his chest. I feel his arms snake around my back. Closing my eyes, I take a deep breath, pulling him into my lungs.

We stand there, holding each other, for several minutes. Not once do I think of Adam. I don't wonder if he is watching or if he'll be mad. I don't think about the future or someday. All I can think about is now, this moment, and even though it doesn't make any sense, the undeniable fact I will miss Jace.

I don't know how long we stand like this. Maybe minutes or it could be hours, but finally I loosen my hold and take a tentative step back.

"Promise me something."

"Anything, Blue."

"Be careful. No matter where they send you, promise me you'll be careful."

"I promise," he says with a beautiful, crooked smile before lowering his head and kissing my cheek.

This time when he steps away I don't try to stop him. I stand and watch him walk into the night until I can no longer make out his frame in the darkness.

"Goodbye Jace," I whisper.

I remain still for some time, staring into the night where Jace disappeared, until my legs begin to ache and my teeth chatter. With the passing of night into early morning has a chill. Fine dew coats the grass and a light steam rises from the surface of the lake.

I tuck my new memories of Jace safely into the back of my mind and set out to find Adam. I won't be able to sleep until I speak to him, clear the air one way or the other. I only hope he's still here. Approaching the house, my feet become covered with small clumps of wet grass. I find Sam picking up empty cups and bottles, tossing them into a large black garbage bag.

"Hey. Have you seen Adam?" I ask, wiping my soles against the rough patio stones.

"I think he crashed inside."

Worrying my bottom lip, I nod.

"Hey," he says, setting the bag aside. Coming closer he wraps his arm around me and pulls me against him.

"Is everything OK? You've been different lately. Like something is bothering you. What did Adam do? Do I need to kick his ass? He may be my best friend, but you're my sister. I have to love you more," he teases, but I know, deep down, he would disown Adam if he ever hurt me.

I laugh, but it comes out wrong and sounds more like a strangled bird. "No. You don't need to hurt Adam, but I'm glad to know you have my back."

Sam ruffles the top of my head in that annoying way only a big brother can do. "Anytime."

Tiptoeing quietly, I walk through the house and up the stairs to my bedroom. Standing at the end of the hall, in the dark, I see a faint glow coming from underneath my door. Pressing an ear against it, I strain to hear what, or who, is on the other side but there's only silence. Slowly, I turn the knob and nudge the door open, peeking inside. Adam is lying on my bed, sound asleep. His chest is pressed into the mattress and his face rests on my pillow.

I creep inside, trying not to wake him, and get ready for bed. After washing my face and brushing my hair and teeth, I change out of my jeans and hoodie and pull on a pair of cotton shorts and a thin tank top, both smaller than I would like. Standing at the edge of the bed, I attempt to pull the comforter back and make a small amount of space for myself. Climbing in, I lean across Adam and set my alarm to go off in a few hours, so I can drive him home. My dad may be lenient, but letting Adam spend the night in my room is not something he is going to let slide.

Finally settling back, I stare up at the glowing stars stuck to my ceiling. One by one I begin to count them until somewhere around one hundred and twenty seven my eyes become heavy and I begin to drift asleep. There in the blackness I'm greeted by warm, milk chocolate eyes.

"So beautiful," I hear echo in my mind but it dissolves when the sound of my name crashes in to my subconscious.

"Miranda?"

My eyes spring open and my head rolls to the side. In the darkness I can make out Adam's silhouette sitting beside me, wide shoulders and thick chest, a shadow in the night. His frame and size are bigger and broader than Jace's. The comparison makes me cringe with guilt.

"Babe, I am so sorry," he says patting the sheets, searching for my hand. When he finds it, he squeezes my fingers gently before he continues. "I'm so sorry. I acted like a complete asshole earlier. I was just ... well, I was surprised. When you said we needed to talk I thought it was about Boston and how difficult it was going to be for us to be that far away from each other. I honestly never expected ..." he trails off.

I push myself up and rest my back against the padded headboard, the setting moonlight streaming a swath of light across my face.

"I'm sorry, too. It's just I didn't know what to say. I didn't want to tell you over the phone. It didn't seem right. I needed to see you, but you've been so busy these last few weeks."

"I get it. I don't like it, but I get it." He swipes a few strands of hair from my eyes and tucks it behind my ear. "Babe, we will figure this out and we will get through this. It's not the end of the world. This will not break us. If anything it will make us stronger."

"Adam, I'm not sure if I can do this. I mean, if we can do this."

He moves closer, until his bent knees touch the side of my leg. Drawing in a deep breath, he speaks quietly, but shockingly calm. "Miranda. I've loved you since before I knew what love was. I know we're young and I know this is crazy, but marry me."

The instant the words hit my ears I gasp. The roar of my heartbeat is so loud I almost don't hear what he says next.

"It has always been you, Miranda. You're it for me. We've talked about getting married. It was always in our plan."

"But," I try to interrupt him. He can't really mean it. How can he? Can we really do it? Now? Whether he hears me or not, he doesn't pause. He keeps talking.

"Marry me and from here on out it's you, me, and," he places his hand on my slightly swollen stomach, "my son."

I'm speechless. Tears well up in my eyes and begin to drip down the side of my face. They're a mixture of happiness, sadness, and grief.

"Your son? How do you know it's a boy?" I giggle, trying to wipe the tears with the back of my hand.

"I just know." He smiles warmly. "I love you so much. Marry me Miranda," Adam repeats.

My head nods slowly on its own. I want this so badly. I fall into Adam's arms and my heart feels lighter. With each teardrop the images of warm, brown eyes and crooked smiles are replaced with my future with Adam. A new future filled with a someday I didn't realize I wanted.

Chapter 5
Miranda

It has been a little more than a week since I quit my job and I still don't know what I'm going to do. I've spent hours scouring through postings on job search websites, even submitted my resume to a few, but I haven't heard back from everyone. I've even placed calls to a few previous colleagues, each glad to hear from me, but sorry they couldn't help.

Despite my depressing situation, I haven't mentioned anything to the girls or to Sam. Right now, I don't think Katelyn and Paige need to know, and Sam ... well, I'll put off that conversation for as long as possible. With some stroke of luck it will be after I have a new job. In spite of his best intentions, if Sam should find out before then, he will turn into the overbearing version of my big brother; the one I can't stand. I'll never be able to avoid his lecture.

I can hear it now. He'll start by telling me I should've quit my job long ago, insisting that Jonathan has always been a creep, and then continue to insist I go work for him. The idea will evolve into a job offer and constant nagging – indefinitely – until I finally give in. I love my brother, but I'm not sure I can stand to work for him. Isn't there a saying about working for family?

In order to keep up appearances, I get up every morning to the sound of my alarm at 5:30 as usual. Then Katelyn, Paige, and I follow our same morning ritual. I make breakfast while they bicker. I pack their lunches while they argue. I yell at them to hurry up. They yell back that they can't find their shoes. After years of repeating the same routine on a never ending loop, like characters in *Groundhog Day,* one would think I wouldn't have to endure this every morning and they would learn to get along. I suppose that's the purpose of having siblings, to perfect your ability to argue about the trivial things in life, so when the skill is needed for something important you are prepared. That and to have someone else to blame when you're in trouble.

This morning is no exception to the rule. Shrugging my shoulders, I lean against the front door with my bag and keys in hand.

"Paige, if you aren't down here in the next thirty seconds, with your shoes on, I'll go up there, carry you down, and you *will* go to school without shoes," I yell up the stairs.

"One, two, three." My counting is answered by the sound of scurrying feet above.

Katelyn rounds the corner from the kitchen; white wires hang from her ears and she hums to music only she can hear.

"Katelyn, did you finish your report last night?" I ask loudly. Of course she doesn't answer. Instead her head bobs to the beat.

"*Katelyn,*" I scream. Her head pops up. I motion for her to remove the ear buds and ask again, but before she can answer Paige barrels down the stairs almost tumbling off the bottom step. I catch her just a foot from landing face first on the floor.

"I swear you set out each morning trying to give me a heart attack," I say kissing her forehead. Glancing down I'm relieved to see she has two shoes on her feet and they match. It wouldn't have been the first time I hoisted her up over my shoulder and carried her to the car without shoes, following through on my threat.

After dropping both girls off at school, I debate my options. I can either sit at the coffee shop on Atwells and send out my resume in response to a few ads I saw last night, or blow off some steam. Tapping my fingers on the steering wheel, I look out the windshield at the beautiful blue sky and suddenly there really is no choice to be made. After the last few weeks there's only one thing I know will lift my spirits. Plus, the two waitresses at the cafe are starting to give me odd looks for being there so much.

Standing in the middle of the bustling park, I pull down the hem of my thin lavender blouse and tuck my hands into my dark jean pockets. I stand in place, blending into the scenery, while people move to and fro, scurrying to get wherever they need to be. I scan my surroundings looking for my target. This is something I have only done a few times before and the hunt still makes adrenaline course through my veins. It both energizes and calms me at the same time. The thrill of finding the perfect person on which to unleash my plan is unlike anything I have ever felt before.

Squinting to see through the crowd I finally find my prey. A man in his early fifties, his weathered, leather-like skin making him appear much older, sits on the ground, leaning his back against the round water fountain that is the focal point of this section of the park. His tattered clothes and unshaven face are additional evidence it has been sometime since he has seen a shower. Sunken cheek bones and thin frame indicating he hasn't had a decent meal in just as long.

This man is perfect.

I pick up the remainder of my supplies from a nearby vendor's cart and then make my move. Readjusting the strap across my chest, I stalk across the park. As I approach, my victim doesn't look up, not even when I'm only a few feet away. I don't expect him to. I can only imagine how many people must pass by him every day. I bet most don't even see him and if they do, they surely ignore his presence. But not me. I have him in my sight and he will not be ignored.

I lower myself to sit on the worn, wooden bench beside where he rests. The splintered wood bows under my weight, but I know it won't give out. The heat from the hot coffee in the paper travel cup stings my fingertips and the scent of fresh blueberries wafts from the plain white grease stained bag. I set both down beside me, and then sling the strap over my head and place the case at my feet.

Out of the corner of my eye, I watch the man. The intoxicating scent must have finally reached his nose, because he looks at the breakfast next to me longingly. The corner of my mouth pulls up slightly and I bite my lip to control my features, trying to keep a mask of indifference. Snapping both latches simultaneously, I prop the lid of the case so the back is at my shins and the opening is facing outwards. I reach inside and feel the familiar, thin, steely strings beneath my fingertips. My fingers glide down the neck lightly until finally I wrap my fingers around the wood and pull out my most prized possession: my guitar. The same guitar my father bought me when I was a child after much begging. It has seen me through many times, both good and bad.

I nudge the open case a few inches away from me with my right foot before turning my attention to my guitar. I strum my thumb across the strings once, make small adjustment, and strum again. Satisfied with the tune, I begin to play.

Playing the guitar is as natural to me as breathing and happens as involuntarily. Sometime after the first chord, my constant racing thoughts fade away and are replaced with a peaceful quiet. It's as if my body goes on autopilot. My lungs expand. My fingers stretch and glide from note to note, string to string, with little effort.

Soon my voice follows, exploding from my chest without thought. With each word, each lyric, I feel the weight upon my shoulders lessen until it completely disappears. Somewhere, deep in the back of my mind, I know this weightless feeling is fleeting, that once I stop the worry will return, fast and furious, but for now I am free.

It doesn't take long to get the attention of those who pass. I sing songs from my own youth mixed with current hits, as well as a few of my own. Each time I glance up at the crowd surrounding me, it grows exponentially. I can't see individual faces through the haze I'm in, but it doesn't matter. I don't need to see them to feel their energy. The vibrations rippling off each one fuels me further.

After twenty minutes, I begin to play a song I stumbled upon one night when I was feeling particularly sad – "Too Far Away" by Mary Lambert. As soon as I heard the lyrics I fell in love with the song. It was as if it was written for me personally. Closing my eyes, I lose myself in the lyrics describing the heartache of being separated from someone you love. Words describing only being whole when the other is near and of being only half as good when they are away – two things I know better than most.

Finally, when the last note leaves my lips, the most unusual thing happens. Deep in the pit of my stomach a weird rolling and twisting begins. My skin breaks out in a rash of goose bumps and the hairs on the back of my neck stand on end. Even though there are dozens of eyes on me, I can feel the weight of a single pair. I pry my eyelids open and scan the crowd trying to find the source. From left to right I search, until I see a hint of a crooked smile and warm chocolate eyes in the center of the crowd.

No, it's impossible. It can't be. My heart begins to beat so hard, I fear it might burst from my chest. Despite the cool temperature, sweat trickles between my shoulder blades and down my spine. I blink, clearing the residual haze and focus on the crowd once more, but this time there is no one familiar. Whatever or whoever I thought I saw is no longer there.

Pushing the shock aside, I smile politely at my audience and lean over my guitar. Peering into my case, I grin at the sight of the coins and bills laying on the red velvet. There is easily thirty dollars inside. *Not bad for a little more than twenty minutes,* I think.

Stacking the money in a neat pile and scooping up the coins, I set the guitar inside and snap the lid shut with my free hand before turning. Grabbing the paper cup with my left hand and pinching the bag between my index and middle finger, I crouch in front of my unsuspecting victim and present the coffee and muffin to him.

"Good morning. I don't mean to bother you and I hope you didn't mind my playing so closely." I jerk my head toward the bench.

"Not at all. You have a very pretty voice," the man says in a husky tone, raspy from smoking too many cigarettes. He smiles just a little, showing a hint of brown teeth.

"Thank you. These are for you," I say with a soft smile holding the food and coffee toward him. Confusion floods the man's weathered face. His eyes dart from my offering to me several times, unsure if he should accept.

"Please, take them," I urge.

Cautiously, the man extends a shaky hand and takes the coffee and muffin.

"Thank you," he says, unsure.

"You're welcome. This is also for you," I say offering him the money I collected. The man's eyes widen. He looks at me like I've lost my mind, but little does he know after the stress of the past few weeks, I finally feel sane.

After a little more convincing he finally accepts the money, thanking me at least a dozen times. With my guitar back in its case, I sling it across my chest. Walking away from the bench, I can't help but look to that spot. The spot I swear I saw him. Where I thought I saw Jace, but it couldn't be. I leave the park feeling the stress of everyday life eased, but a new lump in my chest.

Janet Lee

Chapter 6
Miranda
Then

Sitting on the carpeted floor, I rest my aching back against the sofa and let out a heavy breath. Piles of laundry surround me; some clean, some dirty, I honestly can't tell which is which. My darling daughter, Katelyn, who last week turned a year old, sits nearby playing with multi-colored stacking cups babbling in a language only she understands.

Much to Adam's surprise, she was not the son he was adamant I was carrying. He loves her more than anything, though. I joke sometimes that he loves her more than me. It could be true, but I don't care. Seeing him with her makes my heart skip a beat.

It's only eight in the morning, but I've already been up for hours. Normally Adam gets up with Katelyn in the morning, the two of them spending time together, while Adam gets ready for work and allowing me to sleep an extra blessed hour. However, this morning, Adam had to be in the office early, something about covering for his supervisor who is traveling for business. This left me to get up with Katelyn at the crack of dawn. No amount of coffee can replace the hole missing hour of sleep has left in my sanity.

The last few nights she has been miserable. I don't know if she is teething again or is coming down with a cold, but she was awake most of the night, whining and cranky. I tried everything I could think of to get her to sleep, but as soon as I lay her down she would wake and cry loud enough to raise the dead. Around four o'clock I gave up. Instead, I sat down in the pale pink arm chair in her room, rested her against my chest, and sang to her until we both fell asleep. Of course, now that the sun is up, she is full of wet smiles and giggles.

THE SECOND VERSE

A year ago, when my doctor told me my blood pressure was abnormally high and the only way to get it under control before I suffered from serious life threatening side effects was to deliver my daughter six weeks early, I thought my world was ending. I begged them not to do it. It was too soon. She would be too small. But it was no use; they were determined to deliver her whether I wanted them to or not.

As they rolled me down the hall, wires and tubes everywhere, I was so scared. Adam wasn't allowed in the operating room because the doctor was concerned about our condition. He was furious, eyes red with worry and rage. I think, if not for my emotional state, he would've strangled the doctor and all of the nurses. But I clutched his hand, tears streaming down my face, and begged him to stay calm. One of us needed to be and it had to be him. Adam's eyes fixed on me and the lines around them relaxed. The nurses removed the brakes from the bed wheels and began to roll me away. Adam quickly leaned down, pressed a gentle but urgent kiss to my lips, whispered he loved me, and then I was pulled away through a set of double doors.

An hour later my beautiful baby girl was born. Katelyn Ann Cross weighed three pounds, two ounces, and was thirteen inches long. She was a perfect, strong-willed, stubborn little girl. She spent three weeks in the NICU before being released. Those were the longest three weeks of my life. I spent every day at the hospital with her, arriving early in the morning and staying late into the night.

The NICU is one of the strangest places. Everyone walking the halls is either a nurse, has a child staying there, or is visiting a child they know. There is an odd feeling of sympathetic camaraderie, but even so, I often caught people staring when they thought I wasn't paying attention. Some people watched with empathy in their eyes, others with pity. They whispered when they didn't think I could hear them; always talking about the eighteen -year - old girl with the premature newborn. What they didn't know is from the moment I heard Katelyn's tiny little cry, I was no longer a teenager. Somehow in that moment my soul aged a decade, or maybe two. I was a mother and nothing else mattered. My hopes and dreams would always come behind hers and that was all right with me.

Katelyn's early arrival had changed our plans. Once Adam knew I was pregnant, the next step was to tell my father and brother. To say neither of them was happy would be an understatement. Sam threatened to kick Adam's ass for real, and I think my father was willing to help if I hadn't stepped in.

Adam and I were married just before Labor Day weekend, on my eighteenth birthday. There was nothing romantic or fairy tale-like about the day. I wore a simple sun dress and flip flops, and Adam dressed in khaki shorts and a polo shirt. Standing inside a stuffy courthouse room with my father, brother, and Adam's sister, Alisha, we exchanged our vows.

The next day I notified Berklee that, regretfully, I would not be attending in the fall. My heart broke a little the day I made that call. Going to that school was all I had dreamt about since I was a little girl. Adam promised we would figure out a way for me to go in a few years, but now that my days are filled with all things Katelyn, I can't imagine trying to juggle school and being a mom.

As for Adam, he had one year left before he graduated. Originally he planned to give up his dorm room, move into my Dad's house with me, and commute to school every day. My father was less than thrilled with the idea to begin with, but we couldn't afford a place of our own and the university did not have family living arrangements available on such short notice. However, like everything else, those plans changed the moment Katelyn was born. Adam took one look at his daughter and I swear he fell head over heels in love.

While I was confined to a hospital bed, trying not to move for fear my insides may fall out, Adam called around and was able to get an interview at a small mortgage broker in the next town over. The pay wasn't great, but it was better than flipping burgers. Adam dropped all of his classes, packed up his dorm room, and moved into my Dad's by the time I was released.

I was furious. Maybe it was hormones, but I don't think so. I believe I would've reacted the same way when I found out regardless. I argued that he shouldn't have dropped out. He was so close to finishing and both of us shouldn't give up our dreams. I was willing to carry the burden of that sacrifice for the both of us, but he insisted. Adam kept saying it was his responsibility to take care of his family and I have to give him credit, he has been doing his best ever since.

With the sound of the morning news playing in the background, my head falls back heavily against the armrest. I'm really not interested in hearing about the latest weight loss craze sweeping the nation right now. Maybe I can close my eyes for just ... one ... moment.

My eyes sting with fatigue. I fight to keep them open and it's a losing battle, but as my lids drift closed two things happen. First Katelyn, who was cruising around the coffee table, turns to look at me. I watch through the slits in my eyes as her expression changes from amusement to determination. Seriousness lies in her innocent pale blue eyes. After seeming to weigh her options, she lets go of the table, lifts her chubby little foot, and takes a single step. A cheeky, four tooth smile brightens her face. She releases the tiniest giggle before taking another step, followed by another and another. She takes four full steps before she falls into my arms. I scoop her up and hold her tightly against my chest. I mentally try to freeze time and seal the moment in my mind so someday, when I am old and gray, I can dig up this memory and replay it.

The second unforgettable moment happens while I hold Katelyn and inhale the scent of her lavender baby shampoo.. The familiar tones of a breaking news update interrupt our joyful moment. I peel my eyes from my precious little girl and focus on what can only be described as indescribable. I watch frozen and in horror as the unthinkable happens less than two hundred miles away. As each video clip plays and the images flood the screen, I know deep in my soul the world will never be the same. Instantly images of chocolate eyes and the crooked smile I hadn't thought about in more than a year flood my mind.

"My recruiter told me that unless World War III breaks out I will probably never see any real combat."

I trickle of terror races up my spine. Katelyn squirms in my arms, the excitement of her big moment gone. She begins to whine and fuss, no longer wishing to be held, but I don't let go. I can't. Kissing her on the head, I rock her back and forth, trying to calm her as well as myself.

"Please be careful Jace," I whisper, squeezing Katelyn tighter against my chest.

Chapter 7
Jace
Then

Lifting the amber bottle to my lips, I take a long pull of the icy cold beer. The bitter taste assaults my taste buds and slides smoothly down my throat, beginning to quench my thirst. I won't be twenty -one for a few more years, but the owner of this dive bar near base doesn't bother carding me. The rest of my unit and I spend much of our down time in this dimly lit, little rough - around -the -edges establishment. Pete, the owner, says if we are old enough to serve our country, we are old enough to enjoy a cold beer at the end of the day. I don't think the cops in town would agree, but who am I to argue?

The setting sun shines dimly through the front windows creating streaks of light on the wooden floor, which is littered with dirt, dust, and peanut shells. The room is thick with late summer humidity and the body heat of those all around. In the far corner of the bar, a small group of thirty-something women wearing too little clothing and revealing far too much skin, hang on a couple of guys. Based on their dirty jeans and sweat stained t-shirts, I assume they came straight from working at the construction site just up the street. t-shirts.

I watch from the corner of my eye and cringe. The women swish their hips from side to side with the beat of the country music pouring from the jukebox. I think they are aiming to look sexy, but, to me, they just look trashy. Sexy is a pair of sapphire eyes and jet black hair hidden by an oversized sweatshirt who, even months later, I can't forget.

Taking another swig of my beer, I tune out the rest of the bar and focus my attention on the news station playing on the TV.. Journalists and government officials have been reporting non-stop over the last several days. The images of the worst attack to happen on American soil in decades plays again and again on a never ending loop. Days ago, when I watched as the events unfolded live on national television with the rest of the base, I was sick to my stomach. Adrenaline and honest to God fear churned in my gut. But now, having seen them again and again, the adrenaline is still there, however the fear is gone, replaced with the need for vengeance. Those responsible must pay for what they did. If they don't, what's to say they won't strike again?

I tip my now empty bottle toward Pete, silently asking for another, when the front door bursts open with a thunderous thud. My best friend, Henry, enters with his arms above his head, whooping. Accustomed to his antics, the regular bar patrons barely lift their eyes to see who, or what, is making the ruckus. Those not familiar watch him with curiosity for a moment, wondering what is going on.

"Yeah, boy. We're going you son of a bitch!" He slides onto the stool beside me, slapping me roughly on the back.

I met Henry, otherwise known as Hound, during basic training. I don't even remember how we met. He simply appeared one day and never went away, sort of like a rash or a stray dog. Even when I was selected to join the Rangers, he somehow found a way to come along. I have to admit, months later, I like having him around. I think if I had a brother I would've wanted him to be like Hound.

Under any other circumstances I'm not sure he and I would have become friends. Hound is cocky and arrogant, talks too loud, and never knows when to shut up. He is not very tall, maybe five foot seven, but what he lacks in height he makes up for in mass. If I didn't know any better, I would think he was taking something to be so big, but I know for certain his size is strictly due to hours in the gym. Despite his build and his current occupation, Henry is a romantic at heart, a lover not a fighter, which is completely ironic. However, if provoked, the knight in shining armor can quickly turn into a raging pit bull, ready to tear apart anything or anyone daring to cross his path.

His temper is actually how my dear friend Henry got the nickname Hound. One night, while on leave this past spring, Henry and I found ourselves in a place similar to this one, but near a warm, sunny beach in Florida. We had driven south to spend a few days kicking back when all hell broke loose. While minding our business talking to two very cute blondes wearing tiny shorts and bikini tops, some asshole stumbled over and started harassing the girls. Henry and I tried to diffuse the situation, offering to buy the guy a drink, trying to persuade him to the other side of the bar and away from the girls. The guy agreed, but as he and I began to walk away, the drunk turned around and took a swing at Henry. Most of it's still a blur, but the one thing I will never forget is the growling sound Henry made as he pummeled that asshole. When I finally peeled my friend off the drunken guy and pushed him through the backdoor, narrowly escaping before the police showed up, I saw Henry was actually frothing at the mouth. I couldn't help but laugh. I remember telling him he looked like a rabid dog, like Ol' Yella, to which he lifted his head to the sky and howled into the night. From then on, Henry was called Hound.

Without asking, Pete pulls a bottle from the bin of ice, twists off the top, and places a beer in front of my boisterous friend. Pete leans on his outstretched arms with a white dish rag thrown over his shoulder, listening to Hound continue.

"We're fucking going."

"When?" I ask taking another swig.

"Next week. Not soon enough if you ask me," Hound says draining half his beer in a single gulp. "We're going to teach those fuckers a lesson."

"Where are you boys headed?" Pete asks, an odd tone of worry in his voice.

"Iraq," Hound says casually, like it's not the other side of the world. "We'll teach those assholes not to mess with us."

I nod my head, but let Hound and Pete's conversation on the Middle East fade into the background. My eyes refocus on the screen over Pete's head, but it's not the dusty, desert scenes I see. All I see are a set of sparkling blue eyes.

I reach into my back pocket and pull out my wallet. Opening the leather, my fingers brush against the soft, worn edges of newspaper. Carefully, I pull out the piece of paper and unfold it. I smooth out the creases, my fingers lingering on my only physical reminder of Miranda. It's an article that was published days after her high school graduation. I had found it in my grandmother's house while cleaning a bin in the kitchen, the day after Miranda and I sat on the edge of the dock. The article had been about the graduating class and their accomplishments, but in the center of the page was a picture of Miranda sitting on a stage, guitar in her lap, looking out at the crowd. The photographer was able to capture the light in her eyes and even in the black and white image, I can see their sparkle.

When I found the article and the picture, I couldn't toss it out. I thought about it for several minutes, feeling ridiculous over my want to keep it. Giving in, I gently folded and creased the page, careful not to mar her face, and tucked it safely into my wallet. If I couldn't be with her, I would at least have her with me.

THE SECOND VERSE

Every now and then I let myself look at it, but only for a moment. I wonder where she is and what she's doing. I wonder how her first two semesters of college went. I wonder if she is performing in little coffee shops or maybe in a bar like this. But most of all I wonder if she is happy.

Hound shoves my arm and the blue haze disappears. "What the fuck?" I snap.

"Dude, you had that fucking look on your face again. You were thinking about her, weren't you?" Disapproval is stamped on his face. I ignore him, gently fold the page, and stick it back inside my wallet for safe keeping.

I don't know why I told him about Miranda. Hell, there was hardly anything to tell. But one drunken night after the first week of Ranger training, we had a few too many beers and began reminiscing on the girls who got away. I relived the entire night by the lake, down to the tiniest, little detail. With no one else around to judge our manhood, Hound listened, like a schoolgirl at a slumber party. Shit, if anyone had heard us that night we would have gotten our asses kicked. I could tell he thought I was crazy, missing someone I had only known for a few hours, but he never said it. He simply let me talk.

"Shit Jace, you need to get over here. Seriously, you're like some love sick dog." His eyes move around me and a sinister smile pulls at his lips. "I know what you need. You need to get your dick wet." He nods his head to my right. "She'll get that chick off your mind."

I follow his gaze to the only girl under thirty in this place. She's leaning against the wall watching us. She is sort of pretty. Her long blonde hair is pulled up into a messy bun. Her eyes are lined in thick black makeup, making her look more tired than sexy. The pale pink fabric of her tank top is stretched tightly across her breasts and rides up her waist, leaving nothing to the imagination. Long tan legs stretch from the bottom of her denim miniskirt and lead down to a pair of knee high black boots. If I saw her on the side of the street, I would think she were a prostitute. Hell, for all I know she is one.

I turn my attention back to Hound, whose tongue is practically hanging out of his mouth. "I'm good. She's all yours, buddy."

"You sure? I'll take one for the team if you want to man up."

"Nah, go get 'er."

"Fuck yeah, I will," he says, standing. "Yo sweetheart!" he calls out, before stalking after her.

Downing the rest of my beer, I toss a few bills on the bar. "Hey Pete. Call me if he gets himself in trouble."

43

Pete chuckles and shakes his head. "You know that's inevitable."

I laugh. "Yeah, you're probably right."

"Hey, you take care of yourself, ya hear." All the humor drains from Pete's face and it's replaced with sincerity.

What do I say to that? There is no good come back. Instead, I nod my head and smile tightly. "See ya around, Pete."

"See ya kid."

Chapter 8
Jace

Pressing my hand to the center of my chest, I try to stop the goddamn aching that simply won't go away. With my duffle bag weighing down my left arm, I place my hand against the thick wood of the mantle above the small fireplace in my mother's living room. Slowly, I study the photographs that stand proudly, chronicling my life.

The timeline begins with a photo from the day I was born, me swaddled in a white linen blanket, cradled against my mother's chest. Next, nestled in a simple wood frame, is a shot of a round toddler riding a tricycle with a wide toothy smile. There's a snapshot of me and my mother at a carnival that was taken when I was eight, which sits within a Popsicle stick frame I made the same year. Sprinkled between pictures taken during holidays and vacations are school photographs, highlighting the years between kindergarten and high school graduation. Finally, at the far right, sits a picture of me in formal dress greens, taken the day I received my Ranger tab.

I study that picture the longest. The man is me, bearing the same facial features and broad shoulders, but there's also something unfamiliar about my appearance. Perhaps it's the defiant smirk, one corner of my lips pulled up just slightly. Or maybe it is simply the youthfulness in my jaw and cheeks. But the closer I look, the more I realize the difference between young me and who I am today is the spark in my eyes. Looking at the man in the photograph, I can see naïve pride and foolish invincibility.

If only I knew then what I know now.

"I can't believe you're leaving," my mother's trembling voice breaks the early morning silence.

I release a heavy sigh, hoping to relieve some of the pressure in my chest.

45

Turning my attention toward the narrow staircase that divides the first floor of the small, two bedroom beach house, I take two uneven steps toward her, lowering my bag to the floor. I try not to wince at the dull pain that shoots up from my ankle to my knee, but fail.

"Mom, please," I beg, not wanting to talk about this again. It could be the dim light coming from the lamp in the corner, casting shadows across the room, but I swear the line between her brows looks deeper than I remember.

"We've talked about this. I need to go. I just … it's just …" I curse under my breath, hating that I feel so flustered. I don't get flustered. I've been trained to remain calm, even in the most chaotic circumstances. Anything else could get me killed.

"I need some time," I pause, "to sort through things." I tap two fingers against my temple.

"Sweetheart, I know you still have some things to work out and the doctors said some wounds would heal faster than others, but why do you have to leave? I can help." She reaches for me, but then quickly drops her arms and wraps them her middle instead.

Seeing the fear and concern on her face is one of the reasons why I have to leave Surfside. It kills me to see her like this, knowing I'm the reason she looks as if she's aged a decade in the last year. I can't imagine what happens to a mother when their only son is sent half way across the world time and time again, with very little information to hold on to, only to have them come home battered, bruised, and needing to learn how to walk again.

This house, the place I grew up in, where I learned to ride a bike and play baseball, no longer feels like home. Somewhere along the way, between deployments, or maybe even when I left for basic training, the idea of home changed from a sanctuary to a mirage. Over the years home became a shimmering illusion on the horizon; a figment of my imagination. As much as my mom would like me to find comfort with her in this place, I can't. I've tried, God I've tried, to feel something other than anxiety here, but the longer I stay the more I feel like I'm suffocating.

After three tours overseas and more than a decade of service, I find myself a solider forced to live as a civilian, and I'm not sure I know how to do that. People keep telling me I'm one of the lucky ones. Lucky to be alive with only a limp, a titanium rod in my leg, and a few scars as the only physical reminders of the reason for my discharge. Others aren't so fortunate.

I should be excited, eager even, to start the next chapter of my life, but being alive and living aren't the same thing.

I cross the room, stopping close enough to finally see the tears dripping down her cheeks. "Mom, I promise I'll be alright, but I need to do this. I need some time on my own."

She sniffles, wiping her nose with the back of her hand. Slowly, she nods her head in resignation. "Call when you get there," she says, but it sounds more like a question.

"Of course," I say, pulling her against me, rubbing my hands up and down her arms.

"I love you, sweetheart."

"I love you too, Mom."

Fifteen hours later, I find myself driving down the unfamiliar streets of a town I've thought about a lot over the years, but never thought I would see again. Coming to Belham, Massachusetts the first time, all those years ago, was out of my control. Something my mother had to do and I had to go along with. This time, however, it was the first place I thought of when I knew I needed time to myself.

The drive north took all day. Mile after mile of interstate stretched before and after me. After a while, the white dotted line marking each lane began to blur like a scene from *Black Dog*. My leg cramped a few times and my back started to ache after eight hours, but there was no way I was stopping and I definitely couldn't go back. I had suffered things far worse than a sore muscles.

When I finally pulled in the driveway of my grandmother's house just after 9 p.m., my mind was clouded with fatigue. There wasn't a part of my body that didn't hurt. I barely recall hobbling to the front door and rummaging under the mat for the key before stumbling into the house and collapsing on the sofa. Sleep took me almost instantly.

Sleep is an odd thing. Our bodies need it to survive, like a system reboot. Without it, our circuits overload and before we know it we blow a fuse. Yet, despite the biological need to sleep, my mind fights it tooth and nail. My subconscious is dead set on showing me gruesome images and playing the soundtrack of the most soul crushing screams on repeat, night after night.

After only a few hours on the dusty sofa, I wake with a start. Sweat drips down the side of my face and burns my eyes. My army tan t-shirt is soaked through and clings to my body. I push up, swinging my legs over the edge of the couch, and pull my shirt off, dropping it on the floor. I place my head in my hands and concentrate on breathing, inhaling deep through my nose and counting to three before exhaling out through my mouth. Normally, after a minute or two, the shaking stops and my heartbeat will slow, but tonight I can't stop the panic.

I push off the sofa and stumble across the room. My arms swipe from side to side, searching in the dark for the small table by the front door, but my knee finds it first. Cursing under my breath, I slide my hand across the table top until I find my wallet. Cautiously, I make my way back to my makeshift bed and sit down clumsily. My body aches from head to toe and the tension from the panic attack is not helping. I lean back, open the wallet, and pull out a worn piece of paper.

The moon offers just enough light that I can make out the image of the photograph, but even if I was blind, I could recount every detail. The edges of the newspaper are torn, and the seams where it has been folded over and over again are held together in spots by tape and in others by luck.

Over time this photograph has become my talisman. It has seen me through good times and bad, both overseas and stateside. I truly believe it has brought me luck, even if I didn't always immediately see my fortune. This picture is always close by, tucked in the pocket of my shirt, pants, or wallet. And the day it saved my life, it was nestled in my helmet.

I focus my energy on the thin piece of paper, tracing the smooth lines of her face and the spark in her eyes, until slowly the tension eases and eventually fades.

My panic attacks began shortly after arriving at the rehabilitation center in Virginia. It could've been the shock of my physical injuries or the realization of what had happened. In the beginning, the attacks were hard to control. I felt like I was drowning and no matter how much I tried, I could never find the surface. After two months and near daily attacks, Dr. Roberts prescribed medication, but I refused to take it. I insisted he find another way to help me that didn't include drugs. He told me there wasn't weakness in taking the medication, but if I insisted he would teach me techniques I could use to ease and, hopefully, stop the attacks. At first, the breathing exercises seemed futile, but over time they helped. Within a few weeks, I was able to gain control, each time breaking free of the attack, easier and faster.

There were still moments, though, when nothing seemed to help; times when I would sit on my bed shaking so violently I was afraid to try to stand. One night, I had an attack so severe I thought I might die of asphyxia. I reached for the phone on the side table to call the nurse who was always nearby, but my hand missed the receiver and knocked over a box my mother had brought earlier that day. The contents fell to the floor around my feet and that's when I noticed it: this photograph. Somehow I managed to steady my hand just enough to pick it up. I stared at her face, retracing each line and reacquainting myself with every detail and before I realized it, the panic attack had faded.

Just like now.

Unable to go back to sleep, I sit back on the sofa and watch the sky out the front bay window. When dawn begins to nip at the darkness my phone rings.

"Hello."

"Oh, thank god," my mother's worried voice responds. "Where are you? Are you okay?"

Scrubbing my face with my hand, guilt washes over me. "Yes, Mom, I'm fine. I'm sorry I didn't call. When I got here last night, I was so tired I fell asleep."

She doesn't respond, but I can hear her fighting to remain calm.

"I'm sorry," I whisper, pressing a hand to my chest when the ache begins again.

"It's okay, sweetheart," she sighs, "I'm just glad to hear you made it there and you're all right." She pauses. "Was the key under the mat?"

"Right where you said it would be." I smile and I can hear her smile too as she continues.

"I haven't been there in a year, but the last tenant was an older woman, so I'm sure she took care of the place."

"I'm sure everything's fine. Honestly, I didn't make it any farther than the sofa."

I hear her laugh softly and I feel a little better. "Well, I didn't mean to wake you. I'll let you go."

"I'll call you tomorrow."

"Okay, sweetheart. I love you."

"Love you, too."

Despite my lingering fatigue, I need to clear my head. The only way I know will work is to run. Before my injury, I ran ten miles every morning. If I really wanted a workout I would run up to fifteen or twenty. It was something I had begun when I was in basic training and kept up years later. Now, however, going for a run is a process.

Pushing myself from the lumpy sofa, I stand and stretch my arms over my head. My back and side are still sore and my legs are stiff. Gingerly, I slip my feet into my boots, not bothering to lace them, and go out to grab my duffle bag from the truck.

Back inside the house, I change into a pair of black athletic shorts and a gray t-shirt. I wrap the scarred area of my thigh with a tan elastic bandage before sliding on my black knee brace, strapping it into place. The wounds themselves no longer hurt. In fact, normally, I can't feel much of the entire outer portion of my right leg due to scar tissue. That's until the brace rubs against it the wrong way.

When I first began rehab I had to wear a damn brace every day. It was bigger and clumsier than the one I wear today, and at the time it was just one more reason to be pissed off at the world. I hated that I had to wear the stupid thing and was determined to strengthen my leg on my own and throw the damn thing away. Of course, being a complete asshole, I pushed myself too hard too fast and actually ended up setting my treatment back several weeks after I inadvertently pulled my staples, reopening the incision by trying to move faster than I should. I only had to learn that lesson once, and afterward I learned to trust the doctors and nurses around me.

With my gear in place, I lock the front door and slip out the back, leaving the door that leads down to the lake unlocked. My pace is not as quick as it once was, but it's one I can sustain for awhile. The sun peeks above the horizon offering glimmering possibilities for the new day. There is a chill in the late summer air. It won't be long before the leaves begin to change from deep green to shades of yellow, orange, and red.

Not being familiar with the area, I keep track of my surroundings. I try to tell myself it's so I can find my way back to the house, but I truly know it's out of habit. I catalog the color of the houses and memorize the names of each street. I log each nuance, never knowing when I might need the information.

After turning up and down a few side roads, I come to the entrance of a park. Following a concrete path that runs parallel to a small river, I maintain a steady pace. The sound of my own heartbeat and the air rushing in and out of my lungs is all I can hear. To begin with I don't pass many people, but the brighter the sky becomes the more people begin to emerge. A few runners pass me, paying me little attention, but every now and then I can feel the eyes of others on me.

About five miles in, my leg is screaming for me to slow my pace. Having also learned this lesson the hard way, I comply, slowing to jog. The heavy sound of my heartbeat begins to lessen and it's then that I hear it, the sound of music, or more accurately, the sound of a guitar.

My mind begins to search back, as it often does, for those memories I keep locked away. Memories I try not to think about, but refuse to stay buried. The images of crystal clear blue eyes and raven hair. I mentally slam the door to the invisible room in my mind where those images reside.

The music grows with each step and I decide this is a good spot on the trail to turn back. Just before I round the next bend, I turn on the ball of my right foot but then stop dead. Audible just above the twang sound of the guitar is a voice. No, not just a voice, but a voice so pure it weaves with each note, blending perfectly.

My heart beats so violently it hurts. Could it be? No, it can't be. It's impossible. Isn't it?

I knew coming back to this town I ran the risk of running into her. I kept telling myself the chance wasn't the reason I chose to escape here. Each time I told my mother I needed time to get my life together, I was also trying to convince myself it was the only reason I needed to come to Belham. I think I always knew, deep down, I just needed the chance to see her, even if it was from afar. There was always the possibility she no longer lived in this godforsaken town, but I just needed that small chance.

What are the odds that within hours of arriving I would have the opportunity?

Within seconds my legs are operating on their own accord. The once building pain is now a dull throb, thanks to the adrenaline in my system. The sound of the music has hooked me and is reeling me in. I round a grassy knoll, topped with a large oak tree, and crash into the back of a swelling crowd. Nearly three dozen people stand in a semi-circle. Some stand quietly, listening to the singer croon, while others hold their cell phones over their heads, recording the performance. Some talk in hushed whispers.

Now, being only yards away, there is no doubt in my mind it's her. Miranda. I could never forget her beautiful, soulful voice even if I tried. It's one of the few things to offer me comfort while living in the belly of Hell tour after tour. There were many nights I would lay in my cot, hearing distant gunfire and muffled blasts, trying to queue her voice in my head long enough to fall asleep. I found small moments of peace replaying her performance by the fire on that summer night.

Slowly, I push my way through the crowd. I need to get a closer look, but I want to do so unnoticed. Weaving into the middle of the group, I get my first clear view. God, she's beautiful. I could say she hasn't changed one bit in the last fourteen years, but that would be a lie. Although they are subtle, the differences are there. Her face is fuller, softer around the edges. There are the faintest creases around and between her eyes, and I can't help but wonder what has caused them. Her hair is shorter; the once waist length black hair now skims the tops of her shoulders. She is seated on a wooden bench with a guitar in her lap, so I cannot see the rest of her, but it doesn't matter. She is simply breathtaking.

The song she sings comes to an end and her audience applauds. I see a small smile curl the corner of her lips. She makes a few small adjustments to the tuning pegs, strumming the strings a few times. Seemingly satisfied, she begins to sing once again. It's a fast paced song, but the lyrics are sad, filled with loss and longing. She sings of missing the one person who was her other half and how difficult it is to move on when they are so far away.

As I listen, I hear the emotion in her voice. This is not just a song for the crowd. This song holds meaning for her. The curled smile on her lips has been replaced with a small frown and the crease between her eyes has deepened. My fingers itch to smooth out those lines and erase the pain.

Lost in my thoughts, I don't notice the song has ended until more applause echoes through the park. Breaking free from my stare, I notice her eyes are frantically scanning the mob of people, searching for something. It's then, for only a moment, our eyes meet. I can't help my smile. I've waited so long to see her again. But I shouldn't be here. I have seen her and now it's time to go. Quickly, I duck behind a few people and move out of the crowd, heading back in the direction I came without a second glance.

Chapter 9
Miranda

I busy myself setting plates on the kitchen table as I wait for Sam to bring the girls home. Every Wednesday Sam picks up Paige from school to take her to karate, and then he grabs Katelyn from drama rehearsal before bringing them home. Since I would normally get home about thirty minutes before them, I always fix something simple for dinner. Typically Sam stays since Claire, who is a nurse at the hospital the next town over, works overnight on Wednesdays.

Tonight I have opted for spaghetti and garlic bread. I set the bread on the table just before they burst through the door. Heavy footsteps and loud voices fill the once quiet space.

"I'm telling you Uncle Sam, birthstones are also minerals," Paige says, as she comes skipping into the kitchen, still wearing her gi. She tosses her backpack in the corner.

"Are you sure?" Sam asks, following her. "Hey." He nods his head in my direction.

"It's totally true. Look it up," she insists.

Sam gives me a questioning look, but I simply shrug. I'm not getting in the middle of this debate. I learned a long time ago that my two girls are usually right and, frighteningly, smarter than me. They are too smart for their own good sometimes. I can't help but laugh when I see Sam pull out his cell phone from his back pocket and begin tapping on the screen.

"Huh, you're right, P. Birthstones are minerals," Sam says, shaking his head in disbelief. "When did you get to be so smart?'

"I was born smart. That's why my head is so big," Paige says matter of fact. Sam and I both roll our eyes.

"Where is Katelyn?" I ask, pulling cups from the cabinet.

"She went up to her room. Something about needing to write something down," Paige answers. This time it's her turn to roll her eyes.

"Okay, sweetie, go tell her supper is ready. Oh, take your bag with you and take a quick shower. You are all sweaty from karate. But be quick," I say, kissing her on the forehead.

"Do I have to," she whines.

"Yes, hurry up."

Paige disappears around the corner, muttering under her breath and I begin rinsing out the pots I used. Out of the corner of my eye, I see Sam reach into the fridge and grab a beer, which I keep for occasions like this. Twisting the cap, he takes a long pull before hopping up onto one of the bar stools tucked under the breakfast bar.

"So," he starts, "when were you going to tell me you quit your job?"

My body tense and jaw slacks open. I guess I couldn't keep it a secret from him forever, but I would've liked a few more days to lock down something new. Drying my hands on a damp dishcloth, excuses roll through my mind, but none of them sound good enough.

I turn to look at him. It doesn't matter how old I am or how much has happened in my life, when Sam gives me his mixed look, the one filled with concern, sympathy, and condescension, I can't help but feel like a little girl again.

"Sam, don't look at me like that," I sigh. "I didn't tell you because it's not a big deal. Quitting was the right thing to do, even if it doesn't seem that way in the short term."

Sam snorts into his beer. "Don't get me wrong. Your job sucked and you should've quit a long time ago. That's not the part that bothers me. What gets me is why you didn't say anything. It has been what? Two weeks?"

Damn, how does he know?

"And you haven't mentioned it once. Why?"

"How did you find out?"

"Does it matter?"

"Yes," I insist.

"Earl Johnson's granddaughter Rebecca's best friend Kelly started at the agency three weeks ago as a temp. She was working the day the school nurse called me." He takes another pull from his beer, eyeing me over the bottle. "That's the day it happened, right?"

THE SECOND VERSE

The perks of a small town; everyone knows everything.

"Yes. Jonathan was such an asshole and Paige was hurt. It ... it just happened."

"Like I said, it should've happened sooner. Now, why didn't you tell me?"

"I don't know. I didn't want you to worry, I guess."

"Well, should I? Should I be worried about you?"

"No," I say forcefully.

Sam narrows his eyes and tilts his head to the right, studying me like I'm an algebra equation.

"Is that so? Alright. Have you found something else yet?" He already knows the answer. He sets the bottle on the counter with a smug look on his face.

"Well, no not yet. But I'm sure I will find something soon," I say reassuringly, brushing by him to place the bowl of pasta in the center of the table.

"Why don't you just come to work for me? You know I'm terrible with the paperwork and with the way business has been lately, I can't keep up with it all. I could really use a hand in the office. I'm going to have to hire someone anyway," he explains.

My eyes remain downcast, focused on the table, but I see his heavy work boots come into sight.

"I don't know, Sam. Isn't it bad to work with family?" I'm grasping at straws.

Sam can see right through me and chuckles. "Not when it's family who started the business in the first place. It isn't my company and you know it," he says, adding an extra emphasis on *my*.

He sets his half empty beer on the table and wraps his arm around my shoulder.

"Aw c'mon, I'm not that bad to work for. Just ask some of the guys. Plus, it seems only right you come run the show in the office. It's something you should've done years ago."

Chewing on my lip, I weigh my options. Oh, who am I kidding? I don't have any options. Plus, if I don't find another job soon, I know Sam is going to step in and offer to help me financially. Really, what's the difference?

I look up at my bother and want to smack the grin off his face. Damn him.

"Shit." I run my fingers through my hair in exasperation. There's no getting go out of this. In the long run, it's easier just to give in now.

"Okay. But," I point my finger in his face, "if you try to pull the older brother card at work I will kick your ass."

That does it. Sam starts laughing loudly, holding his hands up in surrender. "Okay. Okay, whatever you say."

"What's so funny?" Katelyn asks, entering the kitchen, taking her normal seat at the table.

"Nothing," I say quickly, before Sam can answer. I shoot him a look, telling him to keep his mouth shut. I think he's about to ignore me, but luckily Paige comes crashing into the room offering a new distraction.

The four of us settle around the table and begin dishing out pasta onto our plates. Of course Paige takes more than she could possibly eat. That child's eyes are three times larger than her stomach.

"So, Uncle Sam, did Mom tell you I signed up to perform in the school's talent show?" Katelyn asks, twirling her fork in her pasta.

"Is that so? No, she didn't, but I'm sure she would've. I think she's had a lot on her mind lately," Sam says, winking at me.

Jerk.

"Like what?" Paige asks, spaghetti sauce stretching from lips to cheeks. She even has a spot on the tip of her nose.

"Nothing," I respond quickly. "Wipe your face, love, you have sauce everywhere."

Katelyn gives me a suspicious look, but continues.

"It's tomorrow night at six. Do you think you and Aunt Claire can make it?"

"I wouldn't miss it for the world, Katie. Claire is working a double today, so she should be off tomorrow evening. I'll text her later, but count me in for sure."

Katelyn tries to stifle her smile, but she can't hide it. I know he has just made her evening. The four of us eat in comfortable silence for a few minutes until Sam speaks.

"So girls, did you hear? Your mom is going to work for me."

If looks could kill, my brother would be dead. Talk about letting the cat out of the bag. I still hadn't told the girls I was no longer working at the agency. I could ring Sam's neck and he knows it based on the chuckle he is trying to cover as a cough.

"What?" Katelyn asks, brows drawn up. "What about your job?"

"You're going to mow lawns with Uncle Sam?" Paige asks with a look of wonder in her eyes. "That's *so* cool."

Pushing my chair from the table, I reach for their plates, scrape off each one, and stack them to carry to the sink.

"I won't be working at the agency anymore. Starting on Monday I'm going to run the office for Uncle Sam. And no, I will not be mowing lawns. Mowing our lawn is more than enough for me."

"So you'll be his boss?" Paige asks.

With raised brows, I look at my brother. "Yup, and he better watch out or I'll fire him."

"Just try it," he warns, jokingly.

"What will you do there if you won't be mowing people's lawns?" Paige asks, still slightly disappointed.

"The same kinds of things I did before. Paperwork, phone calls."

"Oh." She shrugs. "Can I go watch TV now?"

At least I know where this announcement ranks in her priorities.

"Yes, I suppose, but you only have thirty minutes and then it's time for bed," I call after her.

"Well, that's good," Katelyn says leaning back in the chair and crossing her arms over her chest. "Maybe you can help with the hiring, too."

Sam's brows pinch together, the humor fading quickly.

"What do you mean?" he asks.

"I just mean, some of the guys that work there are a little ... a little weird. Benny is alright and Bryce is nice, always talking about Annie and the baseball team. Luis is, well, Luis, but a few of the others ..." Her voice drops off at the end. I return to my seat and give Sam a questioning look.

"A few of the others what?" Sam prods her to continue.

"I don't know. They're just weird."

"Like?"

"When Paige and I waited in the office this afternoon while you ran into the back, a new guy I hadn't seen before came in looking for keys to the Chevy so he could move it."

"Jay," Sam interrupts.

Katelyn shrugs. "I guess so. Tall, big, dark hair."

Sam nods his head, confirming it was who he thought, and she continues.

"When he saw me leaning against the front desk he stopped dead in his tracks and just stared at me. The way he stared at me," she shivers, "it was weird."

"What the hell Sam!" I snap.

"No, Mom. The way he looked at me wasn't in an old creepy pedophile kind of way. It was like ... like he saw a ghost. He looked at me like I was a figment of his imagination. His face went pale. Then, without a word, he turned and left. Like I said, it was weird."

"Don't worry about him Katie. I'll have a talk with him tomorrow, but he's harmless," Sam says, his tone strong and firm. It seems to convince her.

Shrugging, she tucks her long dark hair behind her ear.

"If you say so, Uncle Sam. I'm going to head upstairs to practice." She stands, the wooden legs of the chair scrapping on the tile floor. "You'll be there? Tomorrow?"

"You bet. I'll be the crazy person sitting in the front row cheering obnoxiously," Sam teases.

"Oh god," she groans. "See you tomorrow." She bends to kiss his cheek.

"See you tomorrow, Katie. Sweet dreams."

Once both children are out of the room, I turn my attention to my brother with my jaw clenched.

"Seriously," I growl. "What's wrong with you?"

"Oh, calm down. They were going to find out eventually." Sam stands to pick up the last few items from the table. I follow close behind, wiping the surface with a damp rag. Scraping the last of the plates into the trash, Sam pulls out the bag from the bin and ties the top into a knot.

"That's not what I am talking about. Who's this creepy guy you have working for you who is coming in contact with my children when you aren't around?"

"First off," he holds up one finger, as if it will make his point more convincing, "I was around. I left them in the office for all of three minutes while I ran out back to grab a bag of fertilizer to drop off at Mr. Randal's place on my way home. Second," he holds up another finger, "like I said, Jay seems harmless. Third," he begins, but I stop him.

"What do you mean "seems"?"

"Jesus, Miranda." Sam runs his hands over his face, annoyed. He begins again, this time his voice laced with anger and disbelief.

"Do you really think I would hire someone who was dangerous knowing the girls are there all the time?"

"Well, no but ..."

"You have nothing to worry about."

"How can you be so sure?"

"I just have a gut feeling."

"Really? How long has he worked for you?" I ask, my body shaking with anger.

"Ah, well, he started Monday," Sam says, ducking his head.

"Monday?" I shout. I look toward the living room to make sure the girls aren't listening. "Monday?" I whisper harshly.

"Well, actually yesterday. I hired him Monday afternoon. You know I've been looking to hire more people. He came in and asked about the job. He is a big guy, Miranda. Built like an ox. I asked when he could start. He said immediately. Bada-bing," he finishes, doing some weird snap fist bump thing.

"How can you be so sure he's harmless? Dammit, Sam, don't you do some sort of background check on these people? You just hire anyone off the street?"

"Calm down. You're acting like I'm an idiot." Sam leans his weight against the counter. "The guy was a Marine or something. Those guys don't seem like the type that would do 'creepy' things." He puts air quotes around the word creepy.

"Huh," I make a noise in my throat.

"Trust me."

The seriousness of his tone and the pleading in his eye softens me. I know he loves Katelyn and Paige almost as much as I do.

"Well, I guess I will be the judge of that. I'm sure I'll meet him at some point, now that I'm running the show." I jab my elbow into his stomach.

"*Pft*, I never agreed to you running anything. I said you could work in the office," he chuckles, rubbing his side.

"Umhm."

"Oh Christ, I've created a monster," he laughs. "All right, I should get going. I'll take this out on my way," he says holding up the full trash bag. "I'll see you tomorrow night at the school," he says with one hand on the knob of the back door.

"Okay. See you then."

Chapter 10
Jace

Sitting in my truck, I narrow my eyes, attempting to block out the blinding sun as I wait for the streetlight to turn green. The country lyrics playing on the radio cause my mind to wander to Miranda. After I left Belham for the first time, a couple days after meeting Miranda, I never tried to contact her again. Within three weeks I was in basic training, and just over a year and a half later I was preparing to be deployed to Iraq. I thought about looking her up when I arrived stateside after my first tour, just to get a glimpse of the amazing things I was certain she was accomplishing, but each time I was about to something stopped me. I think there was a part of me that was afraid to see what she had made of her life, a life I could never be a part of, so I forced myself to stay away.

Staying away and not thinking about her are two different things, though. At first, it was almost sickening. I thought I was going crazy. Everywhere I looked I saw her face. Everything I did and everywhere I went she was there. We had only shared a few hours, but it didn't matter. She was embedded in me. After a while I was able to control my wandering mind a little better. Eventually, thoughts of her drifted into the back of my mind. She was still there, but she no longer consumed everything, until one day the only time I thought of her was when she invaded my dreams at night.

When I returned home from my run, the shock of seeing Miranda was almost enough to make me pack my truck and head back to South Carolina. I told myself maybe I could stay in Surfside without actually living with my mother. I'm sure I could find a place of my own, but deep in my bones I knew it wasn't what I wanted to do; it wasn't what I needed to do. No, I needed to stay.

The best way to distract myself was to keep busy, so hours later I find myself exploring town. When I was last here I didn't get to see much of this place, although I doubt I would remember much of it anyway. I have to admit it is a charming town, with winding rural roads lined with hills of green grass and fields of corn, broken up by side streets filled with modest houses. Being a Monday afternoon, the streets were relatively quiet with little traffic.

The sun is still high in the sky and a cool breeze blows. I drive up and down narrow side roads for another thirty minutes before spotting a black and red help wanted sign, just below a much larger sign reading *All Season Landscaping.* In the corner is a logo made of four small joined squares, all different colors, containing the images of a snowflake, a flower, a sun, and a leaf. Several yards away, behind a line of small trees along the embankment, I can make out a large white garage set back from a main street by a gravel driveway.

My truck kicks up a plume of dust that swirls in the air as I pull into to the dirt drive and come to a stop. Parking in front of what I suspect is an office, I kill the engine. I step out and stretch my legs, trying to work out a cramp in my thigh before heading inside. A small bell rings above the door, signaling my arrival. The office within is a small room, containing a single wooden desk in the center piled sky high with papers. A tall gray filing cabinet sits to the right next to a small window. A few framed certificates hang on the wall beside the cabinet. A large, round clock mounted above the door ticks the minutes away. On the left wall is a white door with a large window that leads to a big garage. Next to it are more frames; only these contain pictures of elaborate gardens, flowers, and what looks like a golf course. I step closer to get a better look, examining each one more closely. Whoever designed these is quite talented. I'm very impressed by the different textures and colors used in each layout.

After looking over each picture a few times, I begin to get restless as it appears no one is here. I walk to the door and peek through the window, but the dimly lit garage appears to be as vacant as the office. Deciding no one must be around, I sigh and decide to come back later. Turning on my heels, I head back to the front door when I hear ta sound behind me.

"Oh," a startled voice calls out. "Jesus, you scared the shit out of me. I didn't know anyone was here," a man says as he enters the office.

He appears to be around the same age as me, or maybe a few years older. He's wearing worn jeans, stained boots, and a green t-shirt with the same logo as on the sign outside across the front. His brown hair is covered with a tattered Red Sox cap, the edges torn and frayed from years of wear.

"Sorry about that," I begin. "I saw the help wanted sign out front and thought I'd come in and ask if the position was still available. I can come back later if now isn't a good time."

"Nah, don't worry about it. Now is perfect. I was in the middle of loading some stuff in my truck out back." He points behind him. "I'm Sam, by the way," he says, extending his right hand.

"Jace." I shake his hand and study his face for a moment. There is something oddly familiar about him, but I can't quite put my finger on what it is.

"So you're looking for a job, huh? Are you from around these parts?"

"No sir. I just moved here. I'm originally from South Carolina."

"Sir? Damn, my father must be rolling over in his grave hearing someone call me sir. Please call me Sam," he laughs. "What brings you to Massachusetts? Normally we head south, not the other way around."

"Well, my mother inherited property up here several years back. She tried to sell it once, but wasn't able to, so she now rents it out. She isn't able to come up to see to the place as often as she would like. I told her I would come and check on things for her." I rub my hand over the back of my neck, continuing, "I was recently discharged from the army and need a change of pace."

"I see." Sam nods his head, pulling open the top draw of the filing cabinet, moving folders and pulling out handfuls of paper before jamming them back in.

"Did you serve overseas?"

"Yes, sir. Three tours in total before I was discharged." I see him smirk when I say 'sir' again. I hadn't meant to, but it's so ingrained it slips from my tongue involuntarily. You can take the man out of the army, but you can't take the army out of the man.

"Damn," he says, his expression turning solemn. He closes the drawer with a metal thud, rubbing his palms on his jeans.

"Thank you." He extends his hand to me once again and I am taken aback. I look from his hand to him several times making him laugh again. "Thank you for your service."

I shake his hand, not knowing what else to do. I don't think anyone has ever thanked me for serving before, nor did I ever expect anyone to.

"Tell me, have you ever done landscaping?" Sam steps toward the cluttered desk where he continues to rustle through stacks of disheveled papers, causing a few to float to the floor. He mutters under his breath about needing a secretary and I don't think I could agree more.

"My mom used to make me mow the lawn every Saturday when I was a kid. Does that count?" I joke, but the truth is mowing lawns is the extent of my knowledge.

Sam looks up from the mess and tilts his head to the side. The corner of his mouth twitches. I can tell he is sizing me up, trying to determine if I'm the right person for the job.

"Look, I may not have a lot of experience, but I guarantee you won'tfind someone who works harder than me."

"Well, mowing lawns as a kid is a hell of a lot more experience than some of the other guys had when they started here." Sam bumps a stack of papers causing more to spill on to the floor.

"Shit." He stoops to pick up the fluttering sheets. "The hours aren't consistent. Some days are longer than others. And with fall here, we're working Saturdays to clean up leaves and winterize yards," Sam explains, crouched on the floor.

"That's no problem. I'm used to hard work and difficult hours." I shift my weight to one leg to alleviate the throb that is intensifying the longer I stand here. I don't want to give away my injury.. Despite the pain, I know I can do this job.

Sam straightens, placing the recovered mess of papers unceremoniously on the desk top. "Ah, here it is," he says, pulling a sheet of white and yellow carbon paper from a tall stack.

"Sorry about this." He waves his hands at the disaster before us. "I hate this office paperwork bullshit. Hey, you wouldn't happen to be good at filing would you?" he jokes.

"Ah," I stammer, not sure how to answer.

"No worries, Jay. I'm only kidding."

"It's Jace, sir."

"Huh?"

"My name. It's Jace. You called me Jay."

"I did?" Sam shrugs, not giving it another thought. "So, tell me how long you plan to stay in town?"

"I'm not sure, sir. I have no immediate plans to go back south."

"All right. I try to keep the guys busy during the winter. We have a few plowing contracts around town and we dig out a number of our clients as well, but the work may be sporadic. It will all depend on the weather."

"Understood."

"One last thing. When can you start?"

"Is right now too soon?" I smirk.

Sam laughs. "I like you already. Be here tomorrow at seven and let's see what you've got. I have a job at the high school I need to have done by the end of the week."

I quickly agree to meet him in the morning. I thank him once again, shake his hand, and leave. That went better than I expected.

THE SECOND VERSE

Chapter 11
Miranda

This isn't the first time I've been back in this auditorium in the last fourteen years, but each time causes goose bumps to crawl across my skin and butterflies to flutter in the pit of my stomach. Being here, seeing that stage, brings back so many great memories of a simpler time, when the world was filled with fairy tales and happily ever afters. Memories that, sometimes, I wish I could lose myself in. But tonight is not about the moments I've lost; tonight is about Katelyn's moments to come.

Paige tugs my hand, pulling me down the narrow, crowded center aisle.

"C'mon Mommy. I see Uncle Sam near the front. I just know he saved seats for us," she says, letting go of my hand and racing ahead of me, nearly knocking over someone's grandmother in the process.

"Paige, slow down," I yell after her and offer an apologetic smile to the older woman who scowls back at me. Her eyes silently tell me I should control my child. Based on her set curls and frown lines, I'm sure she raised a whole pack of children to be well behaved and mild mannered. All other kids pale in comparison. I try not to roll my eyes at her.

Finally catching up to Paige, I see Sam, who somehow managed to save two seats at the end of the fifth row for us. Sitting so close will give us a great view of the stage and every performer in the show.

The wood of the stage is worn in places, but still manages to shine under the lights. A simple heavy red curtain is the back drop for tonight's performances. At this angle I can't see what, or who, is behind the side curtains, but I know Katelyn is back there somewhere. She didn't come home from school this afternoon. Instead she stayed here, to practice and to help some of the other performers prepare. Knowing her plans, I made sure I gave her a hug this morning before leaving the house.

"I'm so proud of you," I said, kissing her on the forehead. "You're going to be amazing."

"Yeah, I got this," she said with a small smile.

Unlike me during high school, Katelyn hasn't spent much time performing in front of other people. Besides me, Paige, Sam and Claire, no one else has heard her play or sing. Even though she's a member of the drama club, she mainly works on set design. I doubt even her best friend, Abby, has heard her sing. Tonight is sort of her public debut and she was calmly nervous this morning.

Settling into my seat, I set my small clutch purse in my lap and turn to my brother, noticing he is alone. "Hey Sam. Where's Claire?"

"She planned to come, but there was an emergency at the end of her shift and she wasn't able to leave on time. She's going to try to make it before Katie's performance, but told me not to save her a seat."

"Oh no." I frown. "That's too bad. I hope she makes it in time."

"Uncle Sam, Mommy said we are going to Big Sal's for dinner. You wanna come?" Paige bounces her legs back and forth under the seat.

"Big Sal's? You know I can't say no to that, P," Sam says with a wink and a little too much enthusiasm.

"Woohoo," Paige yells, arms thrown above her head in triumph, earning us a few sideways glances.

"Paige, *shh*," I say, my eyes darting to see if anyone is staring in our direction.

"Ah, let her be. She's fine," Sam says dismissively.

Just as I open my mouth to argue, the lights dim and a short middle aged man comes out on stage.

"Welcome everyone to this year's annual talent show. I'm Kenneth Bollen. By day I am the music director here at Belham High, but tonight I'm your host. The kids have worked very hard over the last several weeks, and I'm certain tonight's show is going to blow you away." He pauses for applause. "So what do you say we get this party started? To begin tonight's show, help me welcome Trisha Lowe."

One by one the students come out on the stage giving the crowd their best effort. Some play instruments; violins to saxophones. Some dance ballet to hip hop. There is a comedian, and boy and girl who perform a scene from Romeo and Juliet. Some of the kids are really good and others not so much, but they all give it their best shot.

As the applause begins to die down after the latest performance, Mr. Bollen comes back out on stage carrying a wooden stool. Setting it down in the center of the stage, he turns to the audience.

"And now, for our final performance of the evening, please give a warm round of applause to Katelyn Cross."

He sets the microphone in its stand, in front of the stool, and turns toward the side of the stage. I follow his line of sight and see Katelyn step out from behind the red curtain. The audience cheers politely, but no one is as loud as the three of us in the fifth row.

I notice Mr. Bollen squeeze Katelyn's elbow has she passes by and a small part of me wishes I could offer her the same reassurance. Reaching the stool, she hops up and scoots back, nestling her guitar on her lap. Her eyes scan the crowd. When they finally land on me, I give her two thumbs up and smile broadly. Her face brightens just a little. I see her chest rise as she draws in a big breath and slowly fall as she releases it. Our eye contact is broken when she fixes her sights on the strings, but I never take my eyes from my girl.

Softly, she begins to strum the opening notes. I recognize the tune immediately and suck in a sharp breath. It's a song I have played many times, alone at night when I have a bad day, when I just want to forget and find the ability to move on and live, instead of simply surviving.

Why on earth would she choose this song for her first performance? "Gravity" by Sara Bareilles is a powerful, soulful, and emotional song, but aside from the beautiful lyrics, Ms. Bareilles is an amazing vocalist. It's extremely daring to try to perform one of her songs. I'm suddenly very nervous on how this will turn out for Katelyn.

Soon all my worries seem misplaced when Katelyn opens her mouth and begins to sing. Her voice is soft during the opening, but as she approaches the chorus, the crescendo builds and builds until it explodes. My body goes cold and a shiver races down my spine, shaking me to my core. My lips tremble and my eyes well with tears. I try to swallow the lump in my throat, but it won't budge. I can feel the weight of Sam's eyes on me, but I don't dare look away. She is absolutely beautiful. Mesmerizing might be a better word. I've heard her sing a million times, but this, this is like nothing I've ever seen.

Katelyn reaches the most dramatic portion of the song and I hold my breath. She places her hand against the strings so the only sound that can be heard is her powerful voice. Time stands still as she holds the note in perfect pitch. I can no longer hold back the tears. One by one they spill over my lids and stream down my cheeks. Sam reaches across Paige and squeezes my left hand. His hold is strong and comforting, but I can also tell by the small tremor in his thumb as it brushes the back of my knuckles that he is emotional, too.

Katelyn resumes playing and finishes the remainder of the song. As the final note hangs in the air she lifts her head, tucking her long black hair behind her ear, which had fallen to cover part of her face. She looks out at the dazed crowd. No one moves. No one speaks. The entire auditorium has been stunned into a frozen silence. Worry flashes in Katelyn's eyes, but quickly morphs into shock as the audience thaws and a thunderous applause shakes the walls. One by one people stand, showing her the adoration her performance deserves.

I force myself to stand on shaky legs. I wipe my face, so she won't see my tears. Next to me Paige whoops and hollers. Sam beams has he claps and whistles. What I can only describe as pride clenches around my chest. That's my baby. My little girl has brought this room to its feet.

Katelyn waves to the crowd and offers a little bow before quickly leaving the stage. Mr. Bollen comes out to thank everyone who performed and the family and friends who came out to support them. Even though each person was here to cheer on one person or another, the murmurings as people file out and spill into the cafeteria are filled with Katelyn's name.

Inside the cafeteria the tables and chairs have been folded and stacked to make space in the center of the large room. Handmade posters for the upcoming pep rally and yearbook sales line the walls. It seems some things never change. Sam, Paige, and I find an empty section near the back wall, under a large round clock, to wait for Katelyn. Sam pulls me against is chest and whispers in my ear.

"You should be proud."

My throat is still tight with emotion, so I don't dare speak. Instead, I nod my head against my chest.

"Hey guys. I've been looking everywhere for you three. This place is a mad house," a familiar voice says from behind us.

"Hey," Sam says, releasing me after giving me one last squeeze. He places his arm around Claire's shoulders, kissing her on the temple. "You made it."

"I did, but by the time I got here the show was over." She frowns. "How was it? How did Katelyn do?"

"It was great Aunt Claire! You should've seen her. She made mommy cry," Paige explains.

THE SECOND VERSE

Claire's dark sympathetic eyes dart to mine. Claire and my brother have been together for nearly ten years. She has seen it all and been with us through everything. She is family in every sense of the word, even if, for some bizarre reason, my stupid brother doesn't put a ring on her finger to make it official.

When she and my brother started dating, I thought they were such an odd pair. My brother is tall, maybe six feet, and lean. His hair is not as dark as mine, more of a light brown, but we have similar bright blue eyes. Lord knows he used those sparkling blues more than once to get what he wanted. When we were kids he was thin, awkward and lanky, but sometime around the age of sixteen he began to fill out.

Claire, on the other hand, is short and petite. Her mother's Asian features blend with her father's Italian genes to create a beautiful combination. Dark narrow eyes are framed with lush lashes. Her high cheek bones and delicate nose make her stunning.

As pretty as she is on the outside, it's her heart that won me over *and* her ability to put up with my brother's antics. When they're together, there is no denying how perfect they are for each other. They balance one another well. After I had Katelyn, most of my friends from high school vanished. It wasn't until Sam started dating Claire that I realized how much I missed having a girlfriend around. I might love her almost as much as my brother.

"She was great," I say, trying to force a smile. Hopefully she will let it go until we aren't surrounded by a hundred people. Lucky for me, Paige offers a distraction.

"Aunt Claire, Uncle Sam is coming to dinner with us. You wanna come too?"

I turn away from the three of them to stand on my tiptoes, trying to find Katelyn in the crowd, but I am too short to see very far. Dozens of people mingle and talk, cheering as their child finally finds their way to them. I'm debating standing on a chair to see over the crowd when Sam calls out.

"There she is." He points to the left. "Katelyn!" he yells waving his hands over his head trying to get her attention.

She must have seen him, because within less than a minute she pushes her way through the crowd and bounces into my arms.

"Oh my god, Mom that was ... I can't believe it. It was ... it was ... Oh my god," she squeals and stutters, squeezing me once more.

"Baby, you were so good. I knew you would be amazing, but that in there," I nod my head back, "was pure magic." I kiss her forehead.

"You were so good, better than everyone else," Paige chimes in, matter of

69

fact.

"Paige," I warn, but she isn't intimidated. She just shrugs and turns back to Claire to talk about what dessert she wants to order tonight.

"Hey Katie, you killed it tonight," Sam says pulling Katelyn into a side hug and kissing her on the temple. "These are for you," he says presenting her with a bouquet of yellow and white lilies.

"Thanks, Uncle Sam. They're beautiful." She sticks her noise into the flowers and inhales deeply. She wraps her arm around his middle and leans her head on his chest.

Claire apologizes to Katelyn for missing her performance and asks for an encore when we get home. I'm just about to suggest we leave to go to dinner when I hear someone speak behind us.

"Hey, Katelyn."

I move to the side to peer around Sam and see a boy standing just a few feet away with his hands tucked into the pockets of his jeans. There is a shimmer of nervousness in his pale green eyes. He's a good looking kid. His dirty blonde hair is cut short on the sides and longer on the top, falling across his brow. A light shadow dusts his jaw line. If I had to guess I would say he was a year or two older than Katelyn.

Katelyn pulls away from Sam and turns to face her admirer.

"Oh, hi Matt," she says, her cheeks turning pink.

"Hi."

"Hi," she whispers.

Oh boy. This is not good. My baby likes this boy. Like, like-likes him.

Sam's easy going demeanor vanishes in a flash and his expression is immediately replaced with something more stern. His eyes dart to mine, giving me a look that screams, "What the hell?" and I ignore him. I mean, seriously, it was bound to happen someday.

Katelyn is a good kid.

Then again, I was a good kid.

What was I doing at her age?

Shit.

"I just wanted to tell you I thought you were amazing," Matt says. "This is for you."

He presents her a single yellow rose, the kind that looks like the edges were dipped in red paint. Katelyn's face lights up like a Christmas tree. She takes the lilies she had been clutching, the ones her uncle gave her, and blindly hands them to me before gently taking the flower from Matt.

"Thanks," she says quietly, her cheeks instantly changing from pink to red.

Sam clears his throat loudly, causing Matt to lift his eyes in Sam's direction, which breaks Katelyn free of her lovesick haze.

"Sorry. Matt, this is my Uncle Sam, Aunt Claire, and my mother," Katelyn says pointing to each one of us. "Guys, this is Matt. We're in the same art history class," she explains.

Matt extends his hand to each of us. Claire and I quickly shake it but not Sam. No, of course he has to be difficult. Sam holds Matt's hand just a tad longer than is polite and by the way the poor kid flexes his hand now, I'm certain he squeezed it harder than necessary. I can't help but roll my eyes.

"Well, I didn't mean to interrupt," Matt says nodding his head toward Sam,. "I guess I'll see you tomorrow."

Katelyn watches him walk away, her eyes fixed on the spot where he had disappeared into the crowd.

"Ew. Why were you looking at that boy like that?" Paige asks in complete disgust.

"Shut up Paige," Katelyn snaps back. Paige, not threatened, sticks out her tongue. Claire quickly steps in and asks Paige something about school, defusing the situation.

"So, you really thought I was good Mom?" Katelyn asks, still holding the single flower against her chest. Her face suddenly looks much younger than her fourteen years. She looks worried, like all her hopes and dreams hang on my response.

"Of course baby, I couldn't be more proud. You sounded so good."

"Really?"

I nod.

"I've heard you sing that song when you're sad and miss dad. I just wanted to sing something tonight for the both of you."

I'm at a loss for words. My eyes dart from her to Sam. I wasn't sure if he had been listening, but based on the way his eyes are bulging out of his head I would say he was. I look toward Paige, but luckily she's not paying attention to us.

"I miss him too," she says quietly.

"Oh baby, he'd be so proud of you," I whisper pulling her into my chest and kissing her hair.

"I love you, Mom."

"To the moon and back."

"Mommy, are you crying?" Paige asks her face pinched with concern.

"No sweetheart," I sniffle, quickly wiping under my eyes and trying to smile.

"Hey P, how about you and Katie ride with me to Big Sal's?" Sam interrupts, coming to my rescue.

"Woohoo," Paige cheers, jumping up and down in place.

"I'm going to go grab my stuff from backstage, Uncle Sam. I'll meet you by the front door," Katelyn says, pulling away from me and also trying to wipe the emotion from her face.

I mouth 'thank you' to Sam before kissing both my girls on the forehead and watching the four of them disappear in to the crowd. Once they're out of sight, I wiggle my way through the people toward a set of double doors I know lead outside. Bursting through the exit, the cool night air hits the moisture of the tears streaming down my face, stinging my cheeks.

Once outside, I can no longer stop the sob that claws at my chest and it breaks free. My hand clutches the cold brick wall for support, but it's not strong enough to hold me. In a matter of seconds I'm on my knees, bent over at the middle, crying uncontrollably.

My beautiful little girl is no longer little, but a young woman who is wise beyond her years. It's easy to forget sometimes that Adam was a big part of her life, perhaps bigger than he was in mine. He would've loved to have seen Katelyn up on stage tonight. He would've been the first on his feet screaming so loudly he could have been heard miles away. When she found us after the show, he would have swept her up in his arms, kissed her cheek, and told her how proud he was. My cracked heart breaks a little more knowing none of that is possible; not only for Katelyn, but for Paige, too.

After several long, excruciating minutes, I calm my sobbing to a silent sniffle. Pulling in long, deep breaths I try to calm my erratic heartbeat. I slump from my knees and sit back on the concrete sidewalk. Tilting my head upward, I study the darkening sky as dusk gives way to night. A light breeze flirts with a strand of hair that has fallen from my loose ponytail. I wrap my arms around my chest, warding off the chill.

My mind begins to wanders back in time. Of course my first few thoughts turn to Adam, as they often do, but eventually they meander to the night by the lake all those years ago. Back to the night I met Jace. It must be the way my mind played tricks on me in the park, but ever since then I can't seem to get him out of my mind.

My phone chirps in my bag, pulling me back to reality. I rummage through all of the loose junk in my purse and finally feel the sleek surface of my phone. Pulling it out, I see almost a half hour has passed since I left Sam inside and the text is from him.

R u OK? If you don't come soon the girls will b eating dessert for dinner. U know I cant say no to P. ;)

I wipe my cheeks again to insure I have cleared all the remnants of my latest breakdown and push myself from the ground. My hands dust off the dirt from my jeans and I cross the dimly lit parking lot when it hits me- the rolling feeling in my stomach. The same nervousness I had in the park. I scan the now nearly empty parking lot, picking up the pace. I glance back a few times, but I don't see anything or anyone unusual. Hitting the key fob, my car lights blink and the doors unlock in time for me to quickly slip inside. I start the engine, turn on the head lights, and put the car in drive.

As I pull out and slowly make my way toward the exit, my heart skips a beat when I think I see a shadow standing near the entrance of the school. The silhouette has wide shoulders tapering to a narrow waist and is all male. His arms hang loosely at his sides. I can't see the man's face, but the hairs on the back of my neck tell me he is staring right at me. Turning right out on to the street, butterflies explode in my stomach. It could be nothing, simply my mind playing tricks on me, but I'm too tired to deal with anything else tonight.

Chapter 12
Miranda
Then

Last night was perfect. I don't think I could've planned a better evening if I tried, but what made it awesome was I didn't organize any of it. Adam, in an unexpected act of spontaneity, surprised me by setting up the whole thing, an entire night just for us, just me and him.

He arranged for Katelyn to spend the night with Sam and his girlfriend, Claire, as if he needed to ask them. Sam practically worships the ground his niece walks on and everyone knows it, including her. She knows if she bats her dark lashes and gives him 'the look', her uncle will give her anything she asks for. Sam spoils her rotten.

I was shocked when Adam first told me he had planned for us to go to dinner at a restaurant we probably couldn't afford and a movie. I know for some people that may not sound like the most romantic night in the world, but for us it was perfect. Last night reminded me of when we were in high school, back when life was simpler, and we used to go to movies all the time. Back then, there were some months when we would go once a week, waiting in line to be the first to see the latest new release. Last night wasn't about that, though. It was about having some time alone to reconnect, and it was amazing.

It's been several stressful months since Adam and I had a night out. At least since before we moved into this small two bedroom townhouse six months ago. After years of living in my father's house, we finally made one giant step as adults and took over the lease from Adam's sister, Alisha, when she moved to Florida to take care of their mother who had suffered a stroke a few months earlier. Sadly, my mother-in-law passed away in three months' time.

It was hard being so far away when Alisha needed us. There were so many things that needed to be done, and Alisha was struggling to do them all by herself. Adam and I couldn't afford for all three of us to travel, and the thought of bringing Katelyn on a four hour flight made my skin crawl, so Adam ended up going alone. He helped his sister arrange the funeral, and then stayed a little longer to resolve a few legal matters.

When he returned home, he quickly lost himself in work. With the down turn in the economy, there was a declining need for the dozen mortgage brokers who worked in his office. Adam worked hard to keep his job, but within a month of returning from Florida, he was let go.

Unemployment on top of the grief of losing his mother was a dreadful combination. Adam was a miserable mess. He spent countless nights seated at the kitchen table, hunched over piles of paperwork, checkbook and calculator nearby. Worrying about our finances became emotionally and physically draining. More than one evening ended with us fighting over what we were going to do next. Even though it's the 21st century, deep down Adam is a complete caveman and feels the need to be the breadwinner. I tried to be supportive, but I also began applying for positions myself, quietly of course.

Soon after, Adam and Sam, who was also between jobs, decided to open their own landscaping business. It started off small, with the two of them mowing lawns and doing regular maintenance to earn a little extra money while they looked for other jobs. However, as they got into it, they both realized they really liked getting their hands dirty. Within six months they expanded from manual labor to designing client's gardens. Soon they became so busy, they actually began looking to hire additional people to help them.

It's nice to finally see Adam doing something he seems to love, not something he feels obligated to do. Lately, he has been happier than he has been in a long time, but as much as he likes what he does, I have been wondering if he has been working too much. I've noticed he's been a little more tired than usual, and he has lost some weight. But then again, with the amount of physical activity he's doing, I'm sure I would be tired and shed a few pounds, too.

Last night, after the movie, we walked along the river. It was nice to see him relaxed. The warmth of the summer was still in the air, but the nip of fall is just at the fringes. We walked hand and hand, talking about everything. It was as if we hadn't spoken to each other in months, even though we have coffee together every morning. I told him about my new job at the advertising agency. Answering phones and filing is not something I ever saw myself doing, but now that Katelyn is in school full time, I'm happy to have something to keep me busy. Adam told me about the new contract he and Sam were hoping to secure, to design and plant the new gardens that were part of the expansion at the arboretum. If they landed this job, it would be their largest to date.

Now, leaning against the bathroom vanity, remembering the excitement in his voice makes me smile. Catching my reflection in the mirror, I lean closer. My skin is glowing, my cheeks are flush, and my eyes shine. I pull my hair from its elastic and run my fingers through my black locks. I look well rested and relaxed, which is a true testament to how amazing the night really was. To say we reconnected more than once would be a fair statement.

The alarm on my phone goes off, reminding me why I'm hiding away in the bathroom while Adam sleeps awhile longer. Quickly silencing my phone, I tiptoe closter to the white wooden cabinet in the corner where I left the little plastic stick that hopefully holds the next stepping stone in our lives.

This time I wasn't sick to my stomach taking the test. This time I am ready. We are ready. We are prepared. We aren't children preparing to have a child. This time we will be beginning this journey together. This time will be different.

I cannot contain myself when I see the two pink lines in the little window. Positive. It's positive.

Tears run down my face and I squeal, swiping the test off the counter. I rush out of the bathroom and toward our bedroom across the hall. I nearly fall as I stumble inside ready to pounce on Adam, no longer caring if he is asleep or not. As I push the door open however, I stop dead in my tracks.

Lying on the bed, curled up in a ball, is Adam. He grips the sheets in his fist so tightly, his knuckles turn white. His face is pinched with so much pain, his brows almost touch his cheeks. I'm not sure how long I stand there frozen with fear; maybe seconds, maybe an hour. It's Adam's agonizing, gut wrenching scream that snaps me out of my daze.

I rush to his side, the plastic pregnancy test falling from my hand, and grab his arm trying to shake him, not really sure what to do. His muscles are coiled so tightly beneath is shirt I can barely nudge him.

"Adam! What's wrong?" I ask, but he doesn't answer. He doesn't even look at me, but instead groans again, less violently this time.

"Sweetheart? Adam, talk to me. What is it?" Still there's no response.

His posture doesn't change. After another minute of begging him to answer me, I give up and grab the phone off the nightstand. My fingers shake so badly I am barely able to dial 911.

"911. What's your emergency?"

"There's something wrong with my husband. We need an ambulance," I choke, trying to keep the tears at bay.

After managing to give the dispatcher my information, I mindlessly listen as she tries to reassure me everything will be all right. She waits on the line with me for five minutes before the paramedics show up. I try to soothe Adam, but I'm not even sure he knows I'm here. He's lost somewhere inside the pain, and I stumble trying to pull him out.

Chapter 13
Miranda

The sky above is crystal blue and there's not a cloud to be seen. A rainstorm rolled through last night clearing the last of the humidity and leaving behind a perfect fall day. Autumn used to be my favorite season; the weather is still relatively warm, but there's a crispness that nips at the night. Not to mention the color of the leaves changing from vibrant green to all different shades of yellow and orange. Recent years have tainted my view of the world during the fall, but I still have to admit it's pretty.

I've been planning this day with the girls for days, ever since I realized neither of them had activities scheduled for this weekend, which is extremely rare. I wanted to do something fun, but most of all I just wanted to spend the day with them. I feel like we spend so much time rushing from here to there that we never really spend time *together*.

Katelyn and Paige were up at the crack of dawn. A cease fire was called, postponing my usual morning battle to get them fed and dressed on time, and Paige chatted animatedly about what she wanted to see at the zoo while stuffing her little face with cereal. The radio played our favorite songs during our car ride, and we sang along loudly and danced obnoxiously in our seats, laughing and giggling.

The girls' cooperation continued once we arrived at the zoo. Exhibit after exhibit they laughed and joked. Katelyn helped Paige stand on the railings to see into the gray wolf habitat. Paige shared her favorite blue cotton candy with Katelyn with no intervention from me. Everything was perfect, simply perfect, until a few seconds ago when Meghan Trainor's "All About the Bass" was drowned out by an annoying sound that could only mean one thing.

"Great," I mutter under my breath.

Slowly, I maneuver the car to the side of the road and throw on my hazards before killing the engine. I'm not familiar with this area and normally wouldn't stop somewhere I don't know, but right now I don't have much of a choice. The street is lined with houses every few hundred feet. In the distance, nestled beneath tall pine tree sand just beyond a stone wall along the curb, there is a small playground. Three simple swings hang from a metal A-frame. The area beneath the swings in covered in pebbles with small wayward, clumps of grass shooting up here and there. A platform leading to a set of narrow hang bars is set to the left of the swings, as well as a dome shaped set of bars behind that. It's nothing over the top, not like at the local elementary school, but it seems to suit its purpose.

"Mommy, what's wrong?" Paige asks from the seat behind me.

"We have a flat tire, don't we?" Katelyn asks from the opposite side of the backseat.

"Great. We're never going to get to get home to play *Minecraft*," Paige says, her voice cracking and tears welling up in her eyes.

"Geez. Calm down will ya. I just need to change the tire," I say, looking back at them in the rearview mirror.

"Do you even know how to change a tire?" Paige asks, like it's the most absurd thing she has ever heard. I can hear her rolling her eyes.

"Sure I do. What do you think I am?" I try my best not to sound concerned, but the truth is I have no idea how to do this. How hard can it be?

"Really? My friend Jackson says girls can't do things like change tires or fix cars, because it's stuff boys do," Paige says. "Is that true, Mommy?"

I turn in my seat to look at her. "No, that is not true. Girls can do anything boys can do," I reassure her and maybe myself, too.

"That's what I thought. I told him boys and girls are the same."

I turn to Katelyn. "Katelyn, why don't you take Paige to that playground? I'll have the tire changed in a few minutes and then we'll go home."

"Okay. C'mon Paige," Katelyn says unbuckling her seat belt. She slides out of the car, rounds the back, and helps Paige out. Paige slips her arms into her pale blue jacket before turning toward the playground.

"Woohoo. Wanna watch me do the monkey bars?" I hear Paige ask as she takes off running. Fingers crossed she doesn't hurt herself – again.

Several minutes later, after emptying all of the junk out of the trunk and spreading it out on the side of the road for the world to see, I find the jack and the tire rod-thingy. After I secure my hair back in to a loose ponytail, I crouch down next to the passenger side front tire and peer under the vehicle, trying to find the right spot to put the jack. Everywhere I look seems to be a bad spot. Who designed this tiny jack anyway? It seems ridiculous that this little thing is strong enough to hold up this entire car.

When I think I've found the right spot, I set the jack underneath the car and, using the lever, begin to lift the car. Once the car is in the air, I take a step back. A proud smile spreads across my face.

"I got this," I say to myself.

Wiping the sweat from my brow with the back of my hand, I shed my tattered but comfortable UMass sweatshirt, one I've owned for more than a decade, and roll up the sleeve of my thin, very worn, beige, long sleeve t-shirt. I refocus on the tire and begin to loosen the bolts. Well, I begin to throw my body weight against the metal wrench, even bouncing up and down, but not a single bolt moves.

Several minutes tick by. In the end my arms and shoulders are sore and none of the bolts are loose. Taking a step back, I look down at my grease covered palms and my dirt covered jeans. The pride I felt a short while ago is gone. Instead, tears of frustration, defeat, and self-pity quickly build and begin to trickle down my face. Moments like this make me feel useless. Just one more thing I should've learned to do at some point in my life, but never thought of it until it was too late. Sam is never going to let me live this down.

I roughly swipe the rouge tears from my cheeks. Tipping my head to the sky, my eyes slip shut, and I draw in a deep breath trying to calm down. All I wanted was one nice afternoon, out of the house, with my girls – together – like a normal family. Was that too much to ask?

"Excuse me ma'am, do you need help?"

A smooth, rich voice startles me and my whole body freezes. Muscles tense, teeth clench, lungs refuse to exhale, eyes snap wide open. A lump the size of my fist lodges in my throat. A swarm of butterflies takes up residence in my stomach and flutter to and fro. I don't turn to see who is behind me. I don't need to. I would recognize that voice anywhere. It's a voice I've committed to memory. A voice I have tried to forget, but failed. Given my current state, for a split second, I believe I may be hallucinating. However, a moment later, when I hear the sound of gravel crunching under the weight of someone's shoe, I know he is there.

"Ma'am, is everything all right? I didn't mean to startle you, but do you need some help?" he repeats.

I close my eyes and attempt to swallow the knot in my throat. Satisfied my tears have stopped and I've regained a small amount of composure, I turn around. I can't stop the small gasp that escapes my lips when I'm greeted with a pair of milk chocolate eyes I thought I would never see again. Eyes that have haunted my dreams since the incident in the park earlier this week.

I think I hear him suck in a harsh breath, but with the roar of my heartbeat in my ears I can't be sure.

"Miranda." He whispers my name in a tone that can only be described as reverence.

My eyes trace the lines of his body, from his black work boots, to a pair of dark wash jeans that fit perfectly across his hips, up to a pale green t-shirt that compliments his olive skin tone and dark features. His wide frame stretches the fabric, making the fit almost sinful. He's big, bigger than he was all those years ago.

Once my eyes travel to his face I find the corner of his mouth pulled up and a twinkle in his eyes, which are shaded from the sun by a tattered tan baseball cap.

"Enjoying the view?" he jokes, breaking my trance.

I roll my eyes, but my cheeks flame with heat. I nervously tug at my sleeve, suddenly very aware of my appearance. I wish I had spent an extra five minutes picking out my outfit this morning. Not that I have many options, but I'm sure I could have come up with something better than my ripped jeans and torn shirt.

How embarrassing.

"Jace," I breathe, trying out the sound of his name on my lips.

Shockingly it feels ... really good. Like I was meant to speak his name. The thought scares me. My heart drops into the pit of my stomach, weighed down by guilt, and beats wildly.

"Wh ...What are you doing here," I stutter, crossing my arms over my chest.

"It's nice to see you, too," he teases, but his faint smile is forced.

"I'm sorry." Releasing a puff of breath, I blow my bangs out of my eyes. "It's just I ... I didn't know you were here. In Belham, I mean."

He nods. "I actually moved here a couple weeks ago. I am staying in my grandmother's old house."

"What? That can't be. An older woman has been living there for years." I should know. I live right next door.

"Sandra?" he asks. I nod. "She moved out at the beginning of the

September. She moved to Kansas to be closer to her daughter and new grandson," Jace explains.

That was almost a month ago. How could I not notice her little blue car was no longer in the driveway? Shit, I guess I won't be joining the neighborhood watch anytime soon.

"So, what seems to be the problem?" Jace asks, stepping closer to peer around me.

"I have a flat tire," I point to the deflated tire and contraption holding the car up, "and apparently I am completely helpless and can't change it on my own," I mutter under my breath.

Jace's eyes move from my face, to my car, and back again. Taking two steps, he closes the space between us. I knew he was tall, but standing this close I remember just how tall. He is easily six inches taller than I am at five-seven. I watch him closely, finding it impossible to take my eyes off of him. His lips thin into a tight line and there is no mistaking the ticking of the small muscles in his jaw. If I didn't know any better, I would think he was mad about something.

"Not being able to change a tire does not make you helpless. In fact, I would bet every penny I have you are anything but."

He raises his hand toward my face. The movement is swift, only a fraction of a second, but I see it in slow motion. I suck in a breath, my body stiffening, as a brace myself for the contact. He must notice the shift in my stance, for as quickly as his raised his hand, it drops to his side.

"You have a little something right here," he says, swiping his index finger against his own cheek.

Heat creeps up my neck to my cheeks again. Jesus, what is wrong with me? Blushing like a schoolgirl. Seriously?

"Thanks," I mutter, rubbing my face with my left hand. Sure enough, there are remnants of black grease on my fingers. Brushing my hand on my jeans, I sneak a peek to my right to make sure the girls are all right. I see Paige dangling from the bars by her knees and Katelyn laughing close by at something she said.

Jace makes a humming noise deep in his throat before squatting near the side of my car, diverting my attention from my daughters. He turns his baseball cap backwards and begins to examine the tire and my handiwork. He wiggles the jack side to side, cranking the handle a few more times. Then he turns his attention to the lug nut I couldn't loosen. Of course, one hard jerk and he has the first one free. The rest quickly follow and are tossed into a small pile. Standing, he lifts the tire free and sets it on the ground. The whole time I am mesmerized by the way his body moves, the flexing and stretching of his tight muscles. It has been so long since ...

"Pop your trunk," he says.

"Huh?" I ask like a damn fool.

"For the spare. It should be in the trunk." I stare at him for a heartbeat before complying.

"Hmm."

"Is 'hmm' good or bad?" I ask, trying to peer around him.

Jace looks up, squinting in the sunlight. Faint lines frame the corner of his eyes and crease his forehead. The light dances in his eyes, making the gold flecks shimmer.

"Well, your spare is missing. Did you have a flat recently?"

Like a deer caught in headlights, I just look at him. I search my memory for the last time I had a flat tire, but don't remember ever having one. Slowly, I shake my head.

"Well, it looks like we aren't changing the tire after all," Jace says, placing a few of the discarded items back inside the trunk.

Tears begin to well up in my eyes again.

Can't anything be simple?

"The good news is it looks like this tire can be repaired," he points toward the ground, "and there doesn't appear to be any damage to the rim. You must not have driven on the flat for too long. That's good." He slams the trunk and turns to me. I swipe the moisture from my face, but it's too late.

"Hey, now. Why are you crying?" His voice softens. "Please don't cry. We can have this fixed in no time."

"Shit. I'm going to have to have it towed. I wonder how much that is going to be," I ramble under my breath before his words sink in. "What do you mean 'we'?" My brows pinch together with confusion. I must have misheard him.

"Well, I'm not about to leave you here alone on the side of the road. Where were you headed? I could give you a ride," he says. I swear I hear the tone of his voice change to sound a little less gruff and a little more optimistic.

"What? No ... Um ..." I stammer. "Thank you for the offer, but I can get a ride."

That's a lie. With Sam and Claire out of town this afternoon attending her best friend's wedding I'm stuck, but I'll figure something out. I always do.

"Why do you need to find a ride when I'm standing right here offering to take you wherever you need to go?" Jace stuffs his hands into the front pockets of his jeans.

"It's very kind of you to offer, but I don't want to impose," I say, trying my best to brush him off without coming off rude. Never in a million years would I have envisioned myself talking to Jace Harper again, never mind turning down his offer.

"Miranda, I never say things I don't mean. Right now, I'm offering to give you a ride and I want to help. I'm not asking."

Damn.

Releasing a heavy sigh, I concede. "I was actually on my way home from the zoo," I say, feeling an uncomfortable heat rush to my face.

"The zoo." He tries but fails to hide the amusement in his voice.

"Yes, the zoo," I laugh nervously. "I spent most the morning and part of this afternoon there." I pause for a moment, debating if I should elaborate further. If he's going to take us home, it's only a matter of minutes before he learns about Katelyn and Paige.

My voice lowers as I explain. "I took my daughters. It's one our favorite places." I lower my eyes to stare down at the flat tire, but not before seeing Jace's eyes widen.

"Your daughters?" he asks, failing to hide the shock in his voice. I glance up in time to his eyes dart down to my left hand.

I nod and can't stop the small smile that forms on my lips. "Yes, my daughters, Katelyn and Paige." I point, toward the girls who are playing several yards away.

Paige giggles while Katelyn pushes her on the swing. My heart swells at the sight. I'm happy to see them getting along. I worry about their relationship the older Katelyn gets and the more pronounced the age difference between them becomes. Soon they won't have much in common.

The sound of Jace clearing his throat brings me back from my thoughts. He rocks back and forth from heel to toe. It's almost like he has too much nervous energy and cannot stand still. It reminds me that, even though our night will be forever etched in my mind, I know very little about him. That night on the dock there was an air of confidence around him. I wouldn't believe his current demeanor were possible if I wasn't seeing it myself.

"All right, let's go," Jace says, interrupting my thoughts.

"What?" I stutter.

"I said let's go. I'll take the three of you home. It's no trouble, really." He shrugs like it is no big deal, but the tightness in his voice isn't convincing and my unease returns.

"Jace. It's really kind of you to offer, but really, it's Okay. I'm going to call someone to change this tire and then we'll be on our way. No worries. I'm sure you have more exciting things to do this afternoon. Thank you, though." I move toward the passenger side door to retrieve my cell phone from inside the car.

Jace takes one step toward me, closing the distance between us by half, and places his hand on the top of the door, stopping me from opening it. Suddenly I feel warm, warmer than I should feel in the cool autumn air.

"It wasn't a request, Miranda. Now get the girls and I'll take you home." His shoulders and arms tense. The strength of his voice weakens my resolve. This time Jace doesn't hesitate to tuck a piece of fallen hair behind my ear. Taking a step back, he stuffs his hands back into his pockets and shifts his weight to his left leg.

I stare at him for a moment before he lifts is brow, silently daring me to argue further.

"Okay," I concede breathlessly.

Breaking free of my stupor, I turn toward the park. Hopping over a fallen section of the stonewall, I walk up dirt path that leads to the swing set.

"Hey, Mom. Who's the guy with the sweet truck?" Katelyn asks nodding her chin toward the street.

Looking behind me, I watch Jace pace back and forth near the side of my car. Even from this distance I notice him limp and instantly my heart drops, wondering how he hurt himself checking under my car. I hadn't really paid attention to his vehicle before, but now my eyes hurt to look at it, partly because it's so beautiful compared to my piece of junk, and partly because the shine reflecting off the pristine paint job. Just looking at his Jeep makes me feel uncomfortable and further confuses me about why he is still waiting for me.

"He's my ..." I pause turning my attention back to the girls and thinking of what I should call him. What do you call someone you have only spent a few hours with, but have spent years thinking about? An acquaintance? No, that sounds too informal. I may not know much about him, but he is more than an acquaintance.

"He's my friend, Jace." My voice comes out strange, a little choked, when I say his name. Paige doesn't give it much thought, but I see the corner of Katelyn's mouth twitch and her eyes narrow.

"Did your friend fix our car Mommy?" Paige asks, pumping her legs back and forth, swinging higher and higher.

"No, not yet, but Jace," I point, "has offered to take us home. Is that Okay?"

Katelyn looks from Jace to me and back. Her eyes glimmer with mischief, but she gives me her best non-committal look. Paige, on the other hand nods her little head and smiles brightly. Pumping her legs twice more she launches herself from the swing and lands at my feet.

"Jesus, Paige, you are going to be the death of me, I swear."

"Is Jace your friend from work?" Paige asks not skipping a beat.

I glance toward the road. Jace is still standing near my car, but now his back is facing us, offering me a view of his glorious backside. *Oh god, where did that thought come from?*

I look into Paige's waiting face. "No. Jace and I knew each other when we were younger."

She smiles brightly. "Did you know boys and girls can be friends without being boyfriend and girlfriend?" She acts like it's the most profound concept. "We call them 'friend-boys'." Out of the corner of my eye I see Katelyn smirk and roll her eyes.

"No, I did know. I think that is a great description. I like it," I say, making her smile wider. I lower my voice to just above a stern whisper. "Now you are to be on your best behavior, do you hear me? Please and thank you. Jace didn't have to offer to take us, so please be extra nice. Got it?" I ask, looking at each of them and giving them my perfected 'I'm serious' look. Immediately, both nod their heads in agreement. I say a tiny prayer that they listen to me this one time.

Together, the three of us walk back to the car; Paige holding my hand and Katelyn following close behind. Katelyn helps me grab a few things out of the back seat. I told Paige to stay near me, but of course, before I know it, she wanders near where Jace is standing along the curb. I quickly scurry over to her, wanting to be there when they meet for the first time. I never know what will come out of her seven -year -old mouth.

I catch up to her just in time to hear her say, "Hi, my name is Paige," in a singsong voice. She sticks out her hand for Jace to shake.

Jace looks down to her and smiles. Gingerly dropping to one knee, so they are eye level, I notice his face pinch with pain for a heartbeat before he takes her little hand in hers and gives it a gentle shake.

"It's very nice to meet you, Paige. My name is Jace."

"Yeah, I know. You're Mommy's friend-boy," she says, looking toward me.

Jace's eyes meet mine. For the first time this afternoon he flashes his crooked smile. I feel my insides begin turn to mush and then instantly feel guilty. Why am I letting him make me feel like a silly girl? I can't feel this way, but the stupid butterflies in my stomach did not get the message.

"That's right. We're friends." He winks at me. "So I hear you went to the zoo today," he says animatedly, giving Paige his full attention.

The excitement and smile on his face appear genuine, but I find it hard to believe. Despite this, my daughter eats it up. Paige smiles and bounces on the balls of her feet.

"We did. I love the zoo. Do you like the zoo? Mommy doesn't take us very often, she's always too busy. But I still love her," Paige blurts out so quickly it's difficult to make out exactly what she said. "Did you know an elephant can eat up to six hundred pounds of food a day? That's a lot," she informs him, placing an emphasis on 'a lot'.

Jace's smile broadens. "You know, I didn't know that. That's pretty cool."

Leave it to Paige to break the ice.

"Yup," Paige says, popping the 'P'. "So do you?" she asks, resting her hands on her little hips.

"Do I what?"

"Do you like the zoo?"

"Well, it's been a very long time since I've been to the zoo, but I liked it when I was a kid."

"You really should go to the zoo. Maybe you can come with us the next time we go!" she says bouncing and clapping her hands. "Mommy, can Jace come to the zoo with us next time?" she begs, folding her hands and batting her lashes.

This is my cue to redirect this conversation. Standing closer to Paige, I place my hand on her arm and pull her back against my front.

"We'll see, sweetheart," I say to Paige, but mouth 'I'm sorry' to Jace.

He shakes his head and slowly stands. I notice he winces again when finally upright, but he quickly masks his expression.

Motioning for Katelyn to come closer, I stand between my girls with my arm around Katelyn's and my hand still resting on Paige's chest. I use their warmth to ease my nerves. I can't explain exactly what I am nervous about. It's probably nothing, but it could be everything.

My mind continues to reel with questions. Why is he here? Why did he offer to help? How am I going to afford to have the tire repaired? Why is he still standing there? What am I doing?

I break free of internal dialogue and turn my attention back to Jace, introducing him to the two most important people in my life.

Chapter 14
Jace

I can't believe she's standing in front of me. After all of these years, I thought I'd only get to see her face in the worn photo I keep in my wallet. I thought I'd never see her in person again, and now I've run into her twice in one week. I must be the luckiest son of a bitch in the world. She's still as beautiful as I remember. There are subtle changes, but she's still as I recall. Maybe a little tired, but there is still a sparkle in her eyes.

What is completely blowing my mind is she has children. I don't believe she is married. If she is, she's not wearing a ring. Yes, I looked. I didn't think about checking; it was more like a reflex. A wave of relief washed over me when I saw the ring finger on her left hand was empty. Not only that, but there was no tan line or telltale sign of an indent, like a ring recently resided there.

"Jace, these are my daughters, Katelyn," Miranda sounds apprehensive as she looks to the older girl at her side, "and Paige." She nods her head down toward the little spitfire in front of her. "Girls, this is my friend, Jace."

I can't help but lift one brow at hearing her use the word 'friend'. Something stirs in my stomach. Using more effort than should be necessary, I focus my attention away from Miranda and back to the girls in front of me.

"Good afternoon, girls. It's a pleasure to meet you." My eyes pass from the little one, to Miranda, to the oldest, and then it clicks for both of us. She sucks in a sharp breath, which startles Miranda.

"Katelyn, what's wrong?" she asks.

"Oh my god, you're that guy. You were at Uncle Sam's shop this week," she states.

I open my mouth to explain, certain I looked crazy that day. When I walked into the office late Wednesday afternoon and saw her, I thought I had officially lost it. Her hair, her face, and those eyes ... I thought I was seeing things. My heart stopped beating for a second. I could barely blink. Convinced I had finally driven myself mad and not knowing how to explain my behavior, I left as quickly as I had entered. Seeing them side by side now, it's still unnerving. The girl could be her mother's clone.

"What do you mean?" Miranda asks, looking at her daughter and then me. "What does she mean?" she repeats, stepping in front of Paige, putting extra space between us.

"Yes, that was me," I admit.

Miranda puts her hands on her hips, silently telling me to continue. Damn she looks good. She looked great all those years ago; the memory of her and those few hours permanently imprinted in my mind. But time has been kind to her. The roundness of her curves and the fullness of her hips is all woman. Gone is the girl that once resided in her body. My mind flashes with images of me running my hands down those soft curves. Jesus, I'm screwed.

"Let me explain," I say holding my hands up, taking a cautious step forward. "I moved to town this past weekend. I was driving around, trying to find my way around town, when came across this landscaping company up on route 12 with a help wanted sign out front. I talked to the guy in the office and he hired me on the spot. I started the following day."

The tension in Miranda's body visibly loosens, so I quickly continue, wanting to reassure her further.

"I was in the shop on Wednesday, dropping off a few items, and I went to the office to leave paperwork in the drop box. I didn't know Sam had come back. He left the job site earlier in the afternoon and didn't mention where he was going. When I walked in the office and saw her," I nod my head to the left, "I was shocked. I mean, damn, she looks just like you, Miranda. I thought I was seeing a damn ghost." Or dreaming, I mutter under my breath. Avoiding Miranda's reaction if she heard me, I turn toward Katelyn.

"I'm sorry if I scared you or made you uncomfortable. I know I must have looked like a creep."

Katelyn laughs and I hear snickering coming from behind Miranda.

"It's okay," Katelyn says.

"Wait. You work for my brother Sam?" Miranda asks, confused.

"Yes. Well, I didn't know he was your brother. Now that I do I can see the resemblance."

THE SECOND VERSE

"Huh."

The four of us stand on the side of the road in an uncomfortable silence for a moment longer. Paige remains shielded by her mother while Katelyn studies her and sneaks glances at me out of the corner of her eye with a sly smile. Miranda's eyes search my face for something before dropping to the ground. Her teeth worry her lip. Wanting to break the tension and needing to get them away from the street and home safely, I clap and rub my hands together. "Let's go get this tire fixed."

"Wait. We can't go right now," Miranda begins to argue.

"Why not? It shouldn't take too long."

"The closest shop that's open on a Saturday afternoon is across town and the four of us waiting for the tire to be repaired is going to be difficult. I mean, have you ever waited in one of those little offices for your car to be fixed? It's bad when enough you're alone. Doing it with two kids, well, that's like hell on earth," she rambles and the girls protest behind her.

"No, no. Just take me home and I will figure out how to have it fixed. Worst case I'll call Sam and he can help."

I'm about to argue, when Katelyn pipes in.

"Mom, Uncle Sam won't be home until tomorrow morning. You know he's staying on the Cape with Claire at her friend's wedding. Why don't you two drop us off at home? I'll watch Paige for you." She looks toward me with a sneaky smile. I like this girl already.

"You're offering to watch your sister?" Miranda asks, her eyes wide in disbelief.

Katelyn shrugs. "Yeah. Sure. It's no big deal. She owes me a rematch in that dance game we were playing last week anyway."

"Yay! I love that game," the little one cheers.

"Then it's settled?" I ask.

Miranda looks at all three of our smiling faces before releasing a resigning sigh and nods. "All right girls. Let's go."

Five minutes later, Katelyn and Paige are in the backseat, singing along to some pop song on the radio, and Miranda is beside me. My fingers itch to reach out and hold her hand, but I shake the idea from my mind. What the hell is wrong with me? I barely know her, but being this close to her, seeing her again, is doing crazy things to my head.

"So which way?" I ask, glancing at the girls again in the rear view mirror.

"Keep following this road for another few miles. You will pass a convenience store on the left and then you want to take the third left," Miranda explains.

My eyes leave the road for a second to glance at her. She has a small smile on her face.

"What's so funny?" I ask.

"Oh, nothing."

After a few minutes the convenience store appears and the landmarks begin to look familiar - really familiar. I pass the first, then the second street, and I am complete disbelief.

"You're kidding?"

"What?" She laughs.

"You're still living next to my grandmother's house?"

Her smile widens and it's the most beautiful thing I have ever seen. "We are."

"Unbelievable. How did I not notice?"

"If it makes you feel better I hadn't noticed you had moved in or Sandra moved out, so I think we're even," she teases as I pull into her driveway and place my truck in park.

"'Bye, Jace. Let me know when you want to go to the zoo," Paige says cheerfully before popping the door open, making me laugh a little.

"You bet," I call out after her.

"Paige, wait," Miranda yells before she unbuckles her seat belt and swings the passenger side door open. "I'm just going to let them in the house."

My attention is focused on Miranda chasing after Paige when Katelyn comes up to my window.

"Listen. I know I'm just a kid and you probably won't listen to a word I say, but be nice to her. It's time she had a little happiness."

Tossing her long dark hair over her shoulder, she stalks off toward the house, disappearing inside without a backward glance. It doesn't take a brain surgeon to figure out what she is trying to tell me. Miranda is alone. Just the thought makes me want to punch someone or something. My knuckles turn white as I grab the wheel. If I ever meet the bastard that left her, that hurt her, I will hurt him twice as bad.

Two minutes later, Miranda reappears and slowly walks back to the truck. Pulling herself up into the cab, she plops into the seat and nervously rings her hands in her lap. Her eyes are lowered so I can't see her face, but the way she is chewing on her lip I know she is debating something in her head.

"Is everything all right?" I ask, still trying to calm myself down.

"Are you sure you want to take me? Really, Jace, it's no big deal if you don't. Don't feel obligated. You have already done enough taking us home. I could just put the tire in the garage and take care of it tonight or in the morning." Her right hand rests on the door handle, readying her quick escape.

This time I don't second guess myself. I reach out and take her left hand in my right.

"Listen to me and listen close because I won't repeat this again. I told you I would help - that we'd get the tire fixed - and I meant it. To be honest, I'm glad to have an excuse to spend a little while longer with you. Although, now that I know you are living right next door, I may need to come by and borrow a cup of sugar later," I tease. "Seriously, Miranda, it's no problem." I squeeze her hand to further convince her and it must work. Almost instantly I sense the anxiety drain from her body.

"All right," she sighs, relaxing back into the leather seat.

"Good. Now that we agree where to next?" I release her hand only to put the truck in gear. As soon as we are back on the road, I reclaim her palm in mine.

Chapter 15
Miranda

My lungs burn, begging me to exhale the breath caught within, but my body is immobilized. I'm frozen with shock at the sight and weight of our intertwined fingers. His skin is rough against mine. The pad of his thumb is thick with callouses. After a few moments, my body finally thaws and the breath escapes through my lips. My muscles relax into the soft leather seat, but my eyes stay transfixed out the windshield.

A gentle squeeze breaks my trance and I realize Jace has been talking to me. I look up and study the side of his face. He looks so similar to that night so many years ago, but there is hardness around his eyes and jaw that I don't recall. There is also a faint scar across his cheek, which falls into his dimple as he smiles and chuckles. *Shit, what did he ask me?*

"Huh?" I ask dumbly, feeling my cheeks warm. What is wrong with my face? I have never blushed like this before.

"I asked, where's the closest garage?"

"Oh." I look toward the dashboard. "At this time on a Saturday there is only one place that will still be open. At the end of the street take a right. It's on the other side of route 20."

Jace nods and we fall back into silence for the next ten minutes until we arrive at the small automotive shop. We both hop down from his truck. Jace rounds the back to retrieve the tire and I wait by the front.

"Why don't you wait in the truck? It shouldn't take too long," he says carrying the tire with one hand, his muscles stretching the fabric of his shirt.

I don't listen to his suggestion and instead follow him into the dingy

94

office. "Let me see how much it is first."

"Don't worry about it," Jace says, waving his hand dismissively.

"Good afternoon." He turns his attention to the old man behind the counter, explaining the issue.

My mouth falls open. He actually thinks I'm going to let him pay to fix my flat tire. He thinks he can just waltz in here and try to rescue me like I'm some damsel in distress. What the hell?

"No." I cross my arms over my chest.

Slowly, Jace turns to face me. His brows pinch together. "What?" he asks.

"No. I will worry about it. You can't just pick me up off the side of the street and think I'll be all right with you paying to fix me ... I mean my car. I can take care of it myself." I push past him and up to the counter. "How much will it cost to fix the tire?"

The old man looks from me, to Jace, to the tire, and back again, unsure of what to say or who to speak to.

"How much?" I ask again, smacking my hand on the counter in frustration.

Stepping around the counter, he takes the tire from Jace and rolls it across the floor. His fingers glide across the surface like he is reading the lines in the tread.

"Ah, here it is," he says aloud, but I sense he is talking to himself. "I think I can plug the hole. That should do it."

"Great. How much?" I repeat.

"Twenty bucks," the old man says, wiping his hand with a dirty red rag, before stuffing it into his back pocket.

"Perfect." I rummage through my bag looking for my wallet. Pulling it out, I grab a crinkled twenty and slap it on the counter. "How long will it take?"

"Ah, give me about a half hour," the old man says, grabbing the waist of his pants and hiking them up over his very large belly before heading out to the garage.

"That long?" I call after him, annoyed, but my question goes unanswered.

I turn on my heel and stomp out of the office into cool autumn air. Taking a deep breath, I fill my lungs and try to calm down. I don't know what came over me, but I hate feeling helpless and that is exactly how I feel for the second time today.

I feel Jace step outside before I hear him. My stomach twists and the hairs

95

on the back of my neck stand on end. Quietly, he comes to stand beside me. With his hands shoved deep in his pockets. His strong back round and his head hangs low.

"I'm sorry if I upset you. I'm not sure what I did, but whatever it was I'm sorry." His voice is so soft and filled with guilt.

Instantly, I feel bad. It isn't his fault. I shouldn't have snapped at him the way that I did. A normal person would've said "thank you" and smiled politely. As quickly as it sparked, my anger fades.

"No, I'm sorry. I don't know why I acted like that. You were only trying to help." I turn to face him, holding out my right hand. "Truce?"

Jace chuckles "Truce" and shakes my hand.

"So now what?" I ask, adjusting my bag on my shoulder.

Jace looks over the top of my head and nods. "Want to get some coffee?"

Turning around, my eyes widen at seeing Atwell's Cafe. I laugh, "Sure."

Jace studies me for a moment, trying to figure out what I am laughing at, before giving up with a shrug.

"Shall we?" he asks, swiping his hand out to lead the way.

Darting around the oncoming traffic, we rush across the street. I can smell the strong scent of coffee mixed with the sweet scent of vanilla and chocolate on the sidewalk, even before pulling the heavy glass door open. Straight ahead is a long counter with a glass case to one side, lined with little pastries. There are a half dozen or so bistro style tables to the left, and a sofa and two arm chairs to the right. Under the large storefront windows, on either side, are long window benches lined with plush material and covered with fluffy pillows. The walls are a deep maroon and accented with natural woods. The space is warm and inviting, meant to entice people to linger.

"Why don't you get us a seat and I'll order," Jace suggests.

I don't mean to, but before I can stop myself I glare at him. Jace holds his hands up, surrendering.

"It's just coffee."

Guilt and embarrassment wash over me yet again. "You're right. Thank you. I'll go grab us a seat near the window."

"How do you take it?"

"A little milk and two sugars, please."

Nodding his head, Jace repeats my coffee order out loud before turning toward to the counter. I can't help but remain in place and watch him walk away. His body deserves to be looked at. Even though there's a slight hitch in his step, there's a sense of strength in the way he walks. The sway of his shoulders paired with the gait of his step commands attention and, I suspect, instills fear in some.

Before I am caught checking him out again, I turn away and debate where to sit. The two reading chairs, nestled in the corner, seem too intimate. Instead, I opt for a table closest to the door. This way, if I have to, I can make a quick exit.

I pull out a chair causing its legs to scrape against the tile floor. The sound of shrill metal echoes off the walls. Quickly, I drop into the seat and hide my face from a middle aged man sitting across the room who is giving me a dirty look for causing a ruckus. I begin rummaging through my bag looking for my favorite lip gloss. However, before I can find it, Jace returns, setting two paper cups on the table before taking a seat across from me.

I search my mind for something to say, but I come up empty handed. What do you say to someone you've only spoken to once, fourteen years ago, but have thought about many times since? A lifetime has passed and I'm a completely different person. I don't think there is anything in the politically-correct-small-talk handbook for situation like this.

My fingers tap nervously on the side of the paper cup. My mouth is dry, but sipping the hot coffee offers no relief. I wipe my sweaty palms across my jeans and peek across the table through my lashes. Jace is leaning forward in his chair, forearms resting on the table top. He pulls at the folded edge of the slip of cardboard wrapped around the center of his cup.

Is he nervous too, I wonder.

His anxiety fuels my courage. I roll the tightness out of my shoulders and draw in a deep breath before speaking. "So," I start, but like my twin, Jace says the same thing. We both stop and stare at the other before laughing.

"This isn't awkward or anything, is it?" he jokes. This time his smile comes easy.

"Nope, not at all," I laugh.

"Well, now that we broke the ice, the rest should be easy." He winks.

"How long are you in town for?" I ask.

"I'm not sure. This is the first time in a very long time I don't have someone telling me where to be and when to be there. It's new for me. I kind of like not having a game plan," he explains.

"The Army? So you really enlisted?"

"Yes ma'am," he chuckles. "I was in for just over thirteen years before I was discharged."

"Wow. I can't imagine doing that."

"Being a solider is what I was made to do. It's odd not having orders to follow every day. Not having a schedule to live by. I would've remained there until I retired, but," he runs his hand across his leg, "it didn't work out that way."

"You were hurt?" My entire body buzzes with concern. I have to force myself to stay in my seat, when I all I really want to do it rush around the table and wrap my arms around him.

His lips press into a tight line and he nods. "It was a road side bomb. Got us good. I was one of the lucky ones though." His eyes focus on the wall behind me. His voice is distant. Gone is the glimmer of humor.

"World War III," I whisper.

"Huh?" His attention comes back to be.

"That night, the night we met, you said your recruiter told you you'd never see real combat unless World War III broke out. It seemed impossible then."

"Tell me about it."

"Do you think if you knew then what you know now you would have done anything different?" I'm not sure my question is entirely intended for Jace.

"No," he says adamantly. "Life isn't about the destination, but the journey. So far, I have had one hell of a ride." He smiles broadly. "How about you? I have to say I'm surprised to find you're still in this little town, Blue. I thought for sure you'd be some big shot music person traveling around the world. Did you move back after college?"

A lump forms in my throat at hearing the nickname and I force it down. "I never went," I admit sadly.

"What? Why?" he asks, his brows pulling together.

My eyes widen, silently telling him to think about it. A moment passes, but then the realization hits. I know he's made the connection. He put the pieces together and figured out Katelyn was my reason for never going to college or leaving this town.

"Oh."

"Yeah."

A tense silence settles between us. My eyes are fixed on Jace, while his are fixed on his cup. The muscles in his jaw begin to tick and his lips harden into a thin line. A deep crease forms on his forehead as his brow furrows. He's lost in his thoughts, warring with himself over something.

Is he upset I have children? Is that a deal breaker? I imagine for some men it might be. I mean, how many people want to start a relationship where another left off? But more importantly, why do I care? This isn't going to go anywhere. It can't. I don't think I can handle more than sharing an innocent cup of coffee with him.

His eyes lift to mine and he studies my face. His hard features ease just slightly as he opens his mouth, but before he can speak a syllable a large boom crashes outside and vibrates through the plate glass window. Out of the corner of my eye, I see the rear of a tractor trailer passing by and the splash of water from a pothole in the street. What comes next happens so quickly I don't have time to react.

The first thing I notice is searing pain in my arms from my now coffee soaked shirt. My wide eyes travel from the soaked fabric across the wet table top to the unrecognizably crushed paper cup crumbled in the middle. A tiny puddle of brown liquid congeals on the smooth surface.

Next, I see the space where Jace sat across from me is now empty. Instead, his chair has been knocked back several feet and lays on its side. Jace is standing a foot from the chair, frozen in place, eyes fixed at a mysterious spot outside the window. A dangerous intensity rolls off of him and vibrates from his body. His white knuckled fists are clenched firmly by his side. A mix of emotions masks his sweat drenched face, but the most prominent is fear. It's unnerving to see such a large man paralyzed by fear and knowing one wrong move could cause him to strike like a caged animal.

I watch, frozen in my seat, debating what I should do. A young waitress rushes to my side.

"Oh my goodness, look at this mess. Are you all right?" she asks, her voice dripping with concern.

"I'm fine." I force a smile. My eyes focus on her for only a second before returning back to Jace.

"Let me get something to clean this up," she says, her gaze following mine, fixing on Jace. "Is he okay?" she asks.

I don't respond because honestly, I don't know. I have no idea what just happened. I don't know why he reacted the way he did or why he is staring out the window. I don't know why he is sweating so profusely that his shirt is soaked through across his chest and under his arms. I don't know anything where Jace is concerned and it's a sobering realization.

Ignoring the young girls stare, I slowly stand and carefully make my way toward Jace. Each step makes my stomach tie into one more knot, until I am standing inches away from him and feel like I'm full of lead. The tips of my shoes kiss the tips of his. My head falls back so I have a clear view of his face.

"Jace?" My voice cracks under the weight of my nerves.

He doesn't respond. I say his name again, but still nothing.

I lower my eyes and look straight ahead, staring at his chest watching it rise and fall with his rapid breathing. Warily, I move my left hand toward his right. My fingers hover just millimeters from his, twitching with trepidation. Throwing caution to the wind, I close the short distance and intertwine my fingers with his.

We stand like that, letting the rest of the world drift into the background. The waitress comes back, cleaning up the wet mess on the table and setting the chair back in place. I feel the weight of her worried stare on my back, but I don't acknowledge her. My focus is entirely on Jace.

Eventually, he begins to come back. His breathing becomes less erratic and falls into a normal rhythm. The tension in his body begins to fade. All the while I remain still, staring at his chest. Finally, when he squeezes my hand, I know he has broken free from his trance.

"Hey," he says, his voice huskier than before.

"Hey," I repeat, smiling up at him.

His hand tightens around mine again. "I'm sorry."

"It's okay."

"No, Miranda, it's not," he huffs, shaking his head. He lets go of my hand and steps away. A shiver runs down my spine at the loss of his touch. I feel the sweat of his palm still clinging to mine.

Jace runs his hand over his short hair and releases a heavy breath. I think I hear him swear, but I can't be sure. Turning back towards me, I think he's going to offer an explanation. I don't need to know the whole story, but I would like to understand. Instead my heart plummets when he suggests we go check on my car, and he walks out of the cafe without a second glance.

With no other options, I follow behind him, the Jace I remember fading with each step.

Chapter 16
Jace

Early Friday afternoon, standing in the middle of a cul da sac, I can't help but be impressed with myself. Stepping back, I admire the evidence of a day's hard work with pride. The yards of several homes, which I've spent the last several hours working on, look amazing. I've cut back fading flowers, trimmed shrubbery, and cleared leaves. It feels good to accomplish something that didn't involve worrying if my next step would be fatal.

I swear under my breath when the clouds that had been steadily darkening open and a drenching rain begins to fall. The humid summer weather a forgotten memory and instead has been replaced with crisp, cool, damp autumn air. I grab the last few tools I had resting at my feet and dash toward the pickup I have been using all week. Luis, the guy I have been working with, races past me, faster than I thought his short legs could carry him. He jumps in the passenger seat. I quickly follow, ducking behind the wheel before slamming the door.

"*Fodasse*," Luis says in his thick Portuguese accent, his teeth chattering. Water drips from his long, wiry hair, wetting the back of the seat.

Rolling my eyes, I shove his arm. "You're such a pussy."

"*Chupa*," he spits, shoving me back.

I like Luis. For the most part he's quiet. He doesn't fill the time with mindless chatter. When he does talk I have to pay extra close attention. His accent makes it difficult to understand him, especially when he talks fast. Working beside him this last week makes me realize how much I miss being a part of a team. I miss the camaraderie of working alongside someone else trying to accomplish a mission, even if my semi-automatic weapon has been replaced by a leaf blower, and the war zone is now an overgrown garden and not in a miserable desert.

"It doesn't look like this is going to stop anytime soon. I say we call it a day and start the weekend a little early. Whatdaya say?" Luis suggests, blowing into his folded hands.

I shrug. It doesn't matter to me whether the weekend starts now or in a few hours. My only plans are to go home and to avoid looking out the window toward Miranda's house. Over the last several days I've had to keep the blinds drawn on that side of the house, so I wouldn't be tempted to check on her every two minutes.

"Do you mind dropping me at my truck up the street? I don't wanna walk back there in the rain," Luis says, adjusting his tired Red Sox hat.

I bring the truck to life and put it in gear without a word.

After dropping Luis off, I head back to the shop. I need to return some equipment before going home. Well, at least that's what I tell myself. Truth is Sam won't give a shit if I keep the truck over the weekend. In fact, it would probably save time on Monday, not having to go all the way to the garage before heading back to the job site, but I need an excuse.

After my episode in the coffee shop on Saturday, I'm certain of one thing - I need to stay far away from Miranda. She's too good for me and there's no doubt in my mind I'll ruin her. I saw it in her eyes when she looked at me. She was looking for the eighteen -year -old kid she met all those years ago. Looking for a glimmer of the person I once was. I don't want to see the look in her eyes when she realizes he's gone.

Unfortunately for me, Miranda began working for her brother on Monday. I didn't need to see her to know she was there. I could feel her presence. That first morning when I went in to pick up the job slips for the day, I felt her eyes on me. She bore a hole in the back of my head and I knew she was trying to get my attention. I ignored her, but it nearly killed me. It took every ounce of strength I had not to turn and look into her pleading blue eyes. But, even if I don't speak to her, I need to see her, just for a moment. If I can just catch a glimpse, I'll be able to make it through the weekend without going crazy.

Pulling into the driveway leading to the garage, the first thing I notice is Miranda's car. My eyes fall to clock on the dash. She should be leaving any minute. She's left every day around three pm, not that I've been paying attention or anything.

I round the building and park in the back. The rain still falls, but it's no longer pouring. I press the button on the wall, opening the large garage door, and pop the tailgate of the truck. There are several bags of winterizing fertilizer, a couple rakes, and a leaf blower that need to be brought inside. One by one, I carry the items, setting each in their rightful place. I jog back outside to swipe the paperwork resting on the dash and rush to put it in the office.

I pass several rows of metal shelving that reach from the concrete floor to the ceiling. All hold various tools and pallets of materials. Rounding the corner, just as I'm about to take the stairs, I hear a scraping noise. I stop and listen closely. Several seconds later, I hear the noise again. Setting the paperwork on a nearby counter, I walk slowly across the space. All my senses are on high alert and my training involuntarily kicks in. My eyes sweep back and forth, surveying the area. I make mental note of every fine detail, until I find the source of the noise and my heart drops.

Perched precariously on top of a ladder, I find Miranda. She stands on the tips of her toes on the second to the top rung, body stretched, her left hand holding on to the ladder, and her right arm reaching for a box on the shelf. The fabric of her black t-shirt lifts, revealing a silky smooth strip of flesh across her back and belly. I lick my lips as images of licking that little piece of skin flash through my mind. I think I could spend hours kissing her stomach.

A curse falls from her lips, freeing me of my dirty thoughts. I step closer, ready to grab ahold of the ladder and yell up to her, but before I can say anything, I watch as her fingertips brush against the box and her right foot slips. I stare, frozen in place, as she teeters for a moment before she loses her balance and begins to fall. A desperate squeak rips from her lungs.

I know the fall only took a fraction of a second, gravity pulling her small frame to the Earth, but my mind slows the moment allowing me to react. I leap forward and catch her, just feet from the hard concrete floor. Her body folds against my chest and I collapse to my knees, causing a searing pain to shoot through my thigh. My heart hammers in my chest, both fear and adrenaline coursing through my veins. The muscles in my arms tighten, pulling her even closer.

Miranda is quiet for several minutes. Her breathing is shallow and ragged. She nuzzles her face into the crock of my neck, and I swear I hear her inhale. The thought of her sniffing me causes my lower half to stir to life, but I force the indecent thoughts from my brain. This is not the time or place.

After what feels like an eternity, I break the silence. "Are you okay?"

She nods against my chest. "Yes, I think so."

Lifting her head, she looks up at me with her beautiful blue eyes. Fuck, I could spend the rest of my life getting lost in those eyes.

I feel her pull away just slightly, so I loosen my hold but don't let go. I know this is wrong. I know I'm no good for her, but shit I'm not ready to let go yet.

"Thank you for ... for catching me. If you weren't here ..." Her voice fades, not finishing the sentence, but she doesn't need to. We both know what would have happened if I hadn't shown up when I did.

Knowing she's all right, that she is safely on the ground, I can't stop the anger that bubbles up. How could she be so stupid? I don't stop myself from asking just that.

Miranda pushes hard against my chest, freeing herself from my hold. She stands on still shaky legs.

"Screw you," she hisses.

"Screw me?" I ask, rushing to my feet. I glare down at her. An evil laugh rushes past my lips. "Screw me? Christ, sweetheart, you have a funny way of showing your appreciation. You could've killed yourself. So yeah, I think the right question is how could you be so goddamn stupid?"

Her hands rest on her hips. Her icy eyes meet my stare. Shit, she may be pissed, but it's sexy as hell. Images of throwing her over my shoulder and spreading her wide on the counter behind us have me hard in an instant.

"That box has Sam's financial paperwork in it. I need it to review his past tax filings," she huffs, as if that is a good explanation.

"And the circus balancing act was what?"

"I had it under control."

I laugh. "Yeah, looked like it. Why didn't you just wait and ask someone to get it for you?"

Miranda rolls her eyes. She pushes past me, bumping her arm into mine, but my arm doesn't give under her small frame and she winces.

"I don't need help."

Damn, she is stubborn. "I beg to differ, Blue."

"Right," she says, dragging out the word with extra sass. "Everyone has gone home early and Sam won't be back until later tonight. See? No one's around to help. I had it under control," she repeats.

I release a heavy breath, trying to calm down. "What about me?" I shove my hands in my pockets, rocking slightly on my heels.

"What about you?" she asks, crossing her arms across her chest, drawing my eyes to her breasts. Shit, I'm in trouble.

"You could've waited until I got back."

"Ha! Yeah right." she scoffs.

"Jesus, you're stubborn," I mutter under my breath, but she must hear me, because her eyes widen slightly.

"You haven't even looked in my direction, let alone talked to me, all week. Yeah, I should wait around for you to get your shit together, so I can ask for your help." Turning, she stalks off toward the office. The heavy sound of her feet against the cold stone floor is in time with the beating in my heart.

"Wait," I call out, but, of course, she doesn't stop. I jog to catch up with her, reaching out and grabbing her elbow. She stops in her tracks and spins around. Her glare moves from my hold on her arm up to my eyes. With a strong jerk she breaks free.

"What?" she hisses.

"I'm sorry. I'm an asshole."

"Yes, you are."

"Look," I begin, rubbing a hand over the back of my neck, "I'm not good for you, Blue. I'm not the boy you thought you knew. That boy is gone and left is a man that you won't like."

"How about you let me make up my own mind? No one remains the same person they were at eighteen. Not you," she lowers her voice and her eyes drop to the floor, "and certainly not me."

With two fingers I hook her chin and gently raise her eyes to mine.

"Truce?"

The corners of her mouth twitch. "Truce."

Miranda's eyes fall to my lips. I watch her pale pink tongue swipe across her own, leaving a trail of moisture. It takes all my restraint not to move closer to taste her.

"Go out with me tomorrow night," I say.

Despite what she said, I know I should still stay away, but I can't. Maybe I can keep my shit together long enough just to spend a small amount of time with her. I survived fourteen years after only spending a few hours with her. Perhaps I can survive a lifetime after a single date.

Her eyes widen and she sucks in a sharp breath. She pulls her bottom lip between her teeth and nervously worries it back and forth. The slightly swollen flesh pops free and is replaced with her thumb nail.

I'm about to tell her to think about it, or maybe say I was just kidding, when she finally answers with a simple "Ok".

That small, two letter word causes something to relax inside me, and I realize I was nervous she might say no.

Chapter 17
Miranda

The morning sunshine streaming through the window brightens the room and wakes me from the most peaceful night's sleep I've had in a long while. I lie on my back, snuggled under the covers, staring up at the ceiling. The memory of yesterday afternoon plays on an agonizing, endless loop. My mind continues to wander to what could have happened if Jace hadn't been there. I try not to let myself think about it for too long, though. Instead, I focus on what happened after the fall and the warm sensation swirling in my chest. I replay the weight of his strong arms around my body as he held me tight. I remember the feel of his defined muscles beneath his damp shirt. I couldn't resist the urge to smell him while cradled in his arms. The musky scent of man mixed with the lingering odor of gasoline from the power tools he used all day was a heady combination.

Obviously he was upset over what happened, or more importantly what could have happened, but I didn't expect him to be as mad as he was. The anger that vibrated from him after I was safely standing on my own two feet was frightening. Even though I was grateful he was there, I wouldn't allow Jace to treat me as if I was a careless imbecile. I've spent years taking care of myself and my family. I don't *need* to be rescued. However, somehow in less than a week, Jace has swooped in and saved me – twice. If I'm honest, I'm ashamed to admit it feels nice.

The warm feeling I was just basking in cools a little, as twinges of guilt bubble up. Closing my eyes, I see Adam's adoring face smiling back at me and the muscles around my lungs constrict, causing each breath to be more painful than the next. Somewhere, in the back of my mind, I know Adam wouldn't want me to be alone forever; in fact he told me as much, but that knowledge doesn't diminish the sensation of betrayal squeezing my heart.

Pushing aside my blankets along with my thoughts of Adam, Jace, and things that were and could be, I sit up and stretch my arms over my head. Familiar dull thuds echo from downstairs, followed by clanging of dishes. Groaning, I force myself out of bed to see what kind of mess the girls have made.

Much to my surprise, when I round the corner to the kitchen, I'm only greeted by a half empty cereal box laying on its side, round morsels splayed on the counter, and a few splashes of milk nearby. Not the worst mess in the world. One day last month, I came down to find pancake batter splattered everywhere: on the floors, walls, and fridge. There were even little footprints leading from the kitchen down the hall into the living room. Luckily, Paige's attempt to make me breakfast stopped before actually turning on the stove. I swear she probably would have burned the house down.

After making quick work of cleaning up the kitchen, I settle at the table with a piping hot cup of coffee, my cold hands instantly warming on the hot ceramic surface. The sound of Paige's cartoons blends with the gentle, never ending strumming of Katelyn's guitar. Glancing at the time on my phone for the tenth time in a measly two minutes, I decide it's late enough to call Claire. Even if it's not, that's too bad. I can't wait any longer.

Swiping my thumb across the screen, I press Claire's number and wait, tapping my fingers on the table.

"Hello," she answers on the third ring, her voice heavy with sleep.

"Good morning. I hope I didn't wake you."

"Nah, I need to get up anyway. The damn dog has been staring at me for the past five minutes and your brother is pretending to sleep and not notice the whining." I hear a muffled smacking sound followed by my brother's laugh.

"I'm up. I'm up," I hear him groan in the background.

Claire laughs. "So, what's up? I haven't talked to you all week."

"I know. Sam said you were working mostly nights lately."

"Yeah, Lisa needed someone to cover for her this week. Her son was home from college and she wanted to spend some time with him."

"That was nice of you to volunteer. Are you working tonight?"

"No, thank god. I have the next three days off."

"Nice." I pause, debating making small talk first or launching right into why I am calling.

107

Janet Lee

"So, what's up? Is everything alright?" Claire asks, noticing my hesitation.

"Yeah, everything is fine. I was just wondering ... uh ... do you and Sam have any plans this evening?" Suddenly I feel bad I might be interrupting their weekend.

"None at all. Why? What's going on?"

"Well ..." I stutter. "I sort of have ... a ... a date and I was wondering if Paige could spend the night," I rush the end. I don't know what kind of reaction I expected, but when all I hear is silence it makes me wonder if the call dropped.

"Hello? Claire?"

"Holy shit," she whispers before repeating much louder. "Holy shit!"

"*Shhh.* Jesus Claire, don't scream. Sam doesn't need to know," I say, but it's too late. In the background, through the muffled phone, I hear Sam ask what's wrong and Claire tell him I have a date.

"This is amazing. I'm so happy for you! Of course Paige can stay over. What about Katelyn? Who is he? Where is he taking you? What are you going to wear?" She rattles so fast, I barely catch it all.

"Katelyn is staying at a friend's tonight. I don't think you know him. I don't know where we are going and I haven't even thought about what I'm going to wear."

I don't know why I don't tell her about Jace. I think it's partly because I don't want Sam giving him a hard time, although I know I can't prevent that forever. I want to see if this is more than a date before I give anyone the details.

"Are you sure you don't mind taking Paige overnight?"

"Don't be silly. We love it when she visits. We can have a girls' night. Do our nails. Sam's too," she teases. I hear him groan and I can't help but laugh. Poor Sam, he is surrounded by women.

"I'll come by around three to pick her up. I just need to run to the grocery store beforehand. Sam has been surviving on ramen all week."

"Perfect. I'll see you then."

"Miranda, I'm very happy for you. You deserve this," she says, the humor gone from her voice. I don't know what to say, so I stay quiet. "I'll see you this afternoon," Claire says before ending the call.

I sit at the table, staring at my phone for a few moments, before Paige saunters in to the room. As she rummages through the refrigerator drawer filled with apples and oranges, I hear her voice.

"So you have a hot date with Jace tonight." It's not a question, but a statement.

I tense and my eyes snap up from my phone. Paige takes a big bite of apple and hops up onto one of the bar stools tucked beside the granite covered breakfast bar. Katelyn leans against the door jamb, her arms across her chest and her legs crossed at her ankles. Her eyes watch me with curiosity, but the anger I anticipated is missing.

I'd been thinking about what to tell them. Paige is too young to understand the complexity of adult relationships and she doesn't have any memories of her own of Adam. She only has the images from photo albums and the stories I've told her of her father. To her, he is a figment of her imagination. Katelyn, on the other hand, has years filled with memories. She remembers sitting on the floor playing Barbie's with him and the piggy back rides he used to give her when he put her to bed at night. For Katelyn, Adam is not an imaginary figure, but a real person. I never want her to feel like I am replacing him. No one could ever take his place. I think that's part of the reason I've never dated anyone in the years since. That and no one worthy has come along. I can't help wondering if Jace is worth it.

My eyes pass from Paige to Katelyn and back again. Drawing in a deep breath, I sigh. "Yes, I'm going on a date with Jace tonight. Is that okay with you girls?" I ask, my voice soft.

Paige shrugs in indifference. "Sure. Can I stay with Aunt Claire and Uncle Sam? I want to show them the new move I learned at karate this week."

"Yes, Aunt Claire will be her in a few hours to pick you up."

"Woohoo!" she hollers, throwing her hands over head sending the half eaten apple flying to the floor with a juicy thud.

"I'm going to pack my stuff." The bar stool skids across the tile floor as she jumps down.

"Hey, pick up the apple!" I call after her, but she doesn't hear or chooses to ignore me. Her small but heavy feet stomp up the stairs.

Bringing my mug to the sink, I reach down to grab the discarded core, meeting Katelyn's stare when I straighten. She's studying me closely. I can't translate the expression on her face. Drying my hands on the slightly damp dish towel, I break the growing silence first.

"Sweetheart, are you okay with this?"

"You going out with Jace? Or dating in general?"

"Either I guess."

Katelyn pushes herself from the wooden door frame and steps closer to me. I'm not sure what to expect, but my tension eases when she smiles brightly.

"Of course, Mom. You've been single for too long. You spend all of your free time with me and Paige. I think it's great you are going to go out and have some fun for a change. You deserve it."

Her words cause tears to pool in my eyes. Just when I think she couldn't amaze me anymore, she goes and does it again. I pull her into my chest as a single tear rolls down my cheek.

"I love you, Mom."

"To the moon and back," I whisper into her hair.

Hours later, after Katelyn left to spend the night at a friends and Paige waits impatiently downstairs for Claire to show up, I stand in my bedroom staring at the heap of clothing thrown on my bed. I have been staring at the same outfits for the last forty five minutes. A little while ago, Paige came in to offer me her advice.

"Which one do you like?" I asked Paige who sat with crisscrossed legs on my bedroom floor.

In my right hand I held a conservative navy blue dress with small pale blue and white flower pattern that starts thicker at the knee length hem and thins as it flows upward to the high neckline. In my left hand was a cute little black number. The A-line skirt and tight bodice are accented by a red belt that makes it fun and flirty. I bought it years ago for no reason other than it looked amazing on me. Unfortunately, I never had an excuse to wear it.

"I choose that one," Paige said, pointing to the black dress.

"Are you sure?" I asked.

I can't believe I'm placing my fashion decisions in the hand of a seven year old.

"Definitely. Every woman should have the perfect little black dress and that," she pointed at the dress again, "is little and black."

My eyes widened and my mouth fell open.

"Paige, where did you hear that?"

Paige twirled the end of her hair with indifference. "Aunt Claire told me a girl's closet isn't complete without a little black dress."

Note to self, discuss the dos and don'ts of fashion advice with Claire.

A light rap at the door brings me back to the debacle at hand.

"Hey," Claire starts, but stops almost immediately. "Whoa, what happened in here? Did your closet throw up?" she teases.

"Ha, ha, very funny," I say dryly. "god, Claire, what am I even doing? I can't do this. I mean, this is crazy, right?" I ramble, running my hands through my hair, tugging at the roots. "Help me," I beg.

"Breathe, Miranda. Just breathe. It's going to be all right," she says, stepping closer and rubbing a small circle between my shoulders. "You can do this and more importantly, you should do this. This will be good for you, to go out with another adult you aren't related to."

"But, we - " I begin, but she stops me.

"*We* are sisters. If not by blood then, hopefully someday soon, by marriage. Go out. Have a little fun."

Closing my eyes I breathe deeply as Claire instructed. "Fine, but I have no idea what to wear," I say, collapsing onto the edge of the cluttered bed.

"Oh sweetie, sure you do. Let's see what we have to work with."

Claire crosses the room and begins to sift through the dresses, skirts, and tops I have tossed everywhere. She hums and haws as she goes.

"Did he say where you're going?" she asks, looking at me out of the corner of her eye, not willing to take her attention off the task at hand.

"No, he didn't. Oh god, I have no idea where we're going. How am I going to know what to wear?" I bury my face in my hands.

"Calm down. It's going to be fine. Aha, here it is," she proclaims proudly, holding up the same black dress Paige picked out earlier. A laugh erupts from my chest causing Claire to look at me like I have lost my mind.

"What's so funny?"

"Nothing," I say, calming my breathing and taking the dress from her. I hold it up to my chest and stand in front of the floor length mirror.

"Are you sure?" I ask, meeting her eye in the mirror.

"Absolutely. Wear these shoes and take this sweater with you." She holds up both and then sets them on the foot of the bed.

I turn side to side, studying the dress in the mirror. I hope it's not too much. I don't want to look like I am trying too hard.

"So, are you ever going to tell me who this mystery man is?"

"His name is Jace. We knew each other when we were teenagers. He recently moved back to town and we bumped into each other," I tell her, shrugging like it's no big deal.

"I'm so happy for you. Really." She pauses, like she wants to say something more on the subject, but doesn't. "All right, Paige and I are going to leave. Time to get the mani and pedis started. Sam is going to be so excited," she says sarcastically. "Call me tomorrow and let me know when to bring Paige home. I don't want to interrupt anything," she teases, wagging her brows.

"There will be nothing to interrupt," I laugh as I push her out of the room, both of us laughing.

"Bye Mommy!" Paige calls up few minutes later.

Rushing to the top of the stairs, I blow her a kiss and watch her and Claire disappear through the front door.

There is something unnerving about being in an empty house. The creak of the floorboards is angrier. Every tick of the clock is more deafening. Each memory is clearer. The unease churning in the pit of my stomach is a combination of rarely being home alone coupled with it never being this quiet when we are.

With my outfit decided, I can no longer put off the inevitable. Stripping off my large t-shirt and comfy jogging pants, I start the shower, letting the hot water steam the mirror before stepping in. I spend longer in the shower than I have in almost a decade. Like most mothers I have perfected the five minute shower. In, wash, and out. There isn't really a need for much else. My hair is usually pulled back in a ponytail, so conditioning is an unnecessary step. My legs do not see the light of day after Labor day and rarely before, so shaving is not a priority. As for other areas, well, let's just say they're on display once a year for an annual exam and nothing more.

After a long twenty minutes, soon after the water runs cold, the scent of lavender with a hint of vanilla fills the air. Every part of my body has been scrubbed, rubbed, loofah-ed, buffed, shaved, rinsed, and repeated. My straight hair has been blown dry with a round brush adding volume. A thin swipe of liner and a bit of mascara frames my eyes. There is a hint of blush on my cheeks and a gloss to my lips.

Standing in front of the mirror, in the dress Paige and Claire picked out, I can hardly recognize the person staring back at me. It makes me smile. I am as shiny as a brand new penny and I feel amazing.

Don't get me wrong. I am certain things between Jace and I will stay innocent tonight. Even if he has other things in mind, I will not cross that line. Despite the fact he will not see all the fruits of my labor, there is an unfamiliar tightness in my belly. Jace's reaction doesn't matter. This is not for him. This, my reflection in the mirror, the straightness of my posture, and the gleam in my eyes, is for me. For the first time in a long time, I don't feel like a mother or a sister. I'm not a wife or a daughter. Not a caregiver. Not the breadwinner. For the first time in forever, I feel like a woman.

And it feels amazing.

Chapter 18
Jace

After asking Miranda out, I quickly realized I had no idea where to take her. I have only ventured out and explored Belham and the surrounding areas a few times, but from what I can tell it's not a hub of nightlife. I tried to search the internet on my phone for ideas, but everything I found just didn't seem right. So, when Luis called me around noon to ask if he had left his hedge trimmer in my truck, I broke down and asked for his help.

"Ah, you have a date," he said in his thick accent.

"Yes. I want to take her some place nice, but not cheesy," I said, hoping he understood.

"Ey, I know just the spot. I took my old lady there once and she was all sweet on me afterward." I swear I could hear him making crude gestures with his hands through the phone.

"Oh. I am not sure if that's what I am looking for," I started but he cut me off.

"No, no. Trust me, she will love it."

"Are you sure?" I asked, because I wasn't.

"Absolutely."

Now, hours later, I stand in my kitchen, keys in hand, staring at the clock above the stove. My weight rests against the counter and the fingers tick the seconds on the linoleum. I told Miranda I would pick her up at six, but I've been ready since five. I've thought about going next door to get her early a few times, but stopped myself. I don't want to seem over eager.

I did a little research and was able to find the place Luis recommended on

113

the internet. I have to admit it looked really nice. The Blooming Hill Arboretum is only about a twenty minute drive and the photos of the gardens were amazing. Shortly after I hung up with Luis, I made a trip to the store and packed us a light picnic dinner, nothing too fancy, but enough so we wouldn't be starving by the end of the night. And, if things go south, I can bring her home, wave goodbye, and try to forget about the whole thing.

My leg throbs, reminding me of the punishing ten mile run I did this morning when I couldn't fall back to sleep after waking, like a kid on Christmas morning with a ball of nerves in my stomach. I shift my weight to the other leg to ease the pain. I've been wrapping it with a bandage under the brace I wear to work the last few days. One night earlier this week, I couldn't even lift my leg to climb the stairs to get to my bedroom. Instead, I had to sleep on a decade old mattress in the spare bedroom on the first floor.

Shit, what the hell am I thinking? This date is a bad idea. I should have listened to myself and stayed as far away from Miranda as I could. She deserves someone who can give her the world, not someone who has been damaged by it.

Feeling my aggravation rise, I push off the counter and stuff my keys in my pocket. If I wait any longer, I will talk myself out of going and I have a feeling I will hate myself for it later. I kill the lights throughout the house, heading toward the front door. Stepping on to the front porch, the chilled air fills my lungs and begins to cool my anger. My eyes drift to the left, toward Miranda's house, and my breath catches as I see Miranda step outside. Even from this distance she's beautiful, and my need to be near her intensifies, drowning my doubts.

The pain in my leg all but forgotten, I hop down the three steps that lead to the gravel walkway. Popping the door of my truck, I slide inside and bring the engine to life. I sneak another peak toward Miranda. Her eyes lock on the truck and her face is scrunched up in confusion. I can't help but chuckle as I back out of the driveway. I drive the fifty feet to her driveway, pull in, and park in front of her garage. I'm out and around the front of the truck before she even makes it to the bottom step. Humor twinkles in her eyes.

"I could have met you at your truck. You didn't need to drive over," she says.

I'm momentarily lost in a haze. God, she is beautiful. Her ebony hair falls loosely around her face. A light shimmer of gray shadows her eyes and makes their blue even more vibrant than I thought possible. A gentle breeze swirls around us and the scent of lavender fills my lungs. There is a hint of pink to her lips, which now turn upward.

"I said I would pick you up at six. I can't very well make you walk to my house on the first date." I wink. "Are you ready?"

"Yes. I'm ready."

I don't know why, and it happens before I can think about it, but I reach out and take her hand, leading her to the passenger side of my truck. Once she is safely tucked inside, I round the front and climb back in. We share a sideward glance before I put the truck in reverse and back out of the driveway, beginning the short twenty minute ride into Springfield.

I peek at Miranda every few seconds. She looks so amazing tonight it's hard to keep my eyes on the road. The cute little black dress she has on shows off her silky skin and gorgeous legs. What I wouldn't give to run my hands over them, but I can feel her nervousness, so I choke back those thoughts.

Miranda's eyes focus straight ahead. I peek over to see her nervously wringing her hands in her lap. Reaching over, I slide my hand in hers and give it a gentle squeeze. Her pretty blue eyes swing in my direction, wide with surprise, before a small smile pulls at her lips.

"So, where are we going?" she asks, finally breaking the silence.

"You'll see. It's a surprise."

Her face puckers. "A surprise? I hate surprises."

"Only people who love surprises say they hate them," I say, looking over to her briefly before returning my eyes to the road. "I wanted to take you some place different, so I asked one of the guys and he suggested this place," I explain.

"Who did you ask?"

"Luis."

"Seriously? You asked Luis, really? This ought to be interesting," she laughs.

Her smile lights up the whole damn truck. Her blue eyes sparkle with humor, and dimples I never noticed before dot her cheeks. I shift in my seat, trying to keep myself under control.

A comfortable silence settles between us as bright streetlights and dark alleys pass by in a blur. It takes less time than I expected to arrive at the address Luis gave me. The Arboretum is surrounded by a high brick wall and thick green shrubs, with a small building made of cement and glass serving as an entrance and welcoming center. The parking lot, with its oak trees standing tall and proud in the medians, is nearly empty, as I thought it would be with most people coming to visit during the daytime.

"This is it," I say as I put the truck in park. Reaching into the back seat, I pull the soft cooler forward. I don't realize Miranda is sitting stiff, her face an unhealthy shade of gray, until I turn forward, reaching for the door handle.

"What's wrong?" I ask, instantly worried Luis was a bad person to ask for advice. I'm going to kick his ass on Monday.

Miranda takes a deep breath, her features smoothing and shoulders squaring when she exhales. "It's nothing. Come on," she murmurs, reaching for her door. Quickly, I reach for her, stopping her from moving.

"Miranda, what is it?" She must see the anxiety building in my eyes because she quickly answers.

"It's nothing. It's just" she stammers, searching for the right words. "I should've realized where we were going," she pauses, breathing deeply again. "If I had been paying closer attention to the roads and not on how ridiculously amazing you look tonight," her cheeks blush a little, "I would've noticed."

"You've been here before? We can go someplace else if you'd like." I move to place the cooler back in its spot, but this time she rests her hand on my arm, stopping me.

"No. I don't want to leave." Her eyes are fixed on mine and beneath the glossy, blue surface I can see she is telling the truth. "This place, this arboretum, was the first big job my brother and," her eyes drop as well as her voice, "Adam designed together. This is where they got their big break."

That wasn't what I was expecting. I wasn't sure what she was going to say, but that was something I never could've imagined. She hasn't spoke of Adam before, but I've heard his name in passing at work. From what I've learned, Adam and Miranda were married for several years and during that time Sam and Adam started Four Seasons Landscaping., No one talks about where he is now.

"What's in the cooler?" Her voice has undertones of emotion, but the heaviness has faded.

"I thought we could have a picnic, if you'd like. But if you want to go somewhere else, we can. I don't care where we go, Miranda, I just want to spend some time with you."

One side of her mouth curls into a smile. "You packed a picnic? I don't think I have ever been on a picnic before."

"Really?" I can't help but smile, glad the tension is fading.

"Really."

"Well, we must change that immediately."

Somewhere from my truck to the building's entrance Miranda's hand finds its way into mine. I can't explain why, but I like it. As we enter through the gate, I can't help but scan the perimeter, count all possible exits, and plot alternative routes to each one. I make note of the man in the far left corner nervously checking his watch and the backpack at his feet.

I'm so lost in surveying the area I don't hear Miranda call my name, but the squeeze of my hand frees me from my thoughts. My eyes find hers, wide and concerned.

"Jace?"

"Yes, sorry. What did you say?" I rub the back of my neck with my free hand.

Miranda nods her head toward the green, leafy archway to the right. "I asked if you wanted to start in the rose gardens."

"Sure." I adjust the strap to the bag and allow Miranda to guide me in whatever direction she wants to go. This is her night and I need to get my shit together before I ruin it.

Together, we duck under the foliage. I glance at the man on the bench once more. At the same time I notice short, blonde woman in tight black yoga pants approaching from the opposite direction. As we pass, the woman's eyes linger on me for a few seconds too long. I quickly determine she is not a threat, but the feel of Miranda tensing by my side indicates she does not agree. Miranda's spine straightens just a little and she moves closer, into my side, sliding her right hand up my forearm and stopping just above my elbow. I have to suppress a laugh. She's claiming me and it's the sexiest thing I've ever seen. Yoga Pants' eyes drop to Miranda's hand and then lower to the stone walkway.

Message received.

"Huh," Miranda huffs and this time I can't stop from laughing.

Lowering my mouth to her ear I speak so only she can hear me. "Don't worry, Blue. She has nothing on you."

She doesn't respond, but the smile on her face is enough for me.

Chapter 19
Miranda

I could hardly believe it when we pulled up in front of this place. Of all of the places in the world, I never imagined Jace would choose this one to take me to tonight. I allowed myself the time it took to walk from the truck to the front gate to reminisce about how excited Adam and Sam were when they got the contract to work on the gardens in the arboretum. All Seasons Landscaping had only been open a few months, and landing this job was a huge deal. This place is essentially where it all began for them.

Once we step through the gates and into the gardens, I push all thoughts of Adam and my past aside, and focus on the here and now. I refuse to allow myself to ruin this evening over things I cannot change. Instead, I take a deep breath and try to relax.

"Wow. This place is amazing," Jace says, his eyes sweeping from side to side, soaking in the beautiful landscaping around us. Rose bushes in all different shades of pink, orange, and yellow blend together in to a flawless pattern of color against a green background.

"It sure is. Wait until you see what is past that bend in the path," I say, pointing ahead to where the stone path disappears around a soft corner.

"I can see why Sam is as busy as he is. This is like art." Jace laughs. "He must have thought I was crazy when I told him my own landscaping experience was mowing lawns as a kid."

I laugh at this too. Sam must've been dying on the inside when he first spoke to Jace, but I know my brother. He took one look at Jace and saw something in him. Something that, no matter how inexperienced, is worth taking a chance on. I know, because I see it every time I look in to his eyes.

"Sam wasn't always this way. To be honest, I'm not really sure how it all began. One day he was out of work, wandering through life, and the next he owned his own business, tied to responsibilities. I really don't know how he learned how to do all of this." I wave my hand. "It just seems to come naturally."

Approaching the turn in the path, I brace myself for what's ahead. This section is one of my absolute favorites. The sweet fragrance of the regal flowers behind us fades and is carried away by the fresh, crisp scent of a trickling brook. Short, clean grass carpets the ground from path to stream. A tall willow tree weeps over the edge, its long wispy branches wave in the breeze skimming the water's surface. Clumps of lily pads float on the water where a small eddy swirls gently.

"Wow," Jace breathes.

"Yeah." A shiver runs down my spine and I tug at the edge of my sweater.

Side by side we stand quietly for several heartbeats, both lost in a moment of serenity. "This looks like a great place to sit for a while. Shall we?" Jace asks nodding his head toward the grass.

"We shall," I tease, taking his arm once again.

Jace spreads out a small blanket I hadn't realized he brought, and we sit side by side nibbling on the snacks he packed. There is a moment of heavy, uncomfortable silence, but soon the conversation begins to flow. We keep the topics light, neither of us venturing too far from safe subjects, and as the sky changes from a day to dusk, I find myself having an amazing time.

"He did not whistle at her." I'm laughing so hard I can barely breathe as Jace explains some ridiculous thing Luis did at work.

"I swear. I couldn't believe it. I thought the woman was going to punch him in the face."

"I would've paid to see that." I laugh harder, my stomach muscles begging for mercy. I wipe my face with the back of my hand and try to get control of my breathing.

Jace leans forward, shrinking the already narrow space between us, and tucks a piece of hair behind my ear. His face is only inches from mine. We are so close I can feel the warmth of his breath on my cheeks and see the golden flecks swirling in his warm, brown eyes.

"I didn't think it was possible," he whispers.

"What?" I ask, taking a deep breath.

The corner of his mouth curls in to his crooked smile I like so much. "You're so beautiful, but when you laugh, your eyes twinkle like sapphires in the moonlight. You're stunning."

I feel the heat rush to my cheeks. My breath comes out in small pants and my heartbeat thunders in my ears.

"Jace," I begin, but stop because I don't know what to say. I should tell him he shouldn't say things like that to me. But I don't want him to stop. Just the opposite, I want him to keep talking.

"I love the way you say my name," he says. "Do you know how many nights I've spent awake trying to recall the sound of my name from your lips?"

He moves a fraction closer. My head swirls dizzily and my eyes dart to either side, trying to gather my bearings. . The garden is quiet except for the trickle of water in the background. No one else is near. We are alone. I turn my attention back to Jace.

His hooded eyes bounce from my eyes to my lips and back again. On impulse, my tongue darts across my bottom lip drawing a low growl from Jace's chest. Quickly, he closes the distance between us, wrapping his arms around me and pulling me near. He lowers his lips to mine, but at the very last second I turn my head, causing his lips to miss their mark and meet my check instead.

I close my eyes as embarrassment sweeps over me. What am I thinking? I can't do this. Oh my god. What am I doing here? Pushing back, I break free from Jace's strong arms. My hair covers part of my face, offering me a small refuge from his stare. I draw in a deep breath before speaking.

"Jace, I'm sorry. I shouldn't be here. I don't even know what I was thinking. Why would I think I could do this again? I can't. I've had a great evening. Really, I have. It's been wonderful, but I should go."

I clamp my mouth shut to stop any further rambling. My blood has run from hot to cold so quickly I can't think straight. Needing to escape, before I embarrass myself further, I push myself from the ground and turn, but before I can move further, his large hand grasps my arm. I stop, but I don't turn to face him. I can't.

"Miranda, look at me," he says, but I don't obey. I shake my head in defiance. "Please," he begs, pushing himself off the blanket.

The tone of his voice grates against my resistance until I have no choice but to give in. I brace myself to see aggravation on his face, caused from being led on and then turned down, but when our eyes finally meet, I'm surprised to see neither. Instead, there's an emotion I can't place swimming in the darkness of his eyes.

"I should be the one to apologize," he says, taking a step towards me. "I lost myself for a moment and wasn't thinking. Well, at least not with the correct anatomy." He laughs.

I can't help it and laugh, too.

"Please don't run away. The last thing I ever want is to make you feel uncomfortable. I just want to spend some time with you. I'm sorry," he says, running the pad of his thumb across my cheek before smoothing a strand of hair from my forehead and letting his finger linger on my jawline.

Once again, I am speechless. It has been so long since I felt the roughness of a man's touch against my skin. The stirring in my belly is something I thought I would never feel again. Something I thought I would never want again. Adam was my one and only. For so long, I was fine with that, but in this moment I'm anything but fine. I press my thighs together to dull the ache and try to push the remorse and guilt I feel into the back of my mind. Both are difficult to do.

"I need a moment," I say.

This time, when I step back, he lets me go. I quickly weave my way through the perfectly shaped bushes and shrubs. I rush up a set of stone steps wrapping my sweater tighter around my body. The night air nips at my skin, but helps clear my head.

Stepping back on the path, I slow my pace. The sound of my footsteps against the smooth, well placed stones, echoes in the night. Coming to a wooden bench, I stop and sit. I tilt my head back and stare at the stars above. The streetlights in the distance cast a pink hue on the horizon, but the brightest stars still manage to peek through. From here, the world seems so peaceful, so serene. The complete opposite of how I feel inside.

I'm not sure how long I'm alone, but soon I hear someone approaching from behind. I should be scared, being out here alone, but I'm not. I don't need to look to know it's Jace. As cliché as it sounds, I can feel his presence and, deep down, I knew he wouldn't let me wander off at night without following.

As he nears, a shiver runs down my spine. My mind races quickly. I search for something to say. Some reasonable explanation for how I reacted. Drawing in a deep breath, to steel my nerves, I open my mouth to speak, but all the words evaporate when Jace gently slips his jacket around me. His intoxicating scent surrounds me once more.

"Wow," he says, taking a seat next to me.

"Beautiful, isn't it?" I respond, thinking he is talking about the view. It's not until I finally turn to look at him do I realize he is staring right at me.

The corner of his mouth twitches. His eyes roam my face, not leaving an inch untouched, before turning is eyes to the sky.

"The stars are different here." His remark catches me off guard. I study the side of his face for a moment, before turning my attention upward as well.

"How so?" I ask.

"The lights, they drown out the darkness. In the desert, where the night swallows every drop of light, the sky is lit with every star imaginable," he says, pausing to draw in a fortifying breath "I saw some things in that place that will haunt me for the rest of my life. Horrible things I wouldn't wish on anyone. Things made of pure evil. But the night sky shining with millions of stars is one image I hope to keep with me forever."

The silence stretches between us until I can't take it any longer.

"Jace." I need to say something. I need to explain. Maybe not everything, but I need to say something. "Look. I don't know how to say this, so I am just going to come out with it. I'm not like the other woman you date. I'm not used to," I wave my hand around, "this. Hell, most days I don't even have a free moment to myself. I don't wear designer clothes or spend hours at the salon. I buy most of my clothing from clearance racks, and I'm lucky if I wash my hair more than twice a week. I don't spend hours at the gym with a personal trainer, because I get a workout just trying to keep up with my life. I had a wonderful time this evening, but this isn't the real me."

Each sentence draws the tears closer to the surface. I can't tell if they are tears of regret or sadness, but I blink them away before I have a chance to find out. All the while Jace watches me intently.

"Blue, I don't care about any of that," Jace says before standing. "I've spent too much of my life toting a gun, following orders, and fighting to see another day." Stepping in front of me, he takes my left hand in his right as he pulls me up so we're standing toe to toe. He bends at the knees so we are the same height before he continues.

"This," he lifts his free hand to gesture between us, "I want this. You and me, Miranda. I want your real. Even though, heaven help me, I should keep my distance. Not because of you, Blue, but because I'm not good enough for you."

For the second time this evening, he has rendered me speechless. I open and close my mouth a few times, hoping to jump start my brain, to voice a response, but it's no use. Instead, I stare into his beautiful brown eyes, which flicker to my lips like before. I swear if he tries, this time, I'll let him kiss me. But Jace doesn't move to close the distance, and I'm shocked at how disappointed I am. Instead, he looks at the stone path.

"C'mon. What do you say we get out of here?"

"We don't have to leave," I assure him. My stomach sinks at the thought of not spending the rest of the evening near him, but it's probably for the best.

"Let's go," is his only response, before locking his fingers with mine.

Before I can fully process what has happened in the last fifteen minutes, Jace weaves us through the gardens, stopping to pick up our discarded picnic.. I can feel the tension building in the inches that separate us, and I don't know what to say to break it.

Once we arrive at Jace's truck, he opens the passenger side door and helps me in before walking around the front of the vehicle and slipping into the driver's seat. The sleek black SUV is barely audible as it purrs to life and we drive away, the arboretum disappearing in the mirror. We continue in silence for several minutes. I roll my thumbs trying to think of something to say.

"Thank you for inviting me tonight. I really did have a nice time. It has been so long since I have gotten dressed up and gone out," I admit.

"The pleasure was mine, I assure you," Jace says covering both of my hands with one of his.

The clock on the dashboard says eight twenty. I'm exhausted from running around with the girls all day, but I am not ready for this evening to end. Would it be too forward to ask him stay out? Of course, it would. God, what kind of woman would that make me look like? I should just keep my mouth shut. Seriously, for all I know he is dying to drop me off, especially after the way I acted. I'm sure he was just being polite earlier. I mean look at him. What would a guy like him see in someone like me, a single mother with two children?

Just then Jace's hand leaves mine and pulls my bottom lip from my teeth. I hadn't even realized I was biting it.

"Penny for your thoughts." His eyes flicker from the road to my face.

"I was just thinking …" I stammer. "You know what? It's nothing."

"I didn't look like nothing. If you bite your lip any harder you'll draw blood."

"Well … I'm not ready for the night to be over," I admit, ducking my chin to my chest. I don't mention that the girls aren't home and I hate being there by myself. The house is too quiet and the memories too loud.

"I was hoping you would say that." He lifts my hand and kisses my knuckles. "I have an idea."

Chapter 20
Jace

The usually busy main street is all but deserted when I pull my truck up to the curb. A flickering red light signals the diner is open, like I hoped it would be. A cold, light rain begins to fall as I step out of the truck and round the front to meet Miranda on the other side. She looks up at the worn sign above the front door and smiles.

"I thought since we didn't eat much maybe we could get some pancakes," I say.

Her smile widens and she slips her hand into mine. "This is one of my favorite places. The girls are always begging me to take them here."

I don't know what made me think of this diner, but when Miranda said she wasn't ready to go home this was the first thing that popped into my mind. To say I was relieved to hear her say she wasn't ready to end our evening would be an understatement. Heaven help me, spending one evening with her isn't going to be enough.

Holding the door open for her, I slip my hand from hers and rest it on the small of her back, guiding her over the threshold. Before tonight, I wanted to hold her, to touch her, but now my want has transformed into a need. Being near her and not feeling her warmth beneath my fingers would be a shame.

Normally, during the day, this place is bustling with patrons. But at this time of the night, it's deserted. The low sound of a radio comes from the backroom, but otherwise it's quiet. We stop at one of the empty booths set beneath the large glass windows that line the front of the diner. The red vinyl squeaks under our weight as we slide in, sitting across from one another. I reach across the table, placing my palms up, inviting her to take my hands. Thankfully, she doesn't hesitate and I am rewarded with her warmth once more.

A middle aged woman wearing jeans and a bright pink t-shirt with the diner's logo on the front pushes through the swinging door separating from the dining area from the kitchen. She looks up from the gray, plastic tote filled with glasses she is carrying to see Miranda and me waiting. She presses her lips into a tight line, matching her narrow eyes. Unceremoniously, she sets the container down on the beige counter, causing the glasses to rattle and clank together.

Miranda glances behind her to see the origin of the noise and turns back to me, amusement dancing in her eyes.

"Someone's grumpy," she whispers, the corner of her mouth twitching, and I laugh.

"Good evening. Would you too like something to drink?" the waitress says, handing both of us a menu.

"I'll have a decaf coffee, please," Miranda speaks up first.

"I'll have the same," I follow.

The waitress nods and leaves without another word.

"Well, all right then," Miranda says under her breath. Her eyes pass over the menu quickly before she sets it on the table.

"Do you know what you want?" I ask, still looking at the selections.

"They have the best chocolate chip pancakes."

"Really?"

"Yeah, they're my favorite."

"Chocolate chip pancakes it is, then," I agree, setting my menu on top of hers. The waitress returns with our coffees. Dumping a handful of creamers on the table, she pulls a pad and a pen from her back pocket.

"So, what'll be?" she asks gruffly, a strand of salt and peppered hair falling into her eyes.

Miranda stifles a giggle and I nudge her leg with my foot, trying to keep a straight face as I order. "We'll both have the chocolate chip pancakes, please."

"Anything else?"

"And a side of bacon," Miranda adds, much to my surprise.

The waitress jots down the order, takes the menus roughly from Miranda and leaves without another glance. Miranda watches her go, a smile on her lips, and then meets my feigned shocked stare.

"What?" she asks innocently, though her smile is bright with embarrassment. Her shoulders lift with a shrug. "Who doesn't like bacon?"

"A woman after my heart," I say, but once the words leave my lips I wish I could take them back. Twirling my spoon, I take a deep breath, stretching the tightness in my chest before meeting Miranda's eyes again. If my statement bothers Miranda, she doesn't show it.

"So, tell me, how is it working for my bother?"

"C'mon, you can't ask me that. It's not fair," I laugh, leaning back into my seat.

"I suppose you're right," she snickers. "Sam can be such a pain in the ass sometimes, but he means well most of the time."

"He seems like a decent guy," I agree, causing Miranda to casually nod her head.

"Sometimes," she teases. "Things will slow down in the next few weeks. He and Claire normally take some time off then, so you're actually lucky. He won't be around as much. Are you ready for your first New England winter?"

"It will be nice to see a white Christmas," I say.

Miranda snorts. "Yeah, right. Do you want to know what will happen? It won't snow at all in December, and then in January we'll get four feet of snow. By the end of March you'll be begging for spring. I swear, it should only be allowed to snow the week before and after Christmas. Then, immediately after the New Year, it should all melt I think," she says, taking a sip of her coffee. "I'm telling you, Jace, you moved in the wrong direction. I would love to move south."

"Then why don't you?"

"My whole life is here. I can't just up and leave. I can't do that to Katelyn and Paige. Someday, maybe."

The second half of the evening goes much better than the first. The food is amazing. Miranda was right, this place has the best pancakes. I'm pleasantly surprised at how much she eats. I hate when a woman doesn't eat. If you're hungry, eat for Christ sake. The conversation flows easily. She tells me more about her daughters. I learn that Katelyn loves music as much as Miranda, but can be very shy, while Paige is a force not to be reckoned with.

"There I am, in the produce section, squeezing oranges, when Bethany Miller, who I cannot stand, comes up to me and asks me if I know what Paige said to her son. Of course I had no idea what she was talking about, so I had to ask what happened. I mean, it could have been something serious. I should have known better." She smiles.

"What happened?"

"She goes on to tell me that her son and Paige got into an argument about whether or not Paige was a girl," she pauses to take a sip of coffee.

"What?" I choke.

"Apparently the two of them got into an argument at recess about Paige liking to do 'boy things', like play sports and do karate, so she must be a boy."

"You've got to be kidding me. But why was she mad? If anything you should've been upset at her son making such a ridiculous comment."

"Well, Paige turned to the little boy and said 'Of course I am a girl. Boys have penises. I have a vagina.'"

I nearly spit my sip of coffee across the table. "She didn't."

"She did. I didn't know what to say. I mean, Paige is right, but she probably shouldn't have said that."

"What did you do?"

She shrugs, smiling, "What could I do? I told Bethany I would take care of it just to get her to leave me alone so she wouldn't call the school. That's the last thing I need. Then Paige and I had a little talk about appropriate comments."

Miranda twirls the spoon in her mug, "How about you? How is your mother? I bet she misses you," she says.

"She's good. I think these last few years have aged her more than necessary, but her boyfriend, Benny, has really helped."

"Boyfriend, huh? Good for her," Miranda teases with a playful wink.

"Yeah, well … boyfriend is an odd adjective to describe a fifty-five year old man who sells life insurance for a living. It could be worse. My mother is happy, so I can't complain."

Miranda explained her mother was still living in a halfway house and would most likely spend the rest of her life in an assisted living facility in one form or another.

"Sam visits her as often as he can, at least once a month, but I haven't seen her in more than a year," she says, her voice just above a whisper.

"That must be tough," I say, pangs of missing my own mother twinge in my gut.

Miranda's eyes fall slightly, but not all the way to her lap. "Sure, I suppose. But we never had a close relationship, even before, when she lived with us at home."

"How old were you?"

"I was five the last time she was home. I remember her locking herself in the bathroom. Being so young I didn't understand what was going on." She begins picking at her cuticles. "I remember my dad telling me 'mommy isn't feel well right now' when I would ask why she couldn't come play with my dolls." She laughs sadly. "My dad would always plop down next to me on the floor and help me brush their hair or change their clothes. Thinking back, he must have looked ridiculous, but that was my dad. Everything he did was for me and Sam."

"Sounds like an amazing father."

"He was. He loved my mother fiercely. I think it nearly killed him having to send her away, but he didn't know what else to do. It had become too much and the last episode she had at home was too much to bear."

I reach across the table and cover her hands with mine. With a gentle squeeze, I silently pass her my apologies and condolences.

"That must have been hard. Even all of the years I've spent away from home, I always found comfort knowing my mom was there, waiting for me."

"How many tours did you serve?" Miranda asks, her tone indicating she is happy to change the subject. Though talking about my service is not my most favorite topic, I oblige when I see her relax.

"I was deployed three times," I say. The waitress takes the opportunity to clear our empty plates and leave the check on the table. Reaching for the slip of paper before Miranda can, I eye the total and toss a few bills on the table.

A shadow of concern clouds her eyes. "Is that where... uh... where you hurt your leg?"

"Yes." One word, that's all I can manage. I don't want to go into the details or see the images in my head. Miranda chews on her bottom lip and I see in her eyes she wants me to continue. Her face is flush with worry, sadness, and, oddly, what looks like guilt.

I draw in a deep breath and keep talking before I can second guess myself.

"I was an Army Ranger. We're trained to be the best of the best, the strongest of the strong. I thought I knew what I was getting into. I went into boot camp a wide-eyed, soft kid and came out a hardened, deadly machine.

"When I was deployed the first time, I was full of piss and vinegar. I thought I knew what to expect, but even with all the training I was still scared shitless. Not that I would admit it at the time," I laugh, shaking my head.

"Rangers do things regular soldiers don't. Our missions are more complex and more dangerous. Jesus, the things I did had to be done; I've never doubted that. I had my orders and I executed them, but the memories and the images still haunt me, even now. I'm sure they will for the rest of my life. Being there was like a living Hell on Earth. That entire first tour, my best friend, Hound, never let me lose sight of our purpose. Shit, that prick kept me grounded through it all."

"He sounds like a good man," Miranda says with a smile, tight smile.

"He was." Memories of my best friend, my brother, flash behind my eyes, intensifying the throb that has begun to thrum in my skull. My head feels too heavy to hold high, and slowly its weight forces my eyes to fall from Miranda's face.

"The second and third deployments were much of the same; more sand, more fighting, and more assholes trying to kill us before we killed them. I like to think we saved more lives than we took, but there is no denying the amount of blood we shed. Our missions grew more dangerous. Each day brought us one foot closer to the evil." I pause, swallowing the large lump in my throat. Focusing on the wadded paper napkin between my fingers, I tear it into little squares and continue.

"It was two weeks before the end of third tour when we finally arrived on its doorstep. That day, I got to look the Devil in the eye and knew, for certain, evil on Earth existed. While my unit patrolled a neighborhood several miles from the center of the city, moving from house to house, door to door, Hound, would not shut up about a girl back home." I manage a smile. "He went on and on about getting home so he could see her. He met a girl a week before we deployed for the first time and had fallen head over heels, turning my best friend into a lovesick puppy. Even after all those years and deployments, they were madly in love. I can't even imagine a love like that," I admit.

"The other guys in our unit were always busting his balls about it, but I never said a word. Hell, he had listened to my bullshit a time or two, so I usually kept my mouth shut. But that day, I was giving him shit about being whipped. Damn, maybe if I had kept quiet, like I had in the past, fate would have worked out differently. Maybe I jinxed us. Maybe I would have seen what was coming if I was more focused on our mission and not talking trash." I clench my fist tightly, causing my knuckles to pop.

"Jace," Miranda whispers my name, covering my fist with her small hands. "It's okay. You don't have to tell me the rest," she insists, but I ignore her.

"As we walked along the edge of a building, I teased him about finally finding the balls to propose to her. I was telling how it was about time he got off his lazy ass and asked her to marry him. Just then, a young boy stepped from the shadows. The kid couldn't have been any older than twelve. His dark hair clung to his sweat soaked forehead in the heat. His eyes were equally dark and vacant. There was no life in them. It was as if Satan himself had sucked the soul from his body.

"It took me a second to realize he was clutching something to his chest. A single second, but even that was too long. Before I could yell to Hound, the loudest, most deafening noise knocked the air from my lungs. I saw flashes of color before everything went black. What felt like a freight train crashed into my chest and sent me flying. My body twisted and bent in ways that seemed impossible. In the distance, mixed with the buzzing in my head, I heard screams before everything went silent and the world faded to black."

I pause, feeling every fiber of my body vibrating. Grief, guilt, and sadness thrum through my veins, saturating my cells, drowning me slowly. My chest clenches, clamping around my lungs, forcing me to take short shallow breaths. Black spots dance on the edge of my vision, and I feel my head being to swim in the dizzy whirlpool building.

After a moment, I feel a gentle squeeze around my clenched fist, the napkin now a wad of unrecognizable paper. My eyes lift slowly and my gaze fixes on two bright blue beacons, shining in the darkness that surrounds me. They call me back from the memories of my past and into the present. Little by little the cloud lifts and my vision clears. Drawing in a deep breath, I force myself to finish.

"Hound died that day, as did three other men in my unit. I will never forget how Mandy, his girlfriend, wept violently in my arms at his funeral and had to be carried away as the mournful sound of "Taps" hung in the air. The final gunshots of a twenty -one gun salute echoed off the gravestones. I think the sound of her wailing still haunts my dreams more than the screaming."

The words linger, but eventually dissipate. Miranda doesn't say anything. She doesn't need to. The look in her eyes and the sullen expression on her face says all I need to hear. Instead, she quietly slides from the booth. Slipping her arms into her sweater, she tucks loose strands of hair behind her ear.

"C'mon, let's get out of here." She nods her head toward the door.

The ride home is quiet. The tension between us is thick. Miranda makes a few comments during the ride, pointing out things in town as we pass through. Whether she does this to break silence or is simply trying to be helpful, I'm not sure. The radio plays softly in the background, filling the rest of the void.

The entire time I know I should say something, but what? After all I've shared, what more could I say? The night had gone so well. At least, I thought it had. I didn't want to end the night with this, this thing between us.

THE SECOND VERSE

Similar to when I picked her up this evening, I pull into her driveway to bring her home. I'm able to put the truck in park and exit, rounding the front to her side, before she is able to get out. Closing the door behind her, I slide my hand into hers, sighing at the comfort of feeling the weight of her hand in mine. Side by side, we walk up the front path to the porch. Only the sound of rustling leaves can be heard above the beating of my heart.

Reluctantly, I release Miranda's hand so she can rummage in her bag for her key. With the lock released and the door pushed open an inch, I know my moment is slipping away. Turning to face me, I notice a tiny tremor run through her body.

"I had a ..." we both begin to say in unison.

"Sorry," she says, blushing. "I had a great time," she finishes. I can't help but notice her eyes dart from my own to my lips. I notice, because mine do the same.

"I did, too," I admit. The pink tip of her tongue traces the line of her lips like it did earlier this evening, leaving a glistening trail in its wake. I want to kiss her, but I also don't want to scare her off again. I know she has things in her past she has not shared with me yet. Hell, she has two children and their father is nowhere in sight.

I lean closer, not able to ignore the need to kiss her, but at the last second I turn my head and kiss her cheek. I already made her run once tonight trying to kiss her. I don't want to risk it a second time.

"Thank you for a great night." My voice is low, and the softness I tried to find was over shadowed by husky need.

A shadow of disappointment passes her eyes. The step back she takes is tiny, merely an inch or so, but it feels like a canyon between us.

"Goodnight, Jace."

Miranda turns toward the door, but before she can cross the threshold, my hand catches hers and I swing her back around. A shocked squeal escapes her throat as she crashes into my chest. Consequences be damned, my lips claim hers.

I meant to be gentle, to start slow and sweet, but the moment her lips touch mine an explosion short circuits my brain and the kiss becomes brutal, bruising even. I hear the thud of her bag drop on the wood planks of the porch seconds before her hands tangle behind my neck. My fingers dig into her hips, pulling her closer. The evidence of my desire now presses against her stomach. I trace my tongue across the seam of her lips, as hers had done just moments before, asking permission. Answering my plea, they part, allowing me inside.

To my surprise, she follows my lead and together we lose ourselves in each other.

After a moment much too short, the frenzy slows until we pull apart, both of us panting. Sliding my hands up her sides, over her arms, across her collarbones, and up to her neck, I cup her face. I place tiny, feather light kisses upon each lip and on each corner, paying homage to the temple of her mouth.

"Wow," she breathes and I have to agree.

"Yes, wow." I kiss her once more, chastely, on the lips. "Goodnight."

"Goodnight."

I watch her enter the house and wait until I hear the click of the lock before heading to the truck. Backing down the driveway, I look out the windshield, noticing a shadow in the front window. I force myself to go home, where I know a cold shower waits.

Chapter 21
Jace
Then

It's always so Goddamn hot in this place. Even when the wind blows there's no relief. I've heard people say the desert isn't so bad, because it's a dry heat. There's no humidity to make the air thick. That might be true, but my mother's oven is full of dry heat, and I don't have any plans to stick my head in it anytime soon. What I wouldn't give for an ocean breeze right about now.

"You really want to play again? I just won three in a row. You ain't got it today," Hound says, scooping up the discarded cards on the makeshift table.

"Blow me," I growl, throwing my losing hand at him. "Just deal and shut up."

"Whatever you say, Sarg," Hound snickers, dealing out five cards to each of us. "But I have to duck out after this hand. I have VTC time at 1700 with Mandy."

"I can't believe she's still with your sorry ass," I tease, looking at another shitty hand. I discard three cards, hoping to get something good in return. As it turns out, luck is not on my side. I get nothing better than what I started with.

"Screw you. I'm a great catch." He flashes me the same smile I've seen him use on girls in the past.

"Yeah, right. I've been stuck with your dumb ass for years and haven't figured out how to get rid of you."

"Fuck you. You know you love me." Hound winks and puckers his lips, blowing kisses my way. "But seriously, sometimes I can't believe it either."

Hound leans over the table and lowers his voice, "Dude, you know I ain't one for hearts and flowers, but," he swallows hard, "I love that girl. She's it for me."

I can't help it. I laugh so loudly a few of the guys throwing darts across the yard turn and look in our directions.

"You can't be serious."

"As a heart attack," he says in a tone I've never heard him use before. "I'm telling you, this love shit just sneaks up on you. One day you're living your life without a care in the world and then *BAM,* it hits you right in the nuts." Hound sounds serious as he throws a card down on the table and takes another from the deck.

"You're so full of shit." A swift gust of wind blows by, sweeping sand in my face.

"Kid, I am telling you. Trust me. We were doing our thing. You know, we went out, we saw a few movies, and she met my dad, things like that. Then one day I was sitting on the couch watching Judge Judy – "

"Seriously?" I cut him off, wiping the sand from my eyes with the hem of my shirt.

"Shut up and listen. For Christ sake, you're annoying as fuck. Anyway, I was watching my girl Judy listen to these two people, who had broken up months before, argue about who should get the Goddamn flat screen TV. It got me thinking - what would happen if Mandy and I broke up? It made me sick to my stomach. Shit, even thinking about it now makes me want to puke my guts out."

I start to laugh again, but the look he gives me makes me stop. I've known Hound a long time, and I've never seen this look in his eyes. Jerking my chin, I motion for him to continue.

"I knew right then I'd fallen in love with her. I knew if the thought of losing her made me feel like I've been punched in the gut, then it must be love. I've never felt like this before." He throws down his hand showing a full house, calling my bluff, before continuing. "I love her, J. I'm telling you, I'm going to spend the rest of my life with that girl. You'll see. One day, you'll find someone who you'd do anything for and the thought of her leaving makes you feel like you've been kicked in the nuts." He stands, wiping his face with his sleeve. "And I can't wait to bust your ass about it."

Chapter 22
Miranda

"Oh God, please make it stop."

Clamping my eyes shut, I try to ward off the pounding in my head. It feels like my brain is ten sizes too large and my skull is squeezing it like a vice. I try to draw in a deep breath, but even the fraction of an inch my shoulders raise causes my head to throb even more. I peel my eyes open to review the paperwork on the desk, but once the small bit of light hits my pupils, tears begin to pool and I slam them shut. Nausea rolls my stomach and bile rises in my throat.

I haven't had a migraine like this in years. The last time I felt like this, Paige was only a toddler. I was locked up in my darkened bedroom for two days while Sam and Claire took care of the girls for me. I thought I was going to die then, and I'm pretty sure I might now. I should've stayed home today, the telltale tingle behind my eyes warning me of the agony to come, but I ignored it, determined to come in and finish the invoices I had left behind last night. Call me dedicated or sadistic, I'm not sure which.

Gingerly, I rest my elbows on the desk and place my head in my hands. Maybe if I just take a break for a second the pain will subside long enough for me to get home. My mind races with all of the things I need to get accomplished today. Between the housework and laundry that's never complete despite my best efforts, helping Katelyn with her English paper, and Paige with her science project last night, I'm exhausted. A small yawn threatens to escape, but I clench my teeth tight knowing the smallest movement will make the pain that much worse.

I start to make a list of the things I need to have done by this evening when I'm nudged in the side. My hand falls from my chin and my head snaps up. A searing pain shoots from my head down my spine making me whimper pitifully. Tears trickle down my cheeks before I can stop them.

"Miranda, are you okay?" a voice shouts.

"Please. Be. Quiet." I bite out.

I try to relax my face, which is screwed up tight, and as I do I feel Jace nearby. Even with my eyes closed I know it's him. His large frame moves in front of me, blocking the sun that shines through the front window. The shadow is just enough relief to allow me to open my eyes into thin slits.

"What's wrong?" he asks, softer this time.

"I have a headache and you are shouting," I hiss.

His beautiful face droops and his lips turn downward. Jace begins to squat, to bring himself down to eye level, but I reach out and grab his forearm.

"Please don't move," I croak, my eyes pinched shut. "You ... sun."

His confused expression melts into realization. "What can I do? Do you need some Ibuprofen?" he whispers.

I want to laugh, because taking Ibuprofen would be like attacking an elephant with a toothpick, but laughing would hurt too much. I shake my head just a little.

"I don't think that's going to help. I have medication at home. I just need to get through the afternoon. I'll be fine, really."

The room goes quiet, but I know he hasn't left. I can feel his presence. Through my eyelids, I see his shadow move and instantly I'm assaulted by bright light. I groan and open my mouth to say something when I feel his arm slide under my knees and the other snake behind my back. In one smooth movement Jace lifts me from my chair and holds me against his chest.

"What are you doing?" I moan, bracing my head against his shoulder.

"I'm taking you home," he says, matter of fact.

"What? I can't leave. I have to finish those invoices. Plus, it's Wednesday. Paige ... karate," I try to explain, but the more I talk the more my stomach rolls.

"You aren't spending the rest of the afternoon in the office like this and you definitely aren't driving yourself home," he says quietly, tucking my head under his chin as we step outside.

Carefully, he opens his truck door and slides me into the passenger seat. I feel his strong arm reach across my chest to secure the seat belt. Then, his hand slides across my collarbone and up my neck, tucking a stray piece of hair behind my ear. All the while I keep my eyes closed. Jace leans forward and places a feather light kiss on my forehead before gently closing the door. My head falls back against the leather headrest.

"But I have to get the girls. Paige will be so upset if she doesn't go to karate," I repeat after we've pulled out on to the main road. Honestly, I just want to go to sleep.

"I'll take Paige and pickup Katelyn after school." The tone of his voice is so nonchalant that, on reflex, my eyes pop open.

"What?" I choke.

With an air of confidence, Jace says, "It's no big deal. I can get the girls and take them where they need to go while you get some rest."

I stare at him. My weakened physical state is wrecking my emotions, causing tears to pool in my eyes. Jace must feel the weight of my gaze, because his eyes leave the road for a moment and meet mine. Quickly, he pulls the truck over, slowing to a stop. In one swift move, he undoes his own seat belt and slides closer to me. Taking my face in his hands, he softly wipes my cheeks with the pad of his thumbs, removing each tear as it falls.

"Aw, Blue. Don't cry. Please. I need to get you home so you can rest. But I can't do that if you're upset," he pleads, leaning closer, kissing the trail his thumbs just made.

Gracefully wiping my nose on my sleeve, I draw in a slow deep breath and nod my head. Jace smiles sadly before moving back to his seat.

I must fall asleep shortly after Jace pulls back onto the street because before I know it, we're in my driveway. I awake to Jace lifting me from the truck. Standing on the front porch, he fumbles with my bag, searching for my keys. On a regular day I might be embarrassed or annoyed that he is going through my things, but I could care less right now. Wrappers and hair ties fall to the ground, along with broken restaurant crayons which land on the wooden porch slats and roll, getting caught in a crack.

With me in his arms, he manages to unlock and open the door. Kicking it closed with his foot, he asks which way to my bedroom. I point up the stairs and snuggle into his warmth. Smoothly Jace carries me up the stairs, as if I were light as a feather, not jostling me once. I assume he looks in each room as we pass, because he doesn't ask which one is mine. Instead he goes straight to the end of the hall.

Once we're in my room, he bends at his knees, pulls the comforter and blanket back with one hand, and sets me down. One by one he pulls off my shoes and then helps me lie back. Feeling the softness of my bed surround me,

I let out a small sigh of relief.

"Where's the medicine?" he whispers.

Squinting, I look up at him. Worry and concern mare his handsome face.

"It's in the bathroom." I point toward the half closed door. "In the medicine cabinet, second shelf from the top on the right hand side."

Without another word he turns, drawing the curtains closed as he passes by. I should be worried about the piles of dirty clothes on the floor and the damp towel hanging haphazardly on the shower rod, but I'm not. I'm not sure if it's because I feel comfortable around Jace, or if it's because of the immense pain I'm in.

Within a minute he returns with the small orange bottle and a little paper cup filled with water.

"Here you go." Jace pops the top, shaking two pills into his hand.

I push up on my elbows and take the pills, popping them into my mouth and washing them down with a sip of water.

"Thank you."

Jace places the bottle and glass on the nightstand and pauses. His head falls to the side and a line forms between his brows. Over the last few weeks I've learned that particular crease forms when he's deep in thought or is trying to concentrate. Curious, I follow his eyes and instantly realize what has his attention. I'm so used to it being there I had completely forgotten about the thick wooden picture frame that sits beside my bed.

"That picture was taken the day Paige was born," I offer, attempting not to speak too loudly. Jace's warm brown eyes glance from the photo, to me, and back again. Lifting it from the nightstand, he holds it in his hands as he sits on the bed at my side.

"Adam was admitted to the hospital two weeks before I went into labor," I begin. "Pancreatic cancer." Two simple words that explain so much.

Jace's eyes fill with sympathy and he swallows forcefully, as if he has something lodged in his throat. Perhaps it's similar to the lump in mine. Pausing, I swallow my grief as my eyes fall back to the photo.

"They tried to keep him out of the delivery room, claiming he wasn't healthy enough to be there and he could catch something and become sicker." I can't help but smile at the memory. "He laughed at them and said 'how much sicker could I get?' Nothing and no one was going to keep him away from us."

I look up from the photo and into Jace's somber eyes. I wonder what he's thinking. I wonder if it bothers him to hear me talk about Adam. I wonder if I should stop, but it's too late now.

THE SECOND VERSE

"After Paige was born the nurse tried to hand her to me, but I insisted Adam be the first to hold her. I knew their time together would be much too short, and I wanted them to have every second they could together. I watched from my bed while Adam sat in a chair beside me, wires and tubes attached to the portable monitors the nurses moved to my room, and listened to him quietly whisper to her." I pause for a moment, blinking back tears. "I don't even know what he said to her. I wanted to ask, but then thought better of it. Whatever it was, it was between the two of them, and I wanted them to share that one small secret. Later that day, Sam brought Katelyn up to the hospital to see us."

I look back to the photo. I'm in a standard white and blue hospital gown. My hair is a mess, half sticking up in a dozen directions and the other half stuck to my face. There's a mixture of fatigue, joy, and sadness in my eyes. Katelyn is sitting next to me, on my right. She looks so young. There's innocence in her expression and her smile is bright. She was so excited to have a little sister and the gravity of the moment was lost on her. Adam sits on my left with Paige, a bundle of pink swaddled in his arms. There are dark circles around his eyes and his cheeks are sunken in from all the weight he had lost in those few short months. The smile on his face was one I had never seen before and would never see again. Sitting there, surrounded by his three girls, he was at complete peace.

"This is the only photo I have of the four of us together. I insisted Claire take a ton of pictures, of Adam and Paige, of him and Katelyn, and of the three of them. But this one, I didn't even realize she had taken it until months later. It's the only one of all of us." I try once more to blink back the tears, but this time I fail. Tiny streams trickle down my cheeks.

"Adam died two days later." The pounding in my head now causes dark spots around the edges of my vision. No longer able to support my weight on my arms, I lie back.

"I'm so sorry," I think I hear him say, but I can't be certain. Cautiously, he sets the photo back in its original spot.

"Get some rest," he says softly, kissing my cheek.

I'm asleep before he even leaves the room.

Chapter 23
Jace

There's pasta everywhere. Even in places I didn't think possible. There are strands on the counter and the floor. Sticky noodles cling to the stove and the front of the fridge. Looking up, there is even one lonely piece hanging from the ceiling. Somehow I can command a unit of over a dozen thick headed men, leading them into the most dangerous places and situations on earth, but making dinner with a child is a complete disaster.

Note to self: don't let the seven -year -old toss spaghetti.

"Oops," Paige giggles beside me, leaning up on her tiptoes to pull a piece of pasta from my shoulder.

"Well, that didn't go like I planned."

After leaving Miranda earlier this afternoon, I went to the elementary school first to pick up Paige. I called Luis on the way to let him know I had something to take care of and I wouldn't be back this afternoon. Sam is down in Connecticut today, so I am certain he won't notice. Even if he did, I don't care. There was no way I was letting Miranda sit in that office for a minute longer. The way her face pinched with pain made me want to punch something. It looked like even breathing hurt. I'm glad she didn't fight me on bringing her home, because she was going whether she liked it or not.

It took much of my strength to leave her alone in her bed. I wanted so badly to lie next to her, pull her against my chest, curl my body around hers, and offer her some comfort. Even after seeing the photo on her bedside table, I still felt this possessive need to protect her and take her pain away.

I will admit it was strange seeing the picture of Miranda with her husband, Adam. Hearing about Adam, knowing he was her husband and the father of Miranda's children, is one thing. Seeing evidence is another. What's even more shocking is it didn't bother me as much as I would've thought. The sting caused by knowing Adam had been with her all of the years I dreamt of her was duller than it should have been. Perhaps it is because I know he has passed on, but I think it has more to do with the shimmer I saw in his eyes as he looked at her in the photo. That man loved Miranda, which was clear as day, so even though she wasn't with me, at least I know she was loved.

After picking up Paige from school, I brought her to karate where I sat on a tiny, uncomfortable wooden bench while she punched and kicked for an hour. I have to admit she is actually pretty good. All the times I've been around Paige she has been a little ball of energy, buzzing from here to there, but she was focused and calm this afternoon. Watching her concentrate was interesting, because as soon as we stepped outside she was back to moving a million miles a minute.

From there, Paige and I drove across town to the high school. Katelyn was definitely surprised to see me pull up to the curb, but once I explained to her that Miranda was sick, she slid into the passenger's seat without another question. I pretended not to notice the slight smile that curled her lips or the way she tried to cover it with her hand.

Once we arrived back to the house, the girls settled in to do their homework, and I rustled through the cabinets looking for something to make for dinner. When I found the spaghetti I felt like I hit the jackpot. I thought spaghetti and sauce would be simple. What I underestimated was my pint-size sous chefs' enthusiasm for all things noodle.

Scraping the last of the tacky pasta from the floor and dumping it in the trash, I begin to rummage through the cabinets once again.

"How about peanut butter and jelly instead?" I call over my shoulder.

"All right," Paige says, sounding slightly disappointed. Out of the corner of my eye, I see Katelyn briefly look up from her lap and nod her head slightly

While Paige and I have been attempting to cook dinner, Katelyn has sat in a kitchen chair, strumming her guitar for the last thirty minutes. She causally hums a tune I don't recognize and jots down something in a worn notebook from time to time. I don't think she would have noticed the spaghetti fiasco if Paige hadn't dropped the metal strainer on the floor.

"What are you working on?" I ask, smearing a glob of grape jelly on a slice of bread.

Katelyn looks up from her lap, biting her bottom lip, reminding me of her

141

Janet Lee

mother. "Nothing," she responses meekly, but I can tell by the pink blushing her cheeks it's more than nothing.

"You've been messing with that thing for the last half hour. That doesn't seem like nothing to me," I prod, pushing a paper plate containing the world's worst looking PB&J across the breakfast bar toward Paige.

"She does that every night," Paige says, taking a huge bite out of the sandwich, humming in approval.

Apparently, looks aren't everything. Never judge a sandwich by the crumbled bread cover.

"I always hear her playing after I am in bed at night," Paige continues, crumbs littering the front of her shirt.

"Shut up Paige."

"You shut up," Paige yells, spitting out a piece of bread.

"Gross," Katelyn utters under her breath.

"Say it, don't spray it," I tease, ruffling Paige's hair. Walking across the kitchen, I sit in the seat across from Katelyn.

"Play me something."

"What?" Her eyes widen, like a deer caught in headlights.

"Play me something," I repeat.

"I can't," she stutters slightly; her voice heavy with anxiety.

"Sure you can."

"I don't know."

"C'mon, please," I beg.

Just as I think she's going to say no and I debate whether to push her further or let it go, she nods her head and takes a deep breath. "Okay."

I watch as she adjusts the clamp on the neck of the guitar, strumming her fingers a few times, testing the sound. Once satisfied with the tone, she begins. I don't recognize the melody at first, but once the first few lyrics leave her lips I know the song instantly. I'm shocked that, played acoustically without any background music at this unique tempo, Katy Perry's "Dark Horse" sounds completely different. In this form, it's more soulful. It's the perfect balance of fierce and delicate.

I'm speechless. Listening and watching her lose herself in the song, I am reminded of the first time I heard Miranda sing all those years ago. Having heard Miranda sing and knowing Katelyn played, I assumed she would be good, but this, this is unlike anything I could have imagined. Her voice is flawless, and it's hard to believe it belongs to a fourteen -year -old. She sounds older. More mature, maybe even wiser.

142

THE SECOND VERSE

A playful smile pulls at her lips as she leads into the second chorus. Her knee bounces slightly to the beat and her head follows. Her voice flirts with higher notes before swinging to meet the lower ones. Then, I'm caught off guard when she transitions into the rap verse of the song. The words pour from her chest, never losing time, flowing perfectly into the ending.

Once the last chord fades, Katelyn looks up from her lap. Her cheeks are still flush and she looks anxious. I sit there, like a fool, staring at her, unsure what to say. Behind me I hear Paige hop off her stool and place her plate in the trash, completely unaffected by her sister's performance. This must be a common occurrence for her, but not for me. I will never be able to listen to this song the same way again. This rendition has ruined the original.

"Wow, Katelyn. That was ...wow. You're amazing," I say finally.

"You think so?" she asks, unsure and unable to make eye contact with me.

"Are you kidding me? That was unlike anything I have ever heard."

"Have you ever heard my mom sing?" She plucks a string on her guitar. "She's really good," she admits.

"I have. But Katelyn that was unbelievable." I move to the seat right next to her and lean closer. "Your mother is good, but," I lower my voice to a whisper, "you're better. Don't tell her I said that."

Her head snaps up and her wide eyes meet mine. A silly smile spreads across her face. Before I have a chance to react, she throws her arms around my neck, crushing the guitar between us, and hugs me.

"Thanks Jace." Pulling back quickly, her cheeks blush once again. She jumps up from her seat and rushes out of the room, an unmistakable spring in her step.

"So Jace," Paige breaks the silence that settled after Katelyn left.. She falls into the chair across from me and folds her arms on the table, leaning forward. She sits as tall as she can and her face becomes stern. "Are you my mom's boyfriend?"

I choke on my tongue. "What?"

"Are you her boyfriend?" she repeats. Her voice is firm and her expression is very serious, completely unlike the restless child that was bouncing off the walls a short while ago.

I stammer searching for an answer I don't have. The best defense is a good offense, so I change the subject.

"Did you finish all your homework?" I ask, quickly standing to clean up the earlier mess. Paige watches me for a moment with a look that tells me she knows exactly what I tried to do.

"Interesting," she says under her breath before skipping out of the room.

A couple hours later, I find myself sitting on the loveseat in the living room, watching some tween show. It stars a blonde boy who apparently is a rock star, his songwriter best friend, who's also the girl he likes, and their two best friends, who keep getting fired from their jobs and appear to be color blind. After fifteen minutes of watching I realize it's like watching a car wreck - you don't want to watch, but yet you can't look away.

Glancing over at Paige, who is stretched out on the sofa, I notice her eyes begin to droop. I'm not sure what her normal bedtime is, but I am ready to call it a night. Based on her expression I believe she is, too.

"Hey, I think you should head on up to bed now."

"Why?" she whines. "I'm not even tired." As soon as the words leave her mouth, she yawns.

I raise one eye brow.

"Fine," she huffs, but without any further fight as she gets up and makes her way upstairs.

"Good night," she calls out, once she is halfway up.

"'Night."

Clicking off the television, I stand and make one last sweep of the kitchen, locking up and shutting off lights as I go. Satisfied any mess we made has been cleaned, all the spaghetti removed, and the dishes washed, I grab my jacket from the back of the chair and head for the front door. A feeling in my stomach stops me with my hand resting on the knob. I can't leave without checking on Miranda one last time.

Hanging my coat on the banister, I creep up the stairs, careful not to make them creak under my weight. As quietly as possible, I walk down the dark, narrow hall to the master bedroom at the far end. Slowly, I push the door open and slip inside.

It takes a second for my eyes to adjust to the dark, but slowly the room comes into focus. Miranda is in a position very similar to the way I left her hours ago, curled up on her left side, only now she is huddled beneath a blanket. From this distance I cannot make out any details, but I try to convince myself she seems all right. My feet do not get the message though, and step by step I get closer. Reaching out, I pull the blanket back so I can see her face. The creases that marred her forehead earlier have disappeared and her eyes are no longer pinched together. She looks relaxed.

I know I shouldn't disturb her, but I sit on the edge of the bed anyway, causing it to dip under my weight. I reach out and run the back of my hand down her cheek. Carefully, I lean forward and place a soft kiss on her forehead.

"Sweet dreams," I whisper.

Her eyelids flutter and I curse under my breath, afraid I have woken her, but she doesn't move. Slipping off the bed I start to stand, but before I can step away, her hand grabs my forearm.

"Don't go," she whispers, her voice thick with sleep.

"Shhh, you need to rest," I say, gently tracing her jaw with my knuckle.

"Please, stay."

I debate with myself for a second. On the one hand, she needs to rest and her daughters are just down the hall. On the other, there isn't anything I want more right now than to curl up beside her.

Miranda must sense my hesitation because she squeezes me arm and asks me once again to stay.

"Please," she begs weakly.

The tone of her voice is my undoing. It's impossible for me to say no, so I don't. Kicking off my shoes, I leave the rest of my clothing on and crawl up from the bottom of the bed. Settling in beside her, I curl my body around hers and pull her back to my front. My knees hook behind hers. My right arm wraps around her stomach and my left snakes under her neck. She fits against me perfectly, like two puzzle pieces coming together. She was made to lie next to me.

"Thank you," she breathes.

I nuzzle my nose into her hair and kiss the top of her head. "Anything for you, Blue. Anything. Now go back to sleep."

Within a few minutes her breathing becomes slow and steady. I try to fight it, but with her snug in my arms, I know it's no use. I press my lips to her head once more before sleep finds me too.

Janet Lee

Chapter 24
Miranda

"Mrs. Clark, I don't think you understand. Paige has been looking forward to tonight all week. Do you realize how much this is going to upset her?"

It takes every ounce of willpower I have to keep the tone of my voice even. Each word is spoken slowly, in order to force back the slight tremor I feel seizing my throat. Having spent the last ten minutes trying to reason with this unreasonable woman, I feel my composure slipping. My hands shake with a volatile combination of adrenaline and rage.

I push through the front door of the office, not bothering to close it behind me and dump an arm full of mail onto my desk. My hair sticks to my forehead, and I brush it back with my free hand. Slumping into my chair, I pass my cellphone from one ear to the other, feeling my anger grow.

"Mrs. Cross, I'm sorry, but it's quite simple," the principal begins in her ridiculous nasally voice. How badly I want to punch her in her face right now.

"Tonight is the annual Father-Daughter Dance," she continues. "It's a night for the young ladies to be escorted by their fathers."

"I understand the concept," I snap, no longer able to control myself. "But you know damn well Paige cannot be escorted by her father." I hiss the word 'escorted', hoping the venom laced word stings her through the phone. "I clearly remember you attending his funeral." The quick intake of breath I hear on the other end of the line confirms my words have, at a minimum, shocked her.

"Mrs. Cross, Miranda, I am sorry, truly I am. Paige is an amazing little

146

girl and it must be hard without her father in her life. But rules are rules. She cannot attend tonight's dance. I'm sorry."

"So am I," I growl, stabbing my index finger on the screen of my cellphone. Slamming phone on the desk, harder than what is probably recommended, I scream, "Stupid bitch!"

Grabbing the nearest thing, I hurl it at the wall. Sheetrock and dust tumble to the ground along with the unsuspecting stapler. The roar of my heart drowns out the sound around me, so I see Jace enter the small office before I hear him. Based on the look on his face and the way his hands are raised in front of him, he fears I've turned into a feral animal. It's easy to assume he heard at least some of my tantrum.

"Uh," he makes an uneasy noise in his throat, "Miranda?" He glances down at the chalky mess on the floor.

Seeing him so flustered would be funny under different circumstances. Watching his brown eyes widen and his brow pull tight might be humorous if I didn't want to kill someone right now. But these are not different circumstances, and any humor that could be found in the moment evaporates immediately under the heat of the scorching anger in my blood.

"What?" I snap.

"Is everything all right?" Jace cautiously steps further into the room, stopping just in front of my desk.

"Yeah, just fucking ducky."

I stand quickly, pushing the chair out from under me with enough force to cause it to crash against the wall behind. I need to get out of here before I do any more damage to this place. I can easily explain the hole in the wall, but anymore and it will be difficult. I jam my phone into my bag and look for my keys, the words spilling from my lips so quickly there is no way to stop them.

"And why wouldn't it be? Rules are rules, right? It's not like she hasn't missed out on enough already. Or that she will have a lifetime of screwed up memories. Why not add this to the list? Don't you have work to do or something? Why are you here? Goddammit! Where are my keys?"

"These keys?" The corner of his mouth twitches, almost curling into the crooked smile I love so much. He manages to keep a straight face, though. He's lucky, because with the way I feel right now, I would probably smack it off.

I reach out to grab the jingling metal in his hands, but Jace holds the key ring above his head, several inches out of my grasp. I jump up to swipe them, but I'm too far away from even grazing them with my fingertips.

"Give them to me." I jump up and down on the balls of my feet.

"Not until you tell me what is going on. What rules? And whose memories are you ruining?"

"Keys. Now."

"No."

I run my hands through my hair, tugging the strands so roughly, almost pulling them out at the roots.

"Jesus Christ, I don't need this bullshit right now." Jace lifts one brow, challenging me. I stare daggers at him, but he doesn't relent.

"Gah," I groan, throwing my hands up in defeat. "There's a dance tonight at Paige's school," I say, but continue to jump, attempting to steal my means of escape. My efforts are unrewarded however, and Jace chuckles.

"You're not getting them back until you tell me what's going on, Blue. If you are in such a rush to leave, then you better hurry up and tell me. What's the big deal with this dance?"

We continue our stare off a moment longer, but if I'm going to have any hope of pulling together a night that will hopefully make up for not being able to go to the dance, I have errands to run before I pick up Paige from school. I don't have time to waste.

"You're wicked annoying, do you know that?" I sigh in defeat. "It's a Father-Daughter dance. I planned to take her myself. We picked out matching outfits. She wanted something green. I look horrible in green, but it's her night, so if my baby girl wants green, green is what we will wear. Well, it's what we would have worn. Instead, I just got off the phone with the principal informing me mothers aren't allowed at the dance." For the first time I let a hint of sadness seep through.

"I can't be Paige's date. Apparently, fatherless daughters cannot attend the stupid dance." My body feels battered and I fall back into the chair, my bag thudding loudly as it hits the floor.

"god, Jace, what am I going to do?"

"That's bullshit."

I can't help but snort. "That's exactly what I said, but it doesn't matter. We can't go. She's going to be so upset." I lean forward, resting my elbows on the desk and my head in my hands.

Jace doesn't say anything further. Instead, silence falls around us. My mind races through my options. Regardless of what I do, Paige is going to be heartbroken. I can't avoid that, but I can lessen it.

With a heavy sigh, I straighten in posture, collect my bag, and stand.

THE SECOND VERSE

"Can I please have my keys now? I have to go to the store before I get her from school."

This time he doesn't withhold my keys. He lightly places them in my hand. I don't stop to question the odd look in his eyes. I don't stop to listen to what he might say next when his mouth opens and closes a few times, chewing on the words stuck in his throat. The only thing I can do is focus on how to minimize the damage to my little girl's heart and gluing the fragile pieces back together when it breaks, all while trying to ignore the cracking of my own.

Chapter 25
Jace

"I don't know, Mom," I repeat for the tenth time in as many minutes, "Traveling that week sounds awful. Maybe I'll just stay here and try my hand at making my own turkey."

"Do you even know how to turn the oven on?" my mother jokes, but it's forced, trying to hide her disappointment.

"I think I can manage," I try to convince her. "It can't be that difficult."

"C'mon, honey. I haven't seen you in months and it has been years since you've been home for Thanksgiving. We'd love to see you. Benny could take you fishing. Did I tell you he is now chartering a fishing boat?"

"You did," I answer dryly, not certain quitting a legitimate job to invest in a charter boat at the end of the season and beginning of winter was the smartest idea. The worst part is she probably invested money, but I haven't the heart to ask right now.

"Look, maybe I'll visit during Christmas."

"Maybe?" she sighs. "What in God's name would make you not want to ..." She stops before finishing her question and begins to shriek. It's a sound I would expect to hear a much younger woman make. "Oh my god, who is she?"

Shaking my head at her excitement I try but fail to keep the smile off my face.

"I don't know what you're talking about," I lie.

"Jace Alan Harper, don't lie to me. Even though I can't see the corner of your mouth twitch through the phone, I can hear it in your voice."

"I don't know what you're talking about," I try again.

THE SECOND VERSE

"You know exactly what I'm talking about. I'm your mother. I know when you're lying," she insists and I know she's right.

I could never get away with anything when I was younger. It's pointless to think I could start now.

"Now tell me who she is."

I sigh in resignation. Tucking the phone between my shoulder and ear, I bend to tie my brown shoes.

"I can't go into all of the details now," I start. "I am actually on my way out."

"I knew it!" she exclaims.

"Do you want to hear this or not?"

"Of course, of course. Go on. I won't say another word."

"I doubt that," I mutter under my breath. "Her name is Miranda. I first met her when we came to clean out Grandma's house that summer after I graduated. She lived next door. Well, I ran into her a few weeks ago. We've been out a few times." I stand, smoothing the front of my shirt. Out of the corner of my eye I see the time on the clock above the stove. Shit, I am going to be late. "Look, Mom, I have to go."

"What? What do you mean? That's all you're going to tell me?" she whines.

"I promise I will fill you in on some of the details later. I have something really important to do tonight and if I don't leave in a few minutes I'm going to be late."

Tucking my wallet into the back pocket of my tan slacks, I swipe a white box from the kitchen counter. Moving the phone from one ear to the other, I pick up my keys and head for the front door.

"Oh, all right, but don't for one second think I'm going to forget about this," my mother promises. I know she is never going to let me get away without telling her every single detail.

"Bye, Mom."

"Talk to you soon, sweetheart."

Disconnecting the call, I toss the phone on the passenger's seat of my truck, place the white box next to it, and back down the driveway. The short drive does little to calm my nerves. I don't know what made me think of doing this. The whole idea is ridiculous, but as soon as it formed in my mind there was no getting rid of it. I only hope it's the right thing to do. It could backfire in more ways than one.

Arriving at my destination, I kill the engine. The anxious nervous feeling

I'm so accustomed to takes hold of my stomach again, and somewhere in the back of my mind I know if I focus on it too much I might have a full blown panic attack. I take a deep breath and hold it until my lungs burn. Releasing it, I look at my reflection in the mirror.

"Now or never," I say to myself.

Wiping my sweaty palms on my pants, I gently pick up the small box and exit the truck.

The walk to the door is short. My feet fall heavy on the wooden steps. Lifting my free hand, I knock on the door twice. Stepping back, I notice dim, blue lights dancing behind the drawn curtains. The sound of murmured voices coming from the television drifts through the window panes. After a few moments, the light thud of footsteps approaches from the other side of the door. Cautiously, the front door creaks open and the younger version of familiar blue eyes appear in the crack.

Katelyn's eyes widen in surprise at first, but then they slowly sweep from my clean shaven face, to my ironed green button up shirt, to my pressed tan slacks, and down to my shined dress shoes. Her gaze travels back toward my eyes, but stops on the box in my hand. A smile curls her lips lightly and humor lightens her face.

"Paige!" she calls, before turning on her heel. I stand on the porch watching her retreat down the hall when a small movement catches my attention.

Shoulders slumped, eyes fixed on the floor, Paige sulks around the corner from the living room and steps into the entry way. It's not until she is at the base of the stairs that she looks up to see who is waiting. When her face meets mine, something weird happens in my chest. My heart halts and beats widely at the same time. Paige's eyes are red and swollen. Her long lashes are wet and clumped together. Her cheeks are streaked with tears, and there is a sheen under her pink nose. Her light brown hair, which is always neatly tucked up in a ponytail, is a knotted mess, stray strands falling in her eyes. Barefoot, she comes to stand on the sage mat just inside the front door.

"Jace?" her voice is hoarse and nasally. "What are you doing here?"

A lump forms in my throat, hearing her meek voice. I have this desperate urge to wrap her up in my arms and never let her go. I want to protect her from the world and all of the harmful things and people in it.

"Well," I begin, clearing my throat before continuing, "I heard of this cool dance at the school tonight." I pause, meeting her eyes, which light with awareness. "I really want to go, but, well, it's a Father-Daughter dance and," I shrug one shoulder, "I don't have a daughter so I can't go."

Paige nods her head, tucking her hair behind her ear. "I can't go either," she sniffles. "Mommy said we could, but my teacher told me I can't." Fresh tears puddle in her eyes.

Bending on one knee, my head is still a few inches above hers, but we are now closer to eye level. I lean real close and lower my voice.

"I was thinking … maybe if you pretend to be my daughter, do you think they'd let me go?"

Her honey brown eyes fix on mine. I watch the emotions within them move from sadness, to confusion, to mischief.

"Do you think if I pretend to be your daughter you could pretend to be my dad and they'd let me go, too?"

I press my index finger to the corner of my mouth and tilt my head to one side, thinking over the situation. Just behind Paige, I notice Miranda standing in the doorway between the kitchen and the hall, her weight resting against the jamb and her arms crossed loosely across her chest. She's wearing a loose pair of cotton pajama pants and a tight, fitted t-shirt. Her hair is pulled haphazardly into a messy bun. I quirk my brows, silently asking permission and her own eyes, damp with unshed tears, answer.

"You know what? I think that might work. But to make it look official, I think we should match. I mean, won't the fathers have matching outfits with their daughters? Do you have anything that will match what I'm wearing or should I go home and change?" I ask shyly.

Paige's eyes, now dry of tears, swim with excitement and fall to my green dress shirt. The shirt I purposely picked out this evening. She nods her head vigorously.

"Yes! Green is my favorite color!" she shrieks, reminding me of the sound my mother made earlier. For a moment I wonder if girls are born able to make that noise.

"Phew," I feign relief, wiping my brow. "That's good. Then these flowers will match, too." I open the white box, still clutched in my hand, revealing a small, child-size corsage. I barely had time to stop and ask the florist to make it for me before she closed for the day. I'm sure I paid extra for making her stay open late, but it the look of awe on Paige's face was worth every penny.

"Those are for me?" she asked softly.

"They are." I present the open flower box like a man would present an engagement ring. "Paige, will you go to the dance with me?"

Paige bounces on the balls of her feet before throwing her arms around my neck. I barely have time to brace myself so we don't go tumbling backward. Never would I have guessed that such a little girl had so much strength, but with her little arms clutched to me tightly, I realize just how strong she is. I pull her close against my chest and before I even think about it, I press a kiss to her cheek.

"Go on. Hurry up and get changed. We have a dance to get to." With that she's gone in a flash.

Straightening to stand, my leg aches in protest. Miranda pushes herself from the wall and walks slowly toward me, her footsteps barely audible on the hardwood floor. Say what you may about short dresses, tight jeans, and stilettos, but there is something sexy about a woman in low hung cotton pants and a snug t-shirt. Her hair falls in small clumps from her messy bun and she tucks them behind her ear.

"Hi," she says, stopping to stand in front of me. I can see her beautiful eyes are wet with tears. "You don't have to do this, you know." Her voice is husky with emotion and not for the first time I second guess my decision. Is she mad?

"I want to." I step over the threshold, closing the door behind me. "It isn't right, them telling you she can't go tonight because her father isn't here. How can they do that to a little girl?" I ask the question, but continue before she can answer. "No, it's not right."

We stand in the foyer, close enough for me to feel the heat from her body, but too far away to touch. I step closer and reach for her hand, which she gives me without protest.

"Do you not want me to take her? I should've asked you first. I don't want to overstep ..." I ramble, but before I can finish Miranda's small hand covers my mouth. A smile tugs the corner of her lips.

"No, I'm not upset." She steps closer, curling herself into my chest. I move to kiss the top of her head. Silence wraps us in a warm embrace, but it is soon interrupted by the sound of stomping and thuds echoing down the staircase. I begin to wonder exactly what is going on up there.

I'm just about to ask Miranda if she would like to go up and check on Paige, when the little girl emerges, rushing down the stairs so fast she almost misses the bottom step. In one movement, I step away from Miranda and catch Paige before she hits the ground. Behind me, I hear Miranda say something under her breath. It was too low to hear clearly, but I think I heard something about Paige breaking her own neck one day.

I set Paige on her feet, flipping her light brown hair back, revealing a smile so big it barely fits on her face. The tomboy little girl I am used to seeing, dressed in jeans and t-shirts, has been transformed in to a pint-sized princess. Her pale green dress with white sweater and matching shoes make her look so innocent. I have to blink to be sure I am really seeing what I am seeing.

"Are you ready?" I ask, smiling down and offering her my hand.

"Yup," Paige says, popping the 'P' at the end. She slides her hand in mine. "'Bye, Mommy. Jace and I are going to the dance. Don't wait up," she says without a backward glance.

The ride to the school is short. Paige is settled in the backseat singing to the sickly sweet pop music she insisted I put on. Her excitement and simple happiness creates an unfamiliar feeling in my chest. It's a mixture of warmth and fizzy bubbles. The smile on her face is all the proof I need to know this was the right thing to do.

Pulling in to the parking lot, I'm surprised to see how full it is. There are dozens of cars lined side by side underneath dim streetlights. With one look it appears every female student in the school is here tonight. Well, at least now every student will be here. In the pit of my stomach I feel a hint of anger swirl once again knowing Paige almost missed this opportunity.

I park my truck in the first empty spot I see. The night is chilly, gripped by autumn, but Paige insisted she did not want to wear a jacket. Miranda was about to argue with her before we left, but I whispered I would take care of it and she bit her lip. Instead, I shrugged off my own jacket and explained to Paige that a gentleman always allows his date to wear his coat. Paige's round eyes twinkled and she nodded vigorously, allowing me to slip my jacket over her shoulders. Now, as we exit the truck, she still has it wrapped tightly around her.

A few yards from the double doors leading into the lobby of the elementary school, we can hear the bass blaring from within. Just beyond the doors the lights are dim, and there are flashes of red and green dancing against the walls to the beat of the music. I pull open the door and gallantly sweep a hand for Paige to enter.

"Milady," I say, in the worst British accent ever spoken. Paige bursts into a fit of giggles.

Side by side, we walk down the short hallway to the gym where the dance is being held. Standing outside the heavy metal doors are two middle aged women, dressed in business suits. I assume they are school staff of some sort who didn't bother to go home and change after the school day ended.

One of the women, an older lady with short salt and pepper hair, red wingtip glasses, and a stern expression, spots Paige and straightens. Her eyes move from my little date to my face and back. She leans closer and whispers something to her companion, whose eyes also study us with a deep frown etched on her face.

Paige and I stop just outside the gym, the entrance now blocked by the older woman.

"Good evening, Paige," the woman says, in a real nasally British accent, making my attempt even worse.

"Hi, Mrs. Clark." Paige's voice is small and missing the normal undertone of humor.

Mrs. Clark. Of course, this is the principal. I heard part of Miranda's conversation with her earlier today. Even with only hearing bits and pieces it was easy to put together what was being said on the other end of the phone. This woman was the one who said Paige could not attend this dance.

Mrs. Clark attempts a smile small, but it looks more like a grimace. I have to wonder if this woman has ever smiled a day in her life. The principal's eyes lift from Paige and fix on me.

"And who might you be?"

"Jace Harper," I say casually offering her my hand, but instead of politely shaking it, the woman crosses her arms over her chest and continues to stare.

"And who are you Mr. Harper? To Paige, I mean?"

"Well, tonight I am her date." I feel Paige's small hand slide into mine. Looking down, I see her smiling up at me and my heart skips.

"I see. You do realize this is a Father-Daughter dance?"

"I do."

"Then I am confused, Mr. Harper, as to why are you here. I explained to Mrs. Cross earlier today that, due to unfortunate circumstances, Paige would not be able to attend tonight's event." She waves a dismissive hand in our direction. "There will be other things later in the school year I'm sure Paige would rather take you to. Now if you will excuse me." She begins to turn, but I speak before she can go.

"Wait." My voice is thick and unwavering. The tone is the same I used when commanding men on the battle field. Even Mrs. Clark, as entitled to power as she may feel, halts immediately. I gently squeeze Paige's hand before letting go and taking a step closer to the principal.

"Listen and listen close, because I will not repeat myself. How dare you prevent a little girl from attending a dance because her father is not here. To punish her for it. You and I know his absence is not because he is some deadbeat who has abandoned his family. In fact, it's the complete opposite. He loved his family very much, but got sick and died. That little girl never even had an opportunity to know him, which is something she can't understand right now, but at some point in her life she will. Now, Paige and I are going to enter that gym and attend this little dance of yours. If you try to stop us, I swear on my life, you will regret it."

Mrs. Clark's eyes widen with a mixture of shock and fear swimming behind her lenses.

"Are you threatening me, Mr. Harper?" Her voice is just audible over the music in the background.

"It's not a threat." Reaching behind me, I take Paige's hand in mine. "It's a promise. Now if you'll excuse us," we walk around the slack-jawed principal, "we have a dance to attend."

Chapter 26
Miranda

Sitting nestled on the sofa under a soft, downy blanket with a glass of wine nearby, I stare blankly at the words of the novel in my lap. I had thought I could use the moment of peace and quiet to lose myself in the pages of the latest Sara Mack novel, but my thoughts are too distracting. I have read and reread the same paragraph at least a dozen times, but the words won't stick in my head.

The house is calm, the normal thrum of energy absent, making the space feel empty. Katelyn never came downstairs after Paige and Jace left. After she finished helping Paige get ready, she disappeared into her room. I thought about checking on her, sensing she was upset, and I wouldn't blame her if she was.

After getting both girls from school and breaking the news to Paige that she would not be able to attend the dance, they were both rightly upset – Paige for obvious reasons, but Katelyn for others. Of course she was upset Paige was disappointed, but I think it went deeper than that. It was one more reminder that Adam wasn't here, and I could see the sadness in her eyes.

It's so easy to forget Katelyn grieves for Adam, too. Even though it's been many years and she was so young when he died, I know she still misses him. From experience I know each passing year the loss lessens, but I doubt it will ever fully go away.

Sitting on the sofa, trying to console Paige, I watched Katelyn out of the corner of my eye. There was sadness stamped on her face, but her eyes were blank, distant. For a long while she seemed lost in her own thoughts, and I couldn't help but wonder if she was remembering the night Adam took her to her first, and only, Father-Daughter dance. It had only been a few months before his death, and he was very sick and weak, but he was determined to take her. He wanted to make that memory for her. It made my stomach curl to know Paige will never have those memories with him, but thanks to Jace she will still have a special memory all her own.

When Jace first arrived, Katelyn seemed amused by his rebelliousness. Now, I wonder if his appearance is part of the reason for her absence since. Is she upset Jace came to take Paige? Does Katelyn feel like Jace is overstepping some invisible line? Invading into her father's territory which has been left unguarded?

I wouldn't be surprised if that's how she felt. To be honest, there is a tiny part of me that feels the same way. I am angry at the universe for taking Adam too soon, but in the same breath grateful Jace has been sent back to me. Am I a horrible person to feel that way? Shouldn't I grieve the memory of my husband for the rest of my life, forsaking anyone who comes along? What *would* Adam think?

My thoughts are interrupted by headlights shining through the front window. The light brightens the wall opposite me before disappearing. I hear the thud of two car doors, almost simultaneously, followed by thudding footsteps and animated chatter on the front porch.

I meet Jace and Paige in the front room. Both are grinning from ear to ear, and Paige is bouncing up and down talking to Jace. Hearing me approach they turn and, before I can brace myself, Paige lunges into my arms, causing me to lose my balance, stumble back, and crash into the wall.

"Whoa." I catch myself before we tumble to the floor. "Geez, Paige. Be careful."

Squeezing her tightly, I feel warmth and the remnants of sweat dampen the back of her dress. I kiss her on the cheek and set her down.

"Did you have fun?"

"It was awesome," she squeals, throwing her hands over her head. Her wide smile transforms into a jaw busting yawn breaks free.

"Wow. That good, huh? You look beat."

"I'm not tired," Paige insists, but yawns again, this one bigger than the first.

"Why don't you head upstairs and get ready for bed? I'll be there in a minute."

She sighs and whines under her breath, but turns towards the stairs. It's not until she reaches the second step that she stops and leaps towards Jace. He catches her easily, becoming used to her daredevil ways. Paige's arms wrap tightly around his neck and she kisses him on the cheek.

"Thank you, Jace."

"It was my pleasure, sweetheart." His voice is soft and filled with reverence. He sets her gently on the floor. "Sweet dreams."

I excuse myself to follow Paige upstairs, but ask Jace to wait for me. Emotions swirl in my chest, leaving little room to breathe. Seeing the way Paige looked at Jace reminds me so much of Katelyn and Adam, making my stomach knot. I want so badly for Paige to have that connection with someone and it scares me how much I want that person to be Jace.

Stepping into Paige's room, only a few steps behind her, I find her already stripping off the only dress she owns. She discards it into the corner and I stoop to pick it up, shaking out the fabric and setting in the black and white laundry basket. Paige pulls on her penguin pajama bottoms and matching shirt Claire bought for her last month.

"So, you had fun?" I ask again, following her to her bed and folding back the blankets for her to climb in.

"Yeah," she starts with a yawn. "It was fun."

"Good. I'm glad. Were any of you friends there?"

After tucking the blankets sung around her chest, I sit on the edge of her bed. I smooth her hair back from her face. Paige rummages under her pillow and pulls out the worn brown teddy bear she still sleeps with every night.

"All of them. Well, all of the girls anyway. You know the boys couldn't go. It was only fathers and daughters. Well, except for Jace and me, but after Jace talked to Mrs. Clark we were able to go in."

I tense. "Jace talked to Mrs. Clark?"

Paige nods, her eyelids beginning to droop.

"What did Mrs. Clark say?"

Paige shrugs and snuggles farther under her blankets with her bear. "I don't know. I heard her say something about not being able to go in the gym, but then Jace got this mean look on his face, kind of like the face that bear made at the zoo when it got stung by a bee. Do you remember Mommy, how it growled and looked mean?"

"I remember," I say, cringing and wondering exactly what happened tonight.

"Jace looked just like that bear. I don't know what he said, it was too quiet, but Mrs. Clark's face looked white after, almost like a ghost. Mrs. Clark didn't say anything to Jace after that."

"I see." *Oh god.*

"We walked around the gym. There were so many people and there were balloons everywhere and someone hung decorations from the ceiling. It was really cool. Then we danced," she pauses, her eyes falling shut for a moment. "Jace dances funny," she giggles sleepily.

"Oh, really? How does he dance?"

"When it was a fast song it looked like he had ants in his pants." She yawns. "You remember the song you played for Katelyn and me last summer at Uncle Sam's pool? Remember when Aunt Claire pushed him in?"

""Billie Jean?""

"Yeah, that one. You should've seen Jace dance when that came on. Me and my friends laughed so hard. It was so funny." She smiles lazily. "Then a slow song came on. My friends went back to their dads to dance. I didn't think Jace would know how to dance to a slow song, but he did." She yawns again. Her eyes drift closed and her breathing begins to even out.

"He picked me up," she whispers, "and set my feet on top his and twirled me around." With a faint smile on her lips she falls asleep. I kiss her softly on the forehead and pull the blanket up to her chin. Taking one more glance over my back, I shut off the light before leaving the room.

When I come back downstairs, I find Jace standing with his back to me. The living room is dimly lit by only one lamp on the small table in the far corner. Music plays softly in the background from my iPod on its stand. It should feel weird having him in my space, but oddly it doesn't. Instead it seems perfectly normal, comfortable even. Of course Jace has been here before. After our date he has come over a few times, but this is the first time we've been alone, more or less.

I try to step quietly into the room, but my feet cause the floorboards to creak. Jace turns and his eyes soften around the edges. His hair has grown longer since he arrived back in town. It's still short, but now visible. I realize I have never actually seen his hair. The first time we met it had been cut in the same close buzz -cut style as when he reappeared in Belham weeks ago. I have no idea if it's straight or curly. Is it as dark as I imagine or does it have highlights? As inconsequential as hair color may seem, it hits me that it's one of a dozen basic things I don't know about him. I'm not sure what frightens me more, that I don't know or that I desperately want to.

"Would you like a glass of wine?" My voice comes out thicker than usual.

Janet Lee

"Sure."

"Let me go grab another glass. I'll be right back."

I quickly duck in to the kitchen to retrieve another wineglass and pause to calm my racing pulse. They say the way to a man's heart is through his stomach, if that's true, then the way to a mother's heart is through her children. Knowing Jace made Paige blissfully happy this evening makes me want to throw caution to the wind. I can over analyze the situation tomorrow.

Returning, I find Jace seated on the edge of the sofa, hands folded, elbows on his knees.

"It seems like you two had a good time," I say, setting the full wine glass on the table and taking a seat next to him.

Even seated he is taller than me, and I have to tilt my head back to look into his eyes. His lids are heavier than normal, fatigue lining the rims, but the gold flecks swirling in the brown pools brightens them.

The corner of Jace's mouth curls slowly into a goofy smile. "We did. Well, I did. I hope Paige did, too." He suddenly sounds a little unsure.

"She did," I quickly reassure him after taking a sip from my glass.

"Good. That's good."

"What did you say to the principal?" I don't know if I really want to know, but I have to ask.

He presses his lips together and an expression I can't quite place crosses his face. "She told you about that?"

"She did. So, what happened?"

"It was nothing." Jace shrugs, his face an odd mixture of amusement and embarrassment.

I lean forward, setting my wine glass on the table, and then turn toward Jace. Crossing my arms over my chest, I tilt my head to one side and lift a brow, calling bullshit.

"Look, let's just say I said no less than I needed to. That woman can take her stupid rules and shove them up her ass. The entire situation was wrong and shouldn't have happened in the first place. When I showed up here tonight and saw the look in Paige's eyes, it nearly broke my heart. Seriously, I might sound like a pussy, but seeing the sadness on her face almost brought me to my knees. It took every ounce of willpower I had not to say more to the vile woman at the school tonight. Paige is a great kid, Blue. They both are. You've done well and they deserve the world." He stands abruptly, like he might explode if he doesn't move. Turning his back toward me, he moves toward a small bookcase where my iPod sits, but not before I hear him say, "You all

162

do," under his breath.

Staring at his back, I'm speechless. In all these years I hadn't realized how much I needed to hear that statement. How badly I needed confirmation that all the sweat, blood, and tears haven't been for nothing. The small acknowledgment makes my heart swell and tears prick the back of my eyes.

The pop song that's playing stops mid-chorus and is replaced by something slower. Jace turns, shrugs off his jacket, and rests it on the arm of the sofa. I watch him move as he crosses the room. I note the sway of his broad shoulders that radiate solid strength. I observe the off balance movement of his hips, caused by his slight limp. He hides his injury so well I often forget about it, but every so often, usually when we're alone, I notice the hitch in his gait and the grimace that seems more pronounced when it's raining out.

"Dance with me," he says, stopping in front of me, holding out his hand.

My mind is assaulted with uncertainty. He wants to dance? When was the last time I danced with an adult? My chest tightens when the answer to that question flashes behind my eyes. Adam. Bittersweet memories wash over me and pull me into the past, but only for a moment. After a few heartbeats, the memory fades and I see Jace's handsome face. It is so different from Adam's but for reasons I can't explain, still causes my stomach flutter in the same way it used to. I stifle the guilt that begins to bubble before slipping my hand into his. Jace places a soft kiss on my knuckles before pulling me to my feet.

Stepping backward, Jace doesn't release my hand. His chocolate eyes meet my blue and I feel him staring into my soul. His lips curl into his crooked smile I like so much. Before I can smile back, he tugs on my hand and I come crashing against his chest. The air in my lungs leaves in a rush. Jace lifts our joined hands, and then slowly trails his free hand down my arm, from shoulder to fingers. Grasping my left hand he places it behind his neck, before retracing the path back up my arm with his fingertips. His feet begin to move to the beat. We are so close, so connected, I have no choice but to follow his lead. After a torturous journey, his hand rests on the small of my back. He tightens his hold, pulling me even closer, as if that were possible.

"Do you remember the last time we heard this song?" he asks, his hot breath causing a rash of goose bumps on my neck.

It takes a moment for the lust fogging my brain to clear just enough so I can think. The country twang of the song is one of my favorite. I would know Mark Wills "I Do" anywhere.

"When?" I ask, shaking my head, admitting I don't know what he is taking about.

Spinning me away from his chest, my knee bumps into the side of the couch. I feel light as a feather. A giggle escapes through my lips as I crash back into Jace.

"You don't remember? Aw, Blue that hurts," he teases, placing our joined hands over his chest. "This song was playing that night. The night we met."

My feet slow until he has to stop moving to the beat. "What?"

"That night, on the dock, this song was playing. You told me it was one of your favorites."

"You remember that?" My eyes widen and my mouth hangs open.

"Of course. I remember every single detail of that night. The way the wind played with the strands of your hair that fell from the hooded sweatshirt you wore. How your eyes sparkled, even in the moonlight, when you talked about your family. I remember how perfect your hand fit in mine and how much I wanted to kiss your perfect, pouty lips." He pauses, his eyes drifting down to my mouth and back up again. "I have replayed every minute, every second of that night over and over. After a while I began to think a night like that could exist only in a dream."

I'm drowning in him. It's all too much. The warmth of his skin sets me on fire. The crisp scent of his cologne fills my lungs making my head swoon. He is everywhere. Tipping my head back, I study his face. It truly is remarkable how handsome this man is. I don't know if any amount of time spent with him will diminish the awe I feel being this close to him.

We begin moving again, swaying to the rhythm of the song. "Your body was made to dance with mine, Miranda," he says so low I almost can't hear him over the thundering of my heart.

"The softness of your curves." His hand brushes from just below my breast to my hipbone. "The sway of your hips. Beautiful," he whispers.

My heart hammers in my chest. His cheek rests just above my ear and I feel his breath hot on my tender flesh. His hips move in time with the beat of the song, slowly turning us in a small circle, and all my previous thoughts of his injured leg go out the window.

I nuzzle my nose in to the small, surprisingly soft spot where his jaw meets his neck and breathe deeply, trying to pull him into my lungs. Jace's hold on my body tightens, and beneath the tight cotton of his shirt I feel the muscles in his shoulders and upper back flex. My heavy breasts ache pressed against his chest, and my thin shirt offers little cover to the tight peaks beneath. Deep in my belly an unfamiliar feeling begins stir from hibernation. Warmth pools in my womb and begins to spread outward, filling my body and limbs.

THE SECOND VERSE

Tonight is different from our date in the park. Yes, that night, being close to Jace, I felt things I hadn't felt in a long time. That first night was like coming home as a kid with a bag full of candy after going trick or treating. The amount of candy is so overwhelming you don't know where to begin, or how to stop eating, and soon you're crashing from a sugar high. This, right now, is like finding a single piece of chocolate after dieting for weeks. You don't want to rush, because you want it to last. Instead, you unwrap it slowly, placing it carefully in your mouth, and enjoy every second of its sinful taste on your tongue.

Feeling my body soften further into his, Jace's chest rises and falls as he sighs. I rest my cheek against his chest and listen to the racing of his heart. He dips his head closer and kisses the edge of my ear before beginning to sing the lyrics, low and soft. His lips on my bare neck cause my skin to prickle with electricity. My heart beats so frantically in my chest I briefly worry I might pass out. Blood and oxygen race through my veins, making my head feel fizzy and my legs feel weak.

I lift my head and our eyes meet. I can see the questions swirling just beneath the surface of his expression. Before I allow myself a second of worry, I stand on the balls of my feet and gently press my lips to his. The kiss starts cautiously, with only a small amount of pressure against his mouth. Jace answers with equal delicate care. Needing more, I wrap my arms tighter around his neck, pulling him closer. My teeth graze his bottom lip before I pull the plump, smooth piece of flesh between them, biting down softly. A low growl vibrates in Jace's chest as he crashes his lips onto mine and his fists tighten on my hips.

I may have started the kiss, but Jace now owns it and, at the same time, claims some ownership over me. The racing thoughts that filled my head earlier are gone, replaced with nothing but the sensation of Jace's tall, strong body. All I can do now is feel.

Jace's lips leave mine and begin to kiss their way across my jaw. His nose brushes the lobe of my ear before he pulls it between his lips, lightly nibbling the sensitive skin. Slowly, he grazes my neck with kisses from ear to collarbone before retracing the same line with his tongue. I think I moan, but I can't be sure. All I hear is my heartbeat mixed with his heavy breathing.

"Please," I whisper, before our lips meet again. I don't know what I'm asking for, to stop or continue.

In one swift move, Jace bends and picks me up, cradling me against his chest like I weigh nothing, which is far from the truth. He begins to walk toward the stairs.

"Jace, put me down. You'll hurt your leg. I'm too heavy."

"I've got you, Blue. I'll never let you fall."

His words go straight to my heart and the fragile muscle seizes. He may only be referring to carrying me, but the tone in his voice hints to something more, something deeper. Something I have been longing to hear.

As silently as possible, Jace and I head up the stairs and down the hall to my room. I quickly glance at both of the girls' bedrooms, checking to make sure their lights are out. Jace nudges my door open and then closed with his foot before setting me on the bed.

I sit on the edge, looking up at him, unsure what to do next. It's been a very long time since I have done this. There was no one before Adam and there has been no one since. The thought alone is enough to almost make me stop, but I force it aside. I don't want to stop. I need this and I need this with Jace.

"So beautiful," Jace speaks softly.

He bends, claiming my lips once again. He rests his knee on the mattress and I move back into the center of the bed. The weight of his body is heavy against mine. Every inch of him calls to me, echoing the same call of desire my own body is creating.

I feel him all over, his warm breath on my cool breasts, the slick moisture of his lips on my stomach, the sticky sweat from his brow against my inner thighs. I feel every glorious inch of his hardness against my delicate softness.

In the seconds, minutes, hours after that first kiss, I lose myself to wave after wave of pure, sinful bliss. I pray to God and the Devil to never let it stop. To instead let me live forever in this state of ecstasy. Neither may have heard my prayer, but I believe Jace heard my plea, for he answered over and over again.

Chapter 27
Jace

I slowly wake from the first dreamless sleep I have had in years. The room is still dark and at first I'm confused by my surroundings. Quickly, however, the images from the night before come rushing back to me. I see her smooth skin and the softness of her curves lying bare before me. Swiping my tongue across my lips, I can still taste her.

Kneeling above her last night I wanted to dive right in. To take what was mine and forget about everything else. I felt like a kid who unwrapped the one present he wanted most of all and wanted nothing more than to play with it for hours. However, I forced myself to go slow. Even though I could see and feel how badly she wanted me, there was still a shadow just behind those sapphire eyes. She needed me to be gentle, to take care of her, so that's exactly what I did.

Stretching my arm above my head, I feel her begin to stir beside me. Rolling to my side, I watch her in the dim light coming through the window. Miranda lies on her side, facing me, with her knees bent and her hands tucked under chin. Her black hair spreads around her on the pillow like a dark halo. Long dark lashes lie upon her cheeks and flutter with the rapid movement of her eyes beneath the lids. Slack jawed and relaxed, she looks very peaceful lost in her dreams.

Carefully, I slide my hand across the sheet and rest it on her forearm. Feeling her, her breath on my face, her warmth beneath my hand, makes me want more. Not more of her body, though I doubt I'll ever get tired of that, but simply more.

I must've fallen back to sleep, because when I open my eyes once again the room is filled with morning light. In the distance, murmured voices and the thud of closing kitchen cabinets break the silence. Next to me, Miranda also begins to wake. Rolling to her back, she stretches her legs, points her toes, and lifts her arms above her head. Her eyes peel open into tiny slits and she peeks at me from beneath her lashes.

"Hi," she whispers.

"Good morning."

"What time is it?" She lifts her head from the pillow trying to find her cell phone.

"It must be after eight." I guess based on the height of the sun outside.

"Eight thirty, actually," she confirms, finding her phone on the floor by the bed. She ducks back under the covers and scoots closer to me. She rests her hand on my chest and I flinch.

"Jesus, woman, you're freezing," I yelp and she laughs. The sound is so pure it knots my insides.

I begin to brush my fingers through her hair and open my mouth to ask her something. Something I have been thinking about, but the noises downstairs grow.

"Sounds like the girls are up," she says with a hint of disappointment. "I don't suppose there is still time to sneak you out the backdoor."

I think she's teasing, but I can't be sure. We never talked about the morning after, or what either of us expected. For a split second I thought about leaving last night. I even started to get up, but Miranda reach out for me, a dreamy, sated look in her eye, and pulled me back down toward her. After that, I fell asleep and, nestled so closely to her, I'm not sure anything could have pried me from her bed.

"Well, I could climb out the window," I suggest. "I think I could make it down without hurting myself, though it has been quite a few years since I tried."

In fact the one and only time I had to climb from a second story window and down a trellis was when I was twenty –two. The boyfriend of a girl I had met the night before came home early from working an overnight shift. In my defense, had I known she had a boyfriend when we left the bar, I would've never gone home with her. Hound laughed hysterically when I told him how my foot got caught on the gutter, when I jumped from a lower section of the roof, causing me to crash to the ground and bruise the side of my face. He told me that was the reason you never go to their place.

"You always take them home with you," Hound said.

By the time the bastard got done telling the rest of the guys in our unit, the story had evolved into me getting the shit beaten out of me by the girl's boyfriend and a group of his friends. Hearing Hound's version it seems I was lucky to survive.

"No, I don't think that will work. I wouldn't want you to hurt yourself." Miranda's drowsy voice breaks up my memory.

"You could go down and distract the girls and I can duck out the front door," I suggest, though my stomach twists with the disappointment she would want me to leave. I have to try to put myself in her shoes, though. If I were her, would I want my daughters knowing I had someone spend the night in my bed? I can't say I would.

Miranda is quiet for a few minutes. I pass my hand up and down the line of her spine. Leaning my head toward her, I rest my cheek on the top of her hair. The scent of flowers and vanilla from her shampoo fill my nose. I close my eyes committing this moment to memory.

"No."

"Huh?" I ask, confused for a moment.

"No, I don't want you to leave." Miranda lifts her head and turns to look at me. "I want you to stay for a little while. If you want, I mean. If you want to go, I could go downstairs. I can distract them. Maybe have them help me make breakfast. I think I could keep them busy so they wouldn't ..."

Before she can continue, I lean forward and seize her lips with mine. I kiss her softly, but with enough force to say *you are mine*. Pulling away, I rest my forehead against hers, our noses brushing against one another..

"I would like nothing more than to stay." I kiss the tip of her nose. "And breakfast sounds good, too." As if on cue, my stomach grumbles, causing her to giggle. It's the most amazing sound in the world.

We both take turns in the bathroom. While Miranda is behind the closed door, I pull on my pants from last night and the white t-shirt I wore underneath my button up. Miranda's arms snake around my middle and she presses her cheek to my back.

"Give me a five minute head start before you come down," she says. "I want to tell the girls you're here first." With her tussled hair in a haphazard ponytail, she pulls a sweatshirt over her tiny tank top, leans up on her toes, and kisses me before leaving.

I sit on the edge of the bed while I wait. Peering at the clock on the nightstand, I begin to count the minutes. My eyes move around the room, touching on all of Miranda's things. It's a very intimate thing, to be alone surrounded by the belongings of someone else. The off-white walls are mostly bare except for a small book case hung on the far wall above a short, comfortable looking arm chair by the windows. The dresser on the wall by the door has a few bottles of perfume and an antique stone jewelry box with a lavender floral design painted on the surface. Everything is neat and organized. The door leading to the small master bathroom has a robe hung on the corner, and there's a small pile of clothing on the floor. There are no pictures, except for the picture on her nightstand.

I stare at the photo for a moment before reaching for it. I feel compelled to look to make sure Miranda isn't around. I don't think she'd be upset with me looking at the picture, but a small part of me feels like I'm invading her privacy.

The first time I saw this photo I was more focused on the story Miranda was telling me than the details of the image. I've always thought she was a strong and courageous person, but listening to her story, the story of Adam and the children, I was blown away and my respect for her grew exponentially. Having served as a solider for many years, I've known my fair share of brave and selfless men and women. People who sacrificed all they had, sometimes including their lives, in order to keep others safe. I'm still amazed by Miranda's ability to put her daughters' wellbeing ahead of her own. I suppose in that way she reminds me of my own mother. Maybe something happens when a woman has a child. Maybe there is a switch in their brains that flips and suddenly their own happiness no longer matters.

Now, sitting here alone, I'm able to take a good look at the picture in my hands. Miranda is seated on a hospital bed, a blue gown hanging slightly off her shoulder. Her hair looks longer than it is now, and it's pulled up into a high ponytail on the top of her head. Sitting beside her is a little girl with the same stunning blue eyes and there could never be any doubt that little girl is Katelyn. On the opposite side of Miranda is a man holding a tiny bundle wrapped in pink - Paige. The man, who I know is Adam, is very thin, and his skin is an unhealthy shade of yellow. His hair is very short, but is also thinned in odd, irregular patterns. The light green t-shirt he is wearing looks to be two sizes too big and swallows him up. It's clear to see he was very sick when this picture was taken.

Despite everything though, it's the look on his face that makes me pause. While Katelyn and Miranda smile for the camera, Adam's eyes are focused on them. Though his cheeks are sunken from weight loss and the bones in his jaw are sharper than they should be, his eyes tell the real story of that moment in time. Those eyes, a similar shade of warm honey like Paige's, glow with happiness and are framed with love. There are no shadows of doubt or sadness, only the light of joy. It's clear as day how much he loved them. How much he loved Miranda.

I wonder what most men in my position would think about this photograph. Maybe I should feel resentment, that after all those years I spent thinking of Miranda, he was with her. Perhaps I should be jealous; he got to hold her in his arms at night and see her smile during the day, while I was half a world away barely holding on to my sanity with only a tattered, grainy slip of newspaper to cling to. Should I hate him or despise him? I don't know. What I do know is I feel none of those things. Instead, looking at him looking at her, I feel glad. If I couldn't have been the one, if we weren't meant to be at that time in our lives, at least she had someone who, by all appearances, loved her deeply.

I carefully set the photo back in its spot on the nightstand and look toward the door. Clattering from downstairs mixing with the sound of laughter floats up through the floorboards. The combination makes me smile.

Deciding I have waited long enough, I make my way down to the first floor. Passing the living room, I glance around. The TV is on, but the sound is off and the room is empty. The clanking of plates pulls my attention to the end of the hall. I peek my head around the corner, and the first person I see is Katelyn seated at the kitchen table. Her head is bent over her notebook and her dark hair hides most of her face. I take one small step and the movement must catch her attention. Katelyn lifts her eyes and they pin me in place. I can't explain it, but the sternness of her ice blue stare almost makes me turn and run.

I don't want to admit it to myself, let alone Miranda, but I feel like I need Katelyn's approval to date her mother. Paige and I have spent time together, even before last night, and in some odd way I feel like we've bonded. Sure she is younger than Katelyn, easier to please and less cynical, but despite that I truly feel she likes me. Katelyn, on the other hand, is older. I can tell there's an old soul looking out from those eyes. She has an adult understanding of relationships and knows what could happen between me and Miranda. Above all, unlike Paige, Katelyn has true memories of her father.

Does she think if this thing between me and her mother becomes serious I will try to replace her dad? Convincing her I would never want to will take a little time. If she told Miranda she didn't like me, or was upset she was seeing me, would Miranda say we couldn't be together? The thought makes me sick.

171

I stand, stuck in place, under the scrutiny of her silent assessment. I keep my posture relaxed, but my eyes beg for her approval. After several heartbeats, the corner of her mouth twitches before curling into a small smile. She breaks her stare with a wink before turning back to her notebook. A breath I didn't realize I was holding rushes from my lungs, and I feel a weight lifted from my shoulders.

"Jace," Paige screeches.

Rushing, she gets her foot caught on the leg of the bar stool she is sitting on and nearly crashes to the floor, but catches herself at the last second. Two steps more and she is leaping into my arms.

"Well, good morning."

"Mommy said you were going to have breakfast with us. She makes the best pancakes and she said I can help her! Do you like pancakes?"

"I love pancakes." Setting her feet on the floor, I follow her to the island in the center of the kitchen where Miranda has a variety of ingredients spread out on the counter. Paige reclaims her seat on the stool and motions for me to sit next to her.

"Mommy, Jace likes pancakes, so we can make them."

"Oh well, I am glad to hear it," Miranda says, looking up from her mixing bowl. "Especially since I already started making them," she adds sarcastically.

"Do you need help with that?" I ask, watching her whisk the batter in the bowl. I have to concentrate on her face to keep my eyes from darting to her breasts which sway to and fro with her movements.

"You know how to make pancakes?" she asks, lifting a brow.

"Well, come to think of it, no, but there must be something I can help with."

"I think the coffee is done and I am dying for a cup."

Needing no further instruction, I slide from my seat and around the counter. During my exploration the last time I was in this kitchen, I know where to find the mugs and sugar bowl. I also know, after watching Miranda make her coffee at the shop, she takes it with milk and two sugars. Moving easily around Miranda as she sets a flat grill pan on the stove and begins spooning batter in small circles on its surface, I grab the items I need and make her coffee, before pouring a cup for myself.

I look toward the table and see Katelyn is still focused on her writing and Paige is absorbed in her handheld video game. Quietly, I move behind Miranda and set her mug beside the stove, making sure to brush my front against her back. She arches into me, as if by instinct, and hums under her

172

breath before straightening.

Her eyes fall to the mug and then back to me. "Thank you."

"You're welcome," I say, taking a sip of my own coffee. "Are you sure there isn't anything else I can do?"

"I don't think so. Paige is going to set the table in a little bit and there really isn't much else to do besides flip pancakes. I'm sure I can handle that." As if to prove her point, with little effort, she flips the four bubbling, doughy blobs revealing a smooth, golden brown surface on the other side.

"Do you do this often?" I ask, nodding my chin toward the pan.

"Every Saturday." She smiles brightly.

Watching her move around the kitchen, mixing, stirring, and flipping, unleashes something within me. The caveman part of my brain likes seeing her like this. I have to remind myself we're not alone in order to keep the lower half of my body in check. There's no doubt in my mind that if her daughters weren't here, I would pick her up, set her on the counter, and have her for breakfast. To hell with pancakes.

"What?" Her voice startles me free from my thoughts.

"Huh?"

"You were staring at me with a look in your eyes," she says, sliding two perfectly golden pancakes on to the plate resting beside her.

"Oh, yeah?" I tilt my head to one side. "What kind of look?"

"Like," her voice lowers to a whisper, "like, uh, you know." She looks down, adding a few more dollops of batter to the pan, conveniently hiding her eyes behind a section of thick, black hair that has fallen free from its elastic. It's not enough to hide the rest of her face, however, and I can see a hint of pink spread across her cheeks.

I take a half step closer. Placing my index finger under her chin, I left her face until her eyes met mine. Lightly, I draw my finger across the curve of her jaw and up to her cheekbone, my skin skimming the surface of hers causing her to shiver. I tuck lose strands of hair behind her ear and lower voice to match hers.

"I'm not sure I do. Tell me. How was I looking at you?"

"Jace." Her voice is shaky and I smile, knowing the effect I have on her.

"Was I staring like you are the most beautiful woman I've ever seen?" I softly kiss her right cheek.

"Or like I've spent almost half my life dreaming of a moment like this?" I place another kiss on her left cheek.

"Maybe like I'm certain that after today, I'll be ruined forever, because

I've had a taste of perfection and there's no way I'll be happy with anything else?"

I hear her draw a sharp breath. Lightly, I kiss the tip of her nose.

"The look I gave you could have said any of those, but if I had to guess, I'd say I was looking at you like I want nothing more than to spend the rest of the day, the week, hell, the rest of my life, getting lost in you."

A tiny whimper escapes her throat and it's my undoing. I lower my head until her soft lips melt into mine, molding to me perfectly. In this moment I know I never want to kiss anyone else for as long as I live.

My kiss starts off very gentle, but almost immediately she wraps her arms around my neck and presses against me, begging me for more. My tongue passes against the seam of her lips and she parts them willingly. Just as my tongue begins to seek out hers, a groan and a giggle quickly remind both of us that we have an audience.

I pull back, my hands sliding down her shoulders and arms, weaving her fingers with mine. Miranda leans to the side, looking at Katelyn and Paige, her cheeks still flush with arousal but also mixed with embarrassment. Releasing one hand, I also turn. If either of the girls had any doubt about our relationship, I think it's gone.

Paige's eyes swim with mischief and interest. From the few things Miranda told me last night, I know she hasn't been in a relationship since her husband passed away. For Paige, that was the first time she has seen her mom kiss someone. Good thing she is too young to really think too much of it.

Katelyn is a different story. For a split second I'm nervous to look in her direction. When I finally do, I'm surprised. I imagined she'd be mad or upset, but she's none of those things. Instead her face is lit with a huge smile and just like that, another weight I hadn't realized was on my chest lifts. I breathe a sigh of relief.

"Ah, I think the pancakes are burning." Paige breaks the silence.

"Oh shit," Miranda says, turning back to scrape the blackened disks from the pan.

174

Chapter 28
Miranda

I lean back in my chair and take in the scene in front of me. I couldn't have imagined this in my wildest dreams. The table is littered with empty dishes. The only evidence of the breakfast I made are the sticky, maple syrup covered plates. Katelyn, Paige, and Jace are huddled together across from me watching some ridiculous cat videos on the internet. Paige is laughing so hard she can barely breathe, while Katelyn and Jace chuckle one moment and share looks over Paige's theatrics the next.

Seeing the three of them together causes butterflies to swarm my stomach. It's the same sensation I get deep down when I feel Jace's eyes on me from across the room, or when I get a glimpse of him leaving his house in the early morning hours to go for his daily run. I won't admit it out loud, but after the first morning I noticed him, in his loose fitting running shorts and tight black t-shirt, round the end of his driveway and jog by, I purposely began getting up twenty minutes early to watch him run every day.

It has been a long time since I felt this way, and my mind immediately wanders to Adam. There is a large part of me that feels guilty for the giddiness bubbling just beneath my skin, like I am betraying him by having some secret affair. Of course I'm not. Adam has been gone for a while, for years, and I've been alone.

In truth, I was alone before Adam even died. Sure we spent as much time together as we possibly could. When we weren't trying to fill a lifetime of memories for Katelyn into a few short months, we would spend time with one another. We laughed about the crazy things we did as children and cried over the moments we wouldn't have together. Side by side we would lie in bed, curled up under the blankets, dreaming of all the places we wished we could've visited and reminisced about all of the places we had been.

Those weeks before his passing is a time I'll treasure for the rest of my life. But – and god I'm an awful person for even having a *but* - looking back now, time has been a blessing. Able to separate myself from the situation a little, I can see that even though I loved Adam, the love changed along the way. Somewhere during that short period of time, we shifted from lovers to best friends. I often find myself lying awake at night, wondering if the transition would have happened regardless of his sickness, or if the cancer that transformed him from a healthy active man into a sickly, weak patient sped up the process and caused our love to change.

I wonder, after having experienced the love of one extraordinary man, if I deserve to experience it again? Is it selfish of me to ask for that opportunity? And more importantly, if it's not selfish, and the universe gives me a second chance, what would Adam think? What would he do if he were me? If I had been the one to die and leave him alone to raise our children, would I have expected him to remain single? To never find someone who made him happy again? Would I have wanted him to be alone for the rest of his life? I want to say I would want him to be happy, even if that meant moving on with someone else, but it doesn't ease the betrayal and guilt I feel.

"Hey. Hey. Hey. Anyone home?"

The sound of Sam's voice from the foyer makes me flinch. Sam knew of my date a few weeks ago, thanks to Claire's big mouth, but he hasn't asked about it, and that makes me nervous. If there is one thing to be said about my dear brother, is he is not shy. I'm not sure how he will react to finding Jace here early on a Saturday morning or if he'll connect the dots. I suddenly feel like a teenager who has been caught sneaking a boy out of the house.

Jace must notice my nervousness, because his foot nudges mine beneath the table. He flashes me a smile and I feel my heartbeat slow just a bit. I try to return the smile, but I cannot make my face cooperate. I move my foot from his and run it up this calf letting him know I'm all right before turning my attention to the doorway.

"We're in the kitchen, Uncle Sam," Paige calls out.

Moments later Sam appears.. Claire follows close behind, so close in fact, that when Sam stops abruptly, she crashes into his back.

"Jesus, Sam. What the hell?" Claire hisses, rubbing her forehead.

When Sam doesn't immediately answer or apologize, she peeks around him and sees Jace seated at the table. Her mouth forms a perfect 'O' in realization. She turns and gives me a knowing smile.

Claire moves past my brother, who is still frozen in place, and stalks toward Jace.

"Hi, I'm Claire, Sam's fiancée," she introduces herself, offering her right hand. "You must be Jace."

"I am. It's a pleasure to meet you, Claire. I've heard a lot about you." Jace flashes a crooked smile, shaking her hand.

"All good things I hope." She winks, tossing her dark hair back.

"Of course," Jace laughs.

"Uncle Sam, you missed the pancakes. I don't think there are any left. They were really good this time," Paige declares, breaking the growing silence.

Sam blinks a few times, before shaking his head, trying to clear it.

"I'm sorry I missed them P," he says, ruffling her hair.

"Maybe next time you and Auntie Claire can come over earlier and eat breakfast with us," Paige suggests.

Claire pulls out the chair next to me. "Would we need to have a sleep over to get here before they're all gone?" she murmurs under her breath, so only I can hear. Well, I think only I can hear her, until Jace coughs to try to hide a laugh.

"Good morning, Sam." Jace pushes away from the table, stepping toward my brother, offering him a handshake.

Sam looks down to Jace's outstretched hand with a blank stare and finally snaps free of his stupor and shakes it.

"Morning." Sam holds Jace's hand longer than acceptable and I can see both their knuckles beginning to turn white. "I wasn't expecting to see you today," Sam continues, a hint of authority in his voice, like an older brother trying to scare his sister's date on prom night.

"And I wasn't expecting to see you so early and unannounced on a Saturday morning," I interject. "So, to what do I owe the pleasure of your visit?" I begin to stack plates on top of one another.

From the corner of my eye I notice Sam stiffen slightly when I say 'unannounced' and Claire giggles beside me. Normally, I wouldn't think twice of random early morning visit.

"I thought I mentioned it yesterday," Sam says, finally releasing Jace's hand, "or maybe it was earlier this week. I wanted to pull out the air conditioners upstairs before the weather gets much colder. I should've done it a few weeks ago, but I've been so busy."

"No, I don't think you said anything about it. In fact, I think I would remember since I planned to try to do it myself this weekend. It was really drafty in Paige's room the other day."

"Why didn't you say anything? I could have done it for you," Jace asks picking up the last few dishes from the table, setting them in the sink. I stare at him for a few seconds.

Feeling my face begin to flush, I look down at the floor. "You shouldn't have to come over and do it for me, but I was afraid I might drop them," I admit. I hate after all this time Sam still has to come help me with things around the house.

"Is there anything else you need me to do while I am here?" Sam asks, putting an extra emphasis on *me*.

"No, that's all I can think of."

"Well, it shouldn't take me too long. I'll be back in a second."

"Let me give you a hand," Jace offers, following behind my brother, not waiting for an invitation. The two men leave the room, their voices becoming quieter the further they get.

"Girls, why don't you head upstairs and straighten up your bedrooms. Dig out all your dirty laundry so I can start a load," I say. My request is instantly met with groans, but they file out of the room and soon I hear their footsteps stomping up the stairs.

I begin rinsing and placing plates and cups in the dishwasher, trying to ignore Claire's stare. Once the dishes are all set, I wipe down the counters and the stove, then tie the trash to take out later. I contemplate sweeping the floor, but Claire is apparently not going to let me ignore her any longer.

"So, you two seem cozy," she starts.

"Please don't make a big deal out of this," I plead, pulling out the chair across from her at the table. Her nearly black eyes twinkle with delight.

"Is he the same guy you went out with a few weeks ago?"

"Of course he is," I insist. "Jesus. What do you think? I went on one date and now I'm picking up guys on the corner and bringing them home?"

"Honey, if I could find a guy like that on the street I'd take him home in a heartbeat." She winks.

"You would not and you know it. I see the way you look at my brother after all these years and he at you. You guys will be together forever."

"I know. That's sad, isn't it?" She tries to pout but fails.

"No, it's great. It's a once in a lifetime thing." I pick at the fringe on the end of the place mat on the table.

"Who says it has to be once in a lifetime?" Claire asks, knowing I'm talking about more than her and Sam. Her voice loses some of its humor and gains seriousness.

"It's seems greedy to ask for more than that, don't you think? Adam and I had a kind of love everyone should have, and I'll be forever grateful I got to be a part of something special. I'll never have that again. I can't."

"Oh sweetie, I wouldn't be so sure. I agree you and Adam had something wonderful, magical even, but I think you could have that again with someone else. I know you were in shock when Sam and I showed up here this morning, but even the two minutes I was in the room with you two I could feel the energy in the air. And I know you probably didn't notice, but I saw how Jace looked at you, even with Sam and me in the room."

"What are you talking about?"

"While you were too busy trying not to look guilty, like you were caught with your hand in the cookie jar," she winks, "I was watching Jace. He was looking at you like you were the center of his world."

"You're crazy." I try to dismiss her comment with a wave of a hand and roll of my eyes.

"Whatever you say, but I would bet my paycheck that man is in love with you."

My mouth gapes open. "What? You can't be serious."

She simply sighs in response. "Anyway, he was here awfully early this morning." She smiles brightly and teases me. "He just couldn't say no to your pancakes?" I know she is not referring to breakfast.

"Actually, he spent the night," I say, just louder than a whisper. I watch her face change from amused, to shocked, then back to being amused.

"He offered to take Paige to the Father-Daughter Dance last night after that vile principal told me I couldn't take her. When they got back we had a glass of wine, did a little slow dancing of our own and, well, one thing lead to another." I feel my cheeks begin to burn. I can't believe I am telling her this.

"Wow," she says in disbelief. "He definitely loves you. There's no chance in hell he doesn't."

"Why does that mean he is in love with me? People who aren't in love have, uh, spend the night together all the time."

"That's not what I mean and you know it," Claire says, crossing her arms over her chest. "C'mon Miranda, seriously? If the man was not head over heels for you, he never would have offered to take Paige to the dance."

"You don't know that," I insist.

"I do. It's obvious."

"No. He can't. It's too soon."

"Love doesn't really come with an itinerary. It will happen when it happens and not a moment before or after. I knew I loved your brother after our first date. I didn't tell him, of course. I let him continue to try to win me over, but I knew."

"Even if that's true, it doesn't matter. It, this thing between us, can't become anything more than this," I say, waving my hands in the air.

"Why?"

I push away from the table and turn to look out the back window toward the lake. The dock where Jace and I first met is still there, the waves lapping lazily at its legs.

"It seems ridiculous to me, so I'm sure it won't make sense to anyone else, but I feel guilty I might actually want to fall in love again. Or worse, that I want to fall in love with Jace. I feel guilty that somewhere in the back of my mind a tiny part of me fell in love with him all those years ago when we met as kids. But most of all I feel guilty because I'm betraying Adam."

Claire comes and stands beside me, putting a hand on my shoulder. "He would want you to be happy, you know. He wouldn't want you to be alone for the rest of your life. He loved you too much to see you lonely forever. He'd want you to find someone to grow old with."

Tears begin to run down my face.

"Adam was the first verse of your life's song, Miranda. It was beautiful and mesmerizing, but even though it has ended, your song is not over yet. Your strength has carried you through this interlude, but now it's time to move on. It's time to start the second verse."

"I don't think I can," I whisper, turning to face her. Claire opens her mouth to say something, but is interrupted before she can speak again.

"All set," Sam's boisterous voice cuts through the emotion in the room. I hear him open the refrigerator, presumably searching for something to drink. I quickly wipe my face before turning around. Jace is leaning against the door jam and as soon as I turn I find his eyes on me. With one look his casual demeanor is replaced with worry and he straightens.

"All of the air conditioning units are out and in the garage. It's supposed to be cold this week, so we pulled out the space heater I bought last year and put it in the corner of the living room. You can always wheel it in here if you want. I know the door is still drafty," Sam continues, pointing toward the backdoor that leads out to a screened porch.

"Great. Thanks," I say trying not to sniffle, but I can't help it. I wipe a hand over my face once again.

"Is everything all right?" Sam asks, his eyes moving from me, to Claire, then Jace before coming back to me.

I push aside all of the things Claire said to me, locking them away in the back of my mind. "Yes, everything is fine."

Sam squints, apparently not convinced.

"Hey Sam, I want to hit the farmer's market before they close in a half hour." Claire saves me from explaining further.

"Really?" Sam asks, his eyes narrowing. "The last time we went there you old me you never wanted to go back because it's too crowded."

"I said that? Are you sure?" She tilts her head, trying to look confused. "I think that was the flea market on Main Street. I really want to see if they have any pumpkins left," Claire says, pulling on her fleece.

"Pumpkins?" my brother asks, thoroughly baffled. "For what?"

"To make pie, of course."

"Pie? You've never made a pie in your life." Sam's face scrunches even more, and he looks at me like I hold some secret clue to what Claire is talking about.

"Sure I have. Didn't I make one for you last year?" Claire grabs her purse from the table.

"I don't think so, and I think that's something I'd remember."

"Well, anyway, I want to make one now. Can we stop there on the way home?"

"Sure, I guess so. Let's go." Sam takes one more swig of orange juice before placing the carton back in the fridge.

I follow them to the front door, fully aware of Jace not far behind. Katelyn bounces down the stairs, laundry basket in hand.

"Uncle Sam, are you leaving already?"

"Your aunt wants to see a man about a squash, or something like that," Sam chuckles, shaking his head.

Katelyn's brows pull together. "Uh, okay. I'm performing the National Anthem at the Thanksgiving Eve football game this year. Do you think you guys will be able to make it?"

"The Thanksgiving Eve game? Wow, that's great," Claire says.

"Congratulations, Katie. I am so proud of you." Sam's face beams with pride.

181

"Thanks. So you'll be there?"

"I'll have to check my schedule at the hospital. With the holiday I'll most likely be on a different rotation," Claire explains. "But I'll be there if I can. I'm dying to see you perform."

Sam's face drops just a little. "Shoot Katie, that's the day for my monthly visit with your grandmother. I can't miss it and you know I can't reschedule it. Damn, I can't believe I'm going to miss you perform."

"That's okay. I understand," Katelyn says, shifting the basket to the other hip. "There's always next year." She smiles.

"That's my girl," Sam says, wrapping his arm around her and pulling her into his side.

"What about you Jace? Think you can come?" Katelyn asks and all four of us turn to look at him.

The corner of his mouth lifts forming that smile I love so much. "I wouldn't miss it for the world."

Katelyn smiles brightly, but what she does next shocks me to my core. Setting the basket on the floor, she crosses the room, wraps her arms around Jace's middle, and hugs him tight before softly saying, "Thanks, Jace."

Tears blur my vision, but I'm able to see him kiss the top of her head. "You're welcome."

Sam clears his throat. He looks as surprised as I feel. "All right, well we are going to head out." Pulling the door open, he waits for Claire to step past him. "Thanks Jace, for your help. With everything," he adds firmly at the end.

"I'll call you later," Claire says stepping over the threshold. "Think about that song," she calls out.

I simply nod and watch them leave, overhearing Sam ask her what the hell is going on. Katelyn retrieves the discarded basket of laundry and heads down the hall toward the basement. I feel the heat of Jace's body as he steps closer, wrapping his arms around me. Leaning into him I feel some of the stress fade. With a simple touch he's able to comfort me. He places a gentle kiss on my neck, just below my ear.

"Well, he didn't try to push me out of the second story window, so I'll take that as a win," he says and I laugh.

Chapter 29
Jace

The sun is already beginning to set, the sky turning a dark shade of navy blue, when the four of us climb into my truck. The full moon is rising above the trees, watching over the darkening world below. Tomorrow is Thanksgiving and the weather has definitely changed. The last of the Indian summer disappeared a little more than two weeks ago and the weather has quickly transitioned right to early winter. I wouldn't be surprised if it snows in the next few days. Of course I've seen snow before, but not as early as November. I have never experienced a New England winter. Oddly enough I'm looking forward to it.

As cold as it is outside, it's equally cold in the truck. I can't pinpoint exactly when it began, but over the last few days there's no denying a building void has formed between me and Miranda. At first I thought I was imagining things, maybe getting in my own head, thinking the whole situation was too good to be true. But as the days went along I realized Miranda really was acting different. Her smile doesn't quite meet her eyes, and she doesn't melt into my embrace like she did before. A tired look has appeared on her face again and I haven't been able to erase it.

We have spent a few evenings together during the last two weeks. Twice the four of us had dinner and once it was just Miranda and me. One of those nights Miranda, the girls, and I curled up in their living room and watched a couple of movies back to back until all four of us fell asleep. I woke up in the early morning with a kink in my neck and an unfamiliar warmth in my chest. Being there, with the three of them, made me long for the type of family I never had. I love my mother with every fiber of my being and without her I wouldn't be the person I am today. But there have been times over the years I've wondered what it would have been like to have my father, or a father in general, around.

Maybe everything is happening too soon. Maybe I said something, did something, to make her feel uncomfortable. I've spent countless hours trying to figure it out, but I have come up empty. I don't know whether to push the issue or give her space. Not being in control of this situation is killing me - and my leg. Trying to clear my head, I've been running farther and harder than I should and it's beginning to catch up to me.

I thought about calling Miranda to tell her I wouldn't be able to make it to Katelyn's performance tonight. I could've made up any excuse, if she even wanted one, but I just couldn't do it. Every time I picked up my phone all I could see was Katelyn's face when she asked me to come tonight. She was nervous at first, but once I agreed the nerves melted away and excitement took over. I can't let her down.

"Then, Mrs. Pine told the class we could have extra recess today because we filled our respect jar," Paige explains, rambling on about her day at school. "I was so excited because I was finally able to climb the monkey bars backwards. Isn't that cool?"

"Wow," Miranda says, her voice thick with mock excitement.

"Jace? Can you do the monkey bars?" Paige asks.

"Absolutely."

"Did they teach you how when you became a solider?"

I laugh. "Nah, I already knew how to do that, but one of the drills we had to do in basic training was sort of similar."

"Really?"

"Yup."

"Wow. Maybe I'll join the army someday."

"I thought you wanted to be a teacher?" Miranda asks, turning back to face Paige.

I glance in the rear view mirror seeing Paige roll her eyes. "Maybe," she says.

"Well, you have a long time before you need to decide," Miranda assures her and turns to face forward in her seat.

"Did you always want to work in an office, Mommy?" Paige asks, but before Miranda can answer, Katelyn scoffs.

"No, sweetheart. I didn't always want to work in an office. It just sort of happened."

"What *did* you want to do when you grew up?"

"She wanted to be a singer, duh," Katelyn interjects, and even though I can't see her eyes, I know she rolled them dramatically.

"Really?"

It's Miranda's turn to roll her eyes but before Paige presses her further, I pull into the parking lot of the high school which is already filled with dozens of cars. I have to circle twice before finding an empty spot.

"I didn't expect there to be this many people already," Katelyn says quietly.

Putting the truck in park, I turn around to face her. Her head rests against the back window as she peers out at the people filing through the gate up to the football field.

"Hey." I reach back and put my hand on her knee. "You're going to do great. No need to be nervous."

She smiles just slightly. "That's easy for you to say."

"I suppose so," I laugh. "But it'll be alright. You're going to blow them away." I squeeze her knee. "Ready?"

Katelyn draws in a deep breath through her nose, holds it for a moment, and then releases it through her mouth. Nodding her head, she undoes her seatbelt and pops her door open. Pulling the keys from the ignition, I catch a glimpse of Miranda out of the corner of my eye. When I turn to look at her, I notice an odd look on her face.

"What?"

"You're amazing, do you know that?"

I know she isn't expecting an answer, but even if she is she doesn't give me a chance to respond. She kisses me gently on the lips. The kiss isn't passionate by any stretch of the imagination, but it's enough to stir that yearning deep down and squelch just a little of the uncertainty I had been feeling.

Katelyn grabs her guitar from the trunk, kisses Miranda on the cheek, and rushes off to get ready. The three of us follow the building crowd up the dirt path leading toward the field. The closer we get to the gate outside the stands, the more condensed the crowd becomes. My shoulders brush against a few people and I'm bumped and jostled by others. Quickly, my anxiety begins to build and I feel an overwhelming feeling of claustrophobia squeeze my chest. Each breath becomes more difficult than the one before it. The muscles in my back tense and before too long they begin to ache. The usual dull pain in my leg amplifies and sharp shocks radiate up through my hip into my spine.

I don't know if she can sense I'm on the edge of losing it or if she simply wants to, but just before I think the walls may cave in around me, Miranda slides her hand into mine. Our fingers intertwine and she squeezes gently. Leading me by one hand and Paige by the other, Miranda guides us to the bleachers, avoiding as much of the crowd as possible by ducking under one section to get to a near empty spot.

"I think we'll have a good view from here," she says, releasing our hands and climbing up a few steps, taking a seat in the second row. She doesn't move all the way down the row. Instead, she stops only a few feet in, so when the three of us sit, I'm right on the edge. It's then I realize she's done this so I wouldn't be surrounded by people on all four sides.

"When is it going to start?" Paige asks.

"I think we have about five minutes," Miranda answers, scanning the crowd with a purpose.

"Who are you looking for?" I ask, but she doesn't answer. Instead she keeps searching until she finds what she is looking for. Standing, she steps up on her seat and begins waving her arms back and forth.

"Be careful. You're going to fall."

She narrows her eyes at me, but steps down regardless. Sure enough, a minute later, Claire comes bounding up the steps.

"Aunt Claire!" Paige screams, throwing her arms around Claire's neck. Claire is so short I imagine within a few years Paige will be taller than her.

"Hello, P. How are you?"

"Good. I thought you told Katelyn you couldn't come tonight."

"Well, I changed a few things around in my schedule so I could make it. I was so bummed I missed the last one," Claire says, setting Paige down on the metal beam. "Hey, Jace," she says, scooting past all three of us and taking a seat next to Miranda.

I nod my chin. "Good to see you."

"So I take it you were able to switch shifts?" Miranda asks.

"Kinda. That witch Michelle wouldn't switch shifts with me, even though I covered for her last month, but Nicole offered to stay late a couple of hours. I told her I wouldn't be too long, but I have to go to work in a little bit."

"Oh, that's too bad. What time will you be working until? Should I move dinner back tomorrow?"

Miranda is cooking Thanksgiving dinner tomorrow afternoon. From what Katelyn and Paige have told me, it seems to be a tradition. They both went on and on about Miranda cooking a big meal and Sam and Claire coming over. Afterward they play Monopoly until it gets too late and they begin to fall asleep or Sam cheats and steals all their money, which ever happens first.

I never told Miranda I turned down my mother's invitation to come home for the holiday, but I also didn't have to think too long when she invited me to join her family either.

"Nah." Claire dismisses the idea with a wave of her hand. "I'll be home tomorrow morning. I figure I will take a nap for a few hours and then Sam and I will come over."

"Are you sure? You know, we don't have to have Thanksgiving dinner tomorrow. We could do it over the weekend."

"Are you kidding me? We have to eat turkey on Turkey Day. What's wrong with you?" Claire asks trying to look offended, but can't seem to control her Cheshire cat smile.

"All right. I'll cook the damn turkey tomorrow."

"Good."

Just then there is a crackle in the speakers overhead and the announcer's voice hushes the crowd.

"Good evening folks and welcome to the twenty -seventh annual Thanksgiving Eve showdown between our neighboring rivals, the Centerville Lions and our beloved Centaurs."

Whistles and cheers fill the air and echo through the night sky. The energy in the crowd surrounding us is almost overwhelming, causing my fist to clench tight in my lap.

"Tonight we have an extra special treat. Ladies and gentlemen, please rise and help me welcome our very own Belham sophomore, Katelyn Cross, as she sings our National Anthem."

The crowd cheers once more and focuses their attention to the center of the field. Katelyn is standing behind a mic stand, and I instantly notice she does not have her guitar with her. In fact, it's nowhere to be seen. Instead, her arms hang loosely by her sides, brushing the edge of her long purple sweater that falls several inches below the edge of the tan jacket she's wearing. Katelyn tucks a stray piece of hair behind her ear before stepping closer to the microphone. Her chest rises, her eyes fall shut, and a moment later her mesmerizing voice begins to pour from the speakers.

Perhaps to the rest of the audience she seems calm, but I can see her fingers twitching with nervous energy. It only takes a few seconds for her to relax, however. By the end of the second line her posture loosens. She opens her eyes and scans the crowd, touching on faces here and there, but not lingering on one for too long. Her voice starts soft and grows gradually with the lyrics, reaching the most powerful part of the song. The power behind the notes causes her eyes to clench shut. Perfectly executed runs bring drama and emotion to the performance.

Hearing the National Anthem always causes a lump to form in my throat. Even before I enlisted in the Army, I felt some unexplainable emotional connection to the song. It's odd, and perhaps it's not a good comparison, but hearing the National Anthem is almost spiritual. It's the same odd sensation I get hearing the hymns preformed at church. It's a mixture of joy, peace, and belonging to something greater than me. Patriotism, whether it felt by civilian or solider, is a powerful thing.

Tonight, hearing Katelyn sing, adds another layer of emotion I wasn't expecting. The joy I normally experience is amplified by an unusual amount of pride. Seeing her stand out on that field, knowing the strength and courage she found to overcome her stage freight to perform is astounding. I'm not only to rush the field and congratulate her, but of Miranda for raising such a brave child. It's all I can do not to rush the field to congratulate Katelyn or pull Miranda against me and kiss her until the sun comes up.

Of course, I do neither. Instead I stand tall, locked in place. I peel my gaze away only for a moment when I feel Paige's small hand slide into my palm. Glancing down, I see her staring at the field with the same look on her face as I assume I wore. I lift my eyes to Miranda and see tears streaming down her face. She must feel my attention on her because she looks in my direction and offers me a weak smile.

Katelyn's voice trails off as she sings the final note and the crowd erupts with cheers, causing me to flinch. My anxiety shoots from zero to sixty in millisecond. Concern drowns the happiness in Miranda's eyes. Her lips part, as if to say something, but she is interrupted by two very loud consecutive blasts followed by a flash of light.

My muscles coil, ready to spring in to action. The racing of my pulse floods my veins with adrenaline, fueling my system for the impending fight or flight. My ears ring and my lungs burn. Images of death and destruction pass before my eyes before my vision clears and the noise of the crowd fades into the background. Sweat begins to run down my back and across my brow. I move in place trying to find the source of the explosion and at the same time potential suspects. The blast must have been close; there's the light scent of smoke in the air, but where?

THE SECOND VERSE

I can't hear Miranda over the roar of my beating heart, but instead feel her pushing against my arm. I have to get her and the girls out of here. I look to my right, toward the narrow staircase we walked up earlier. It's not the most ideal exit, too open but also too confining. I have no other choice; it will have to do.

Blindly, I reach for Miranda's arm and tighten my hold on Paige's hand. With no time to be delicate, I pull them harder than I should and lead them to the stairs, shielding them with my body from anymore potential explosions. Miranda pulls hard against my hold, but I don't slow down. I can apologize for being rough later. Right now, I need to get them to safety. I need to make sure they are safe.

Once we are on the ground below, I scan the area from side to side. Which way now?

"Jace, stop!" Miranda yells behind me. I try to block her out so I can think, but she kicks me hard in the back of the leg causing my knee to buckle.

"What the hell?"

"Stop! What is the matter with you?" she hisses, yanking Paige's hand free from mine before scoping up in her arms. Paige nuzzles her head into the crock of Miranda's neck, sniffling with each breath.

I watch Miranda with Paige confused. My forehead pinches together as I try to figure out why they are reacting this way.

"We need to move as far away from here as possible. We can't stay here."

"What are you talking about? Why?"

"What do you mean why? Did you not see or hear the explosion! Miranda please let me get you out of here."

"There wasn't an explosion."

"I didn't see where, but —"

"Fireworks, it was fireworks," she interrupts.

"We can talk about this later. We have to ... Wh ... what?"

"Fireworks, Jace," she says softly, like she is afraid of spooking me.

Claire appears just behind Miranda and for the first time I realize I had forgotten her. I left her behind. I was so concerned about Miranda and Paige that I forgot to help Claire too.

"Is everything all right, Miranda?" Claire asks, taking a small step forward.

Miranda looks over her shoulder and then sets Paige on the ground. Crouching down so she is eye level with Paige, she speaks in a soft, even tone.

"Why don't you go with Auntie Claire, sweetheart, and see if you can find

189

Katelyn. I'm sure she'll be looking for us," Miranda says, placing a kiss on the top of her head.

Paige sniffles and nods, rushing to Claire who takes her in her arms. Claire gives Miranda a questioning look before flicking her eyes to me.

"I'll meet you by the front gate." It's not a question but a statement.

"I'll be there in a few minutes," Miranda assures her and then turns to me. Her eyes move around my face like she is searching for something. Cautiously, she takes a step forward.

"Are you going to tell me what is going on?" she asks softly.

"I don't know." My voice is hoarse and shaky from the mixture of adrenaline and raw fear. "I, uh, I don't know."

"Are you okay?" Miranda places her hand on my chest.

"Am I okay? Christ, Blue, I nearly tore your arm off and crushed Paige's hand dragging you two out of there like some lunatic. Shit!" I yell, turning away from her, tilting my head to the sky.

"We're all right. It's all right."

"No, it's not," I say under my breath. "Why don't you catch up to Claire? You're right. Katelyn will be looking for you."

"Come with me."

"I think it's best if I don't. I need a moment. I'll find you in a little bit to take you guys home. Unless you would rather Claire dropped you off on her way to work."

"We'll wait for you by the front gate."

Miranda doesn't say anything more, but I can still feel her behind me. I can always feel when she is near. Usually it would be comforting, but right now, I find it unnerving. She doesn't move for several seconds, but eventually I hear her sigh heavily before I hear her footsteps move away. When I can no longer hear them, I count to thirty before turning. Miranda is swallowed up by the crowd walking around the edge of the field.

I turn and take a less crowded, slightly longer path back to the front of the field. This was a terrible idea, not only the football game, but this thing with Miranda too. She was right to be distant the last few days. She must've seen the writing on the wall and noticed this was never going to work. I'm too damaged, too broken. Hell, I have the scars and limp to prove it. I have no right to think I'm good enough for her or her children. They've been through enough. They don't need my bullshit added on top. The best thing to do would be to take a step back and put some space between us.

Nearing one of the large spotlights, I come to a stop, the crowd still moving around me. I reach into my back pocket, pulling out my wallet. My fingers brush against the soft paper and instantly my anxiety lessens. Staring at Miranda's picture, my heart begins to ache and my chest clenches. Deep down I don't believe we are better off apart and there's no use trying to convince my heart otherwise. No matter how badly my head would like to think it's true, it's no use. I fell in love with Miranda all those years ago, sitting on a wooden dock under a clear, starry sky, and I am still in love with her today.

Somewhere in an unfamiliar place only Miranda can reach, I feel a tremendous amount of grief at the thought of losing her. My stomach rolls and bile rises in my throat. My palms sweat, and no matter how deeply I breathe, I feel like I can't catch my breath. If I lost her now, I don't think I would be able to go on.

Suddenly, the need to tell her I love her is overwhelming. I need her to hear those words. I need to say them out loud or else I think my chest will burst. The anxiety I felt before is replaced with eagerness. I have to find her.

Chapter 30
Miranda

I don't fully understand what just happened, but I know better than to push Jace for answers. Either he will tell me when he is ready or he won't. The ball is in his court. If I am honest, he scared the shit out of me back there. I didn't know what was going on as he pulled me behind him. I could hear Paige whining trying to wiggle free, but I was too shocked to try to help her. I just hope Katelyn didn't see our quick exit.

Pushing my way through the crowd of people, I search for Claire and the girls. I told Katelyn earlier I would meet her out front after her performance, and I know Claire and Paige will be nearby. Every now and then I glance behind me looking for Jace. I don't know if I'm relieved or disappointed he is not there, but my stomach drops regardless.

This past week I've been thinking a lot about what Claire said to me. I think she was insane to think Jace is in love with me. It's completely ridiculous to think it's even possible. We have only known each other for a few weeks. It seems totally insane to fall in love with someone in that amount of time. But don't people talk about love at first sight?

The thing is, thinking back, I can't remember when I realized I was in love with Adam. More than one night this week I've laid in bed, staring at the ceiling, trying to remember the moment when I knew I was in love. No matter how hard I try, I can't remember. In every memory I have of Adam there was some level of love.

Of course I remember the first time he said he loved me as if it were yesterday. I was five and had been following him and Sam around the neighborhood on my bike. They tried to hide from me and in my rush to find them, I hit a bump in the street and fell off my bike. Adam ran out from around the side of a neighbor's house and helped me up. He brushed the dirt from my knees and wiped away the blood from my skinned palms with his shirt. His tan eyes looked over me with concern.

"I'm so sorry," he said.

"Whatever."

"No, really. I didn't want you to get hurt. I love you."

"Eww, Adam. You're so gross," I said, pushing his hand from my knee and getting to my feet. I ran the whole way home plotting how I would get them back.

The next time Adam said those three words was on the night he graduated from high school. I'd been so nervous about him leaving for UMass. I knew things were going to change between us and I was so anxious. That night we snuck away from his graduation party and sat out on the porch swing that hung from the rafters wrapped around his parents' house. We talked for hours, but for the life of me I can't remember about what. Just before we had to leave, so he could bring me home before my curfew, he leaned in close, kissed me softly on the lips, and told me he loved me. Even now, all these years later, the memory forms a goofy smile on my face, but I don't think that was the moment I fell in love with him. The love was already there, it just didn't have a name.

If I can't remember falling for Adam, how would I know if I've fallen for Jace? Sure, I feel this deep connection to him. Yes, I've felt more alive in the past few weeks than I have in years. I feel as if I've woken from a really long nap. But I was lucky enough to find love once, which is more than some people get. What right do I have to think I could find it again? I can't help but feel guilty for even thinking it. I had a great life with Adam and he loved me more than I could've ever asked for. No, it's not fair to expect or search for that again. I need to put a stop to this whole thing now before it goes any further.

At the top of the worn dirt path that leads toward the parking lot I stop, searching for any sign of Claire or Katelyn. They both should be here by now. I pull my cell phone from my back pocket to text Claire when a large form steps in front of me, blocking the light from spotlights illuminating the field.

"Hello, sweetheart."

My fingers freeze on the screen. I don't need to look up to know who is standing before me. The scent of cinnamon is enough to make me shiver. Jonathan. I quickly hit the last two keys on the screen before locking and tucking the phone back in my pocket.

"Jonathan." My tone is sharp and I hope it's enough to get my point across. "What are you doing here?"

"My nephew is on the football team. My brother dragged me here to watch the little shit play." He takes a step closer so his thighs brush against my legs and hips. "What about you? Aren't these boys a little young for you?"

"Screw you." I push hard against his chest, but he doesn't move.

"I see your feisty tonight. I like it." He runs the tip of his index finger lightly down my arm. "What do you say you and I get out of here and go have some fun?"

"You can't be serious." I take a step back and move to pass by him, but he mirrors my movement and steps in front of me, blocking my path.

"You hurt my feelings, sweetheart."

"I doubt that. Now, if you'll excuse me." This time when I move he grabs ahold of my arm, which is still tender from Jace's grasp earlier.

"C'mon. You know you've always wanted one night with me. You couldn't have it while I was your boss, although I wouldn't have minded. Now that you don't work for me, I'd like to be over you in other ways."

Jonathan lowers his head and I can feel his sticky breath on my skin. My throat constricts and mouth goes dry. A few yards away people pass by completely unaware of what is going on. I'm sure to them we must look like a couple sharing an intimate moment alone.

I feel my phone buzz in my pocket, but don't move to check it. Instead, with both hands and all my strength, I push against Jonathan's chest.

"Are you deaf or just stupid? I said no. Move. Out. Of. My. Way." I hit my hand on his chest with each word.

"I think you should listen to her." Jace's voice slices through the night, loud and full of venom.

Jonathan takes a step back, turning on his heel to see who's behind him. I take the opportunity to step past him and move toward Jace, but Jonathan grabs my wrist stopping me. A small sob escapes before I can stop it. My eyes are fixed on Jace. Even from this distance, I can see the muscles twitching in his jaw. He opens and closes his fists at his sides.

"Take your hands off of her," he snarls.

"And who the hell are you?" Jonathan spits.

"I'm the person who's going to remove your hand from your body if you don't let go of her."

Jonathan must see the seriousness in Jace's face, because he let's go of my wrist. Quickly, I rush toward Jace.

"Are you all right?" he asks, bringing his hands up to my face.

"I'm fine." I whisper, afraid my voice will betray me.

"Well, isn't that sweet," Jonathan spits. "The bitch isn't worth the trouble."

Jace's eyes dilate until the brown of his irises is only a thin rim around the black pupil. He grinds his teeth together, but leans forward and kisses me gently on the forehead. Then, in one smooth motion, he pushes me behind him and takes a step toward Jonathan.

"What did you say?"

"You heard me," Jonathan seethes, stepping closer to Jace. "That stupid bitch isn't worth the trouble."

I grab the back of Jace's shirt. "Jace. C'mon, let's go. Let's find the girls and go home."

"Yeah, Jace," Jonathan draws out each word, "time to run along. Although, I'd love to have a go at her when you're through with her." He drags his teeth over his lower lip, releasing it with a pop.

Before I can make sense of what is happening, Jace has Jonathan pinned to the ground and he's hitting him over and over. I lunge at Jace, using my entire body and all my weight to try to knock him off, but instead I bounce off like a rubber ball and land on the dirt.

"Jace. Stop!" I yell, tugging on his shoulders and arms, but he doesn't seem to hear me. Desperate to stop him before someone calls the police or worse, he kills Jonathan, I slap him as hard as I can across the face. This seems to free him from his trance.

"Stop."

His blank eyes fix on me and, slowly, recognition fills his face. Jace looks from me to the bloodied and bruised Jonathan who moans beneath him. Shaking out his hands, Jace rolls off the ground and stands.

"Jesus Christ, Jace. You could've killed him. What the hell is the matter with you?"

"You can't be serious. He had his hands all over you and called you a bitch, and you're asking what's wrong with me?"

"You can't just punch people because they're assholes."

"He called you BITCH," he says loudly. "Of course I punched him. Wait. Unless you wanted to go home with him. Is that it?"

"Screw you."

"Screw me or screw him?"

For the second time in two minutes I smack him across the face. This time however, the angle and the force are multiplied. My hand burns from the impact. Jace keeps his face turned not looking back toward me right away. Taking a step back, I see Claire, Katelyn, and Paige approaching.

"Claire, can you give us a ride home on your way to the hospital?" I ask, leaving Jace behind.

Claire's eyes move from me, to Jace, to the lump now stirring on the ground, and then back to me.

"Sure I can, but I need to leave right now or I am going to be late."

"Okay. Let's go."

"No, wait Mommy. I want to ride home with Jace," Paige whines.

"Not tonight, love. Auntie Claire is going to bring us."

"No, I don't want to go with Auntie Claire. I want to go with Jace," she yells. "Jace, take me home with you," she calls out and my heart breaks a little.

"Paige, I said not tonight. Now let's go."

"Jace, tell her! You said we could listen to our song on the way home.." Tears begin to trickle down her face. Hearing the commotion, people several yards away begin looking in our direction.

Jace moves to stand right beside me. The mask of rage he wore a few minutes ago has completely dissolved and has been replaced with one of sadness. He bends down so he is eye level with Paige, who throws her arms around his neck and hangs on for dear life.

"It's okay, darling," he says, peeling her arms free. "Go with your mom and Auntie. I will catch up and if I don't see you tonight before you go to sleep, I'll see you tomorrow." Jace sounds as upset as she is.

"But you promised," she hiccups.

"I know. I'm sorry. Listen to your mom. I'll see you later. It'll be all right." He lifts her from the ground, engulfing her in a huge hug before placing her in my arms.

I see the pain in his eyes and for split second I think about telling Claire to go and let Jace take us home. Instead, I force myself to turn and leave.

Chapter 31
Jace

I stand there like an idiot watching the four of them walk away. Behind me I hear the asshole who had his hands all over Miranda groaning as he tries to get up. He stumbles, kicking loose gravel with is feet, trying to keep his balance. I turn to face him.

"Stay away from her. If I so much as hear you've been looking in her direction I'll track you down and finish what I started tonight. Understand?" He holds up his hands in surrender. I take that as my cue to get the hell out of there.

The ride home feels like it takes much longer than it should. I hit every red light and get stuck behind every slow driver between the school and home. I drum my thumbs on the steering wheel and slam my fist on the dash hoping to make the world speed up for just a few minutes. Just long enough to get me to Miranda.

When I finally pull into my driveway, I see there's only one light on at Miranda's. Katelyn and Paige must have gone to sleep. I sit in my truck, my mind racing, debating what I should do next. Should I let things between us settle down tonight and go over to talk to her in the morning? Should I go over now and beg her to listen? Will she listen to what I have to say?

Right or wrong, I can't let what happened tonight go without trying to explain it to her. I need her to hear the things I have to say or else my head, and possibly my heart, may explode.

Stepping out into the night, I look above. The moon and all the stars are completely blocked from sight by a thick cover of clouds. The temperature feels like it is steadily dropping and evening chill is even more pronounced than it was before.

I tuck my hands in my pockets and lower my chin to my chest to fight off the cold wind as I cross the section of lawn between our houses. The frosted grass crunches beneath my feet and my breath fogs the air in front of my face. Stepping up on the front porch, I catch the sound of a guitar and I hear Miranda's beautiful voice. Hearing her sing comforts me. I want to lose myself in the sound of her voice and never try to find my way out. Not caring how it may seem, I press my ear against the door to listen closer.

I need you; To pull me from this darkness.

I need you; To help me understand.

I need your touch, your warmth, your smile.

I need your hand, your love, your heart.

I need you.

As she holds the final note, I can hear her voice falter, thick with emotion, and I can no longer take it. Raising my hand, I knock on the door with more force than I intended. Silence replaces the sound of the guitar, but soon I hear Miranda approach the door. Slowly, the knob turns and she cracks the door just enough to see who it is before opening it all the way.

"Why are you here?" she asks, crossing her arms over her chest.

I know she's mad at me, but I guess I underestimated just how much.

"I came to apologize," I pause, but Miranda lifts a brow, telling me to continue. "I'm sorry for tonight. For all of it. I'm sorry about the episode after the fireworks. For punching that asshole. For upsetting Paige. For ruining Katelyn's night. For everything."

A gust of wind blasts the back of my head and lifts a few strands of Miranda's. Wearing only a thin t-shirt and cotton pajama pants, the frigid air causes her to shiver. I rub my hands together and blow into them, attempting to warm them up.

"May I come in? It's freezing."

Miranda steps to the side, letting me pass. Closing the door behind me, she walks into the living room. I follow close behind, but stop at the threshold. She bends to pick up her guitar from the floor and sets it aside before turning to face me.

"Blue," I begin, but she lifts a hand to stop me.

"Jace, I don't think this is a good idea."

"Please, just let me apologize. I never meant for any of that to happen tonight."

"That's not what I meant. I don't think this is a good idea," she says, motioning her hand back and forth between us.

My heart stops.

"What? Please don't say that. I know I screwed up tonight. I knew there would be a lot of people there, but I didn't expect that many. I haven't had a panic attack like that in weeks. I thought it was getting better, and it is, but the fireworks, shit, they sounded so much like a bomb going off. My instincts took over before I could even think about what was going on." I try to explain, but I don't know if I am making any sense.

"And the rest of it? You could've killed Jonathan, do you realize that? Jesus, you're lucky you weren't arrested. Hell, you still could be."

"I know," I say with more force then I intended. Lowering my voice, I try again. "I know. I saw him put his hands on you and all I saw was red. I wanted to tear him limb from limb."

"I could've handled the situation myself. I don't need you coming to save me all the time. I've taken care of myself for years."."

"We're back to this? For Christ sake, Miranda, I thought we moved passed this." I run my hands over my hair. "I know you can take care of yourself. You are the strongest person I know, but I want to take care of you. Not because you can't, but because I can. Because … because I … I … I love you."

I hear her take a sharp breath. Her pale, blue eyes grow wide and her mouth gapes open. "Don't say that," she whispers.

"It's true. I love you. I fell in love with you when I was eighteen and I never stopped. I loved you even when I was a half a world away not sure if I would ever make it home, lying in that the god-forsaken desert, staring at your picture from a Goddamn newspaper clipping. When I didn't think our lives would ever cross paths again, and I was certain I would never see your beautiful face, I still loved you."

Eyes still wide, she shakes her head. "You can't mean that."

"Why not?"

"Jesus Jace. You say you fell in love with me way back then, and maybe you did, but I am not the same girl. Hell, I don't even remember who that girl was. Look around you, my life is a complete mess. I'm a widow with two daughters. I'm exhausted most days and I can barely keep it all together." Miranda throws her arms out in exasperation.

"I do remember you, though. I remember you and I still see the girl you were every time I look into your eyes." I take a step closer. "Sure, some things are different, but that doesn't change how I feel. I love you, Miranda. I love you, and Katelyn, and Paige. I love your crazy, messy life, because each time I step through that front door, I feel like I'm home. Your life is not clean and shiny. It's not staged just right with each piece in its perfect position. Your life is cluttered, loud and hectic, but it's lived in. It's a life I want to be a part of."

I place my hands on her shoulders and bend to meet her eyes, which now glisten with fresh tears. "I love you and I can see it in your eyes that you love me, too."

"Please don't say that," she sniffles.

"Why? It's true."

"Jace, please."

"Blue, I know you love me. I can see it the way you look at me when you think I don't realize you're there. In the way you smile at me when I tell you about my day. I can feel it when you touch me, even if it's a brush of your hand on mine."

"I don't. I can't," she insists, taking a step back. The backs of her legs bump against the coffee table.

"That's bullshit and you know it. What are you so scared of? Why can't you just admit it?" My voice is raised. Inwardly I cringe, hoping Paige and Katelyn aren't listening.

"What am I scared of? Are you kidding me? Do you really want to know? I'm scared every decision I make every day is the wrong choice. I'm scared that one day I'm going to drop one of the dozen balls I'm juggling and everything will come crashing down. I'm scared that I'm so busy trying to keep it together I'm missing out on the little things, the things I'm going to regret missing when I'm old and gray." She begins pacing back and forth, her hands waving in front of her as she talks.

"I'm scared I'm messing up my daughters' lives. That they will resent not having their father here, or worse, that they'll forget him. Don't you see Jace? I'm scared of a whole hell of a lot more than whether or not I'm falling in love with you."

"But that's the thing. You don't need to be. Let me help you. Let me be there to catch the balls before they fall. Let me be there so you have time to enjoy the little things without worrying about the big ones."

"You're not listening." She throws her hands up in frustration. "Look. It's been a very long day and I'm tired."

"Fine." I let out a heavy breath. "This conversation is not over. I'll come by tomorrow morning and help you get things ready. We can talk then."

200

"I don't think that is a good idea," she sighs.

"Well, afterward then, when Sam and Claire leave."

"No," she pauses, lowering her eyes to the ground. "I don't think it's a good idea for you to come tomorrow. I'm sorry, Jace, but I need some time to think."

My heart drops. I had been looking forward to my first real Thanksgiving in years. I try not to let the disappointment show on my face, but I know I fail miserably.

"Okay, but this is not over."

I step closer, taking her face in my hands. Lowering my lips to hers, I kiss her like it's the first and last time. She tenses at first but quickly softens, molding herself to me. My body is begging to take this further, and it takes every ounce of willpower I have to force myself to pull away. A tiny sigh comes from Miranda's throat and it's almost my undoing, but somehow I manage to take a step back.

"It's not even close to being over," I say adamantly and walk to the front door.

Taking one last glance back, Miranda is still standing there, her eyes fixed on the spot I just left. Her raven hair falls loosely around her shoulders, and the dim light warms her icy blue eyes and dances on her flush cheeks. My fingers twitch, wanting to touch her, but I force myself to leave, hoping the cold air outside will chill my blood.

Chapter 32
Jace

I stare up at the ceiling. The distant glow of a streetlight creates shadows on the plaster. I follow the swirl pattern over and over again. I have checked the clock on my nightstand every five minutes for the last hour, tossing and turning, trying to fall asleep. My mind continues to playback the evening in a never ending loop.

Finally giving up, I toss the blankets to the side and cringe when my feet touch the chilled hardwood. I should've put the heat on before going to bed, but it slipped my mind. Shaking off the shiver that races up my spine, I head downstairs. The first floor is completely dark except for the little bit of light given off by the digital clock on the oven reading 2:37. Opening the fridge, I duck down and scan the contents. I pull out a beer, twist the top, and take a long pull, hoping alcohol will ease my mind and let me sleep.

Leaning against the fridge, I close my eyes and let my head fall back. Maybe I'm pushing her too hard, too fast. Maybe I'm pushing myself. Maybe she's right. We should take some time to think this through. I feel a twinge of regret in my stomach for not taking my mom up on her offer to go home for Thanksgiving. This would've been my first holiday home in quite some time and I feel like an asshole for disappointing her. I'll call her in the morning and make plans to go home for Christmas. I could probably spend the week there, since Sam said he normally closes the shop.

Taking another swig, I peel my eyes open. It takes me a second to realize something is different. Just moments ago the room was pitch black, but now there's a faint glow. Flickering light dances on the wall, faint at first but growing with each second. I look around, trying to make sense of what I'm seeing, when I hear a gut wrenching scream.

My body moves by instinct. I toss the bottle in the sink and take off running toward the house. Flinging the front door open, I don't stop to put on shoes or grab a coat, I just move down the stairs and out to the front yard. By now it's obvious where the light was coming from - a fire. A raging fire licks the sky as it consumes Miranda's house.

My heart rate spikes and my hands shake. Whether it's from fear, anxiety, or adrenaline I can't tell, but I don't have time to think about it. Another scream breaks through the roaring blaze. I race toward the house, not feeling the cold beneath my feet or the throbbing pain in my leg. I leap onto the porch and throw my weight against the door, causing it to crash inward.

Fire fills the living room and leaks into the hallway. Flames coat the walls, flowing and dripping from the surface. Smoke is heavy in the air, making my eyes water and my throat tighten.

"Miranda!" I yell. "Miranda, where are you?"

No response. Taking the stairs two at a time, I rush to the top. The smoke is even thicker here, rising from below. I crouch down, seeking clean air and call out for Miranda again. I hear noises, but I can't tell where they're coming from.

Miranda's bedroom is at the far end of the hall. Between her room and the stairs are two bedrooms on either side of the hall and a bathroom. The first door on the right is Katelyn's. I push open the door and call her name.

"Katelyn! Are you in here?"

"I'm here! I'm here!" She yells before I see her crawl toward me on her hands and knees. She reaches out and I pull her against my chest. A wave of relief washes over me.

"C'mon, we have to get out of here," I yell, moving her in front of me and pushing her toward the door with my hand on her back.

Once we're out of her room and in the hallway, I finally get a glimpse of Miranda. She's pushing and banging against Paige's door, screaming her name. From the other side I can hear Paige's voice calling for her mother.

"Go outside," I say to Katelyn. "Quickly, go to the street and wait there. Someone must've called 911 by now and the fire department will be here any second. We'll be right behind you. Go!" I shove her toward the stairs.

Her wide eyes look from me to her mother then to the stairs. Without a backward glance she runs down the stairs, disappearing in the smoke.

"Miranda," I call out, crawling down the hall. If she hears me she doesn't acknowledge it. Her face is blackened with soot and smoke with fresh tears streaking across her cheeks.

"Paige!" she screams hoarsely, her now bloodied hand bangs against the door.

I grab her by the wrist and turn her toward me. "Miranda, you have to get out of here."

"No, I've to get her out of there. I think she has something wedged against the door. She was so mad at me when we got home tonight. I have to get her. Let go of me." She fights against my hold, slapping and punching my chest.

"STOP. Get out of here. I'll get her. GO."

"NO."

"Miranda, GO. I promise I'll get her. Go to Katelyn. She's outside" I scream and push her away. She hesitates for a second.

"Bring my baby to me Jace," she yells, before taking off toward the stairs.

"I will. I promise," I say out loudto myself.

Rising to my feet, I take a step away from Paige's door. Not wasting another second I throw my weight against it, but it barely moves. I do it again and again and again, until finally the wood gives, cracking and splintering. I fall into the room, unable to regain my balance.

The smoke is worse now. There's no longer a pocket of clean air and my lungs burn with each breath. The heat is overwhelming and makes me dizzy.

"Paige!" I scream and then cough. I stumble toward the bed, but it's empty. I fall to my knees and lift the edge of the comforter. There I find a pair of little feet, pale against the darkness. Grabbing her ankles, I yank her free and pull her into my arms. Her head lolls to one side.

"Paige!" I cry, tapping the side of her face. I'm rewarded with a small groan. "Thank you." I scoop her up and rush out of the room toward the stairs.

The fire singes the edge of the staircase, making me cling to the wall on my way down. I turn, shielding Paige from the flames as I run out the front door and into the yard. The sound of sirens can be heard in the distance. A small crowd of people has formed across the street.

I quickly find Miranda and Katelyn huddled together at the end of the driveway. As soon as Miranda sees me and Paige she sprints toward us, taking Paige from my arms and falling to the ground. Katelyn joins them and the three of them rock back and forth, sobbing uncontrollably. I place my hands on my knees trying to catch my breath.

Behind me the house is almost completely engulfed in flames. The sirens are getting closer, but by the time they arrive I doubt they'll be able to save anything. Everything in the house will be lost, but at least everyone is safe.

Almost.

I look back to Miranda sitting on the ground with Paige in her lap and Katelyn sitting beside her.

I know what I have to do.

Chapter 33
Miranda

"Shh, it's all right. It's going to be okay," I whisper into Paige's ear rocking back and forth like I used to do when she was a baby. I repeat this over and over until I forget who I'm trying to comfort, her or myself. She opens her eyes a few times, but mostly she rests against my chest.

I don't think I've ever been more terrified in my entire life. If Jace hadn't shown up when he did, I can't even think of what could have happened. A hundred different scenarios played out in my head while I was beating on Paige's door and not all of them ended with her lying safely in my arms.

Flashing lights and deafening sirens come closer until they are right on top of us. There's a flurry of commotion as men jump from the trucks and begin hooking up hoses and equipment. I kiss Paige on the forehead.

"Help is here now. It's all right," I repeat.

Just then, I feel Katelyn tense beside me and then hear her scream. I'm not sure what she sees at first, but then movement catches my attention. I don't remember placing Paige in her arms but somehow I do it, because within seconds I'm on my feet rushing toward the house. I only make it three steps before something hard around my waist stops me.

"You can't go back in there ma'am," someone yells.

"I have to stop him," I scream. "Jace!"

"We have one occupant still in the building," the fireman says into his radio.

"Hold. No one goes in. The structure's not stable," a voice responds.

"You have to get him out of there." I pull against his grasp, but it's no use. He is much stronger than me.

I watch in horror as the house burns. Smoke clouds the air and stings my throat. Suddenly, I feel instead of hear a loud explosion. I'm knocked to the side when the man holding me turns quickly. I fall to the ground. Shattered glass and small shards of wood fly through the air around us.

Behind me I hear Katelyn and Paige scream. I rush to them, ignoring the glass cutting into my feet. I pull them close and turn them so their backs are to the carnage, but unfortunately I give myself a front row seat to our house burning to the ground with Jace inside. Both girls sob into my chest, Paige muttering incoherent words.

Thoughts swirl through my head so quickly I can hardly make sense of them all. How did this happen? What would have happened if Jace hadn't been there to get Paige out? Why did Jace go back inside? Is he alive? How am I going to survive this?

There's activity all around us. Hoses and men scatter across the yard. Everyone moves in synchronized chaos. A few small snowflakes begin to fall, the first snow of the season. Jace told me it was going to snow tonight and I hadn't believed him. My chest clenches and it's hard to breath. A sob climbs up my throat, but I force it down. I need to be strong for Katelyn and Paige. I can fall apart later.

Out of the corner of my eye I notice movement near the side of the house. I squint, trying to see through the blazing heat, and notice a dark form jerking on the ground. It takes me a second, but once I realize what I see, I take off running. The girls scream, catching the attention of a couple firefighters nearby who come after me.

"Jace," I call out, but he does not respond. The jerky movement stops and he lays still.

I pump my legs has hard as I can, collapsing to my knees on the ground once I reach him. I pull his head in my lap and shake him.

"Jace. Jace, look at me. Open your eyes. C'mon, let me see those brown eyes I love so much. Please Jace ... Jace ... please."

One of the men drops to the ground beside me and begins searching for a pulse. I beg and plead for him to open his eyes. Over and over I repeat the words. I lower my face to his hoping to feel his breath on my skin.

"I have a pulse," the man yells. "I need a backboard over here!"

"Thank God," I pray.

"Ma'am, we have to get him away from the house. I'm going to need you to step back."

"No, I'm not leaving him."

He offers me a small, sad smile. "We need to secure him on the board so we can get him to the hospital. He's alive, but his injuries are serious."

I take my first opportunity to look over Jace. His clothes are torn and shredded, barely hanging on to his body. His feet are black and his hands blistered. His face is covered with ash, soot, and blood. His lips and eyelids are swollen and cracked. His short hair is singed in areas and completely missing in others. Patches of red flesh show above one ear. He looks like he just stumbled through the gates of Hell.

Reluctantly, I wiggle backward and carefully lower his head to the ground. I give the paramedics enough space to work, but not an inch more. I watch as they roll him to one side and wedge the backboard beneath him. One of the paramedics tightens a strap around his legs, while the other takes his vitals again.

"Mark," the second paramedic calls out. "What's that on his chest? Can you try to move it? I need to strap him. If it doesn't come free easily, leave it."

The fireman shifts his balance and gingerly pulls on the edge of a dark object stuck to the middle of Jace's chest. I hadn't noticed it moments ago, its blackened surface blending with his charred shirt. As it's lifted a patch of clean fabric is revealed. The man pulls the last corner free and turns it over, taking a look at it.

The paramedic quickly fastens the strap across Jace's chest. Then he and his partner lift him from the ground and place him on a waiting gurney. I'm on my feet in a flash, following after them.

"We need to get him to Baystate."

"I've already radioed it in. They'll have the burn unit waiting for us."

"Start a line and administer fluids."

The paramedics continue to volley information back and forth, relaying stats and giving instructions. They roll Jace into the ambulance, one jumping in the back with him. I move to jump in, but I'm stopped.

"Ma'am, I am sorry, but you'll have to meet us at the hospital."

"I want to go with him," I beg.

"I'm sorry," he says again. Before I can respond, he closes the doors and the ambulance takes off. I watch as its lights disappear around the corner.

The firefighter from before, Mark I think his name is, steps beside me. "I'll see if one of the officers can take you to the hospital."

"Thank you," I sniffle.

He holds out his hand. "This is what he was holding. It must be important for him to have guarded it with his life."

I look down and my knees give out. I feel Mark's hand on my elbow, guiding me to sit on the curb. He's speaking to me, but his voice sounds like I am under water. I can hear the sounds, but cannot make out the words.

In my hands I hold the reason Jace went back into the fire. The reason he is being rushed to the hospital, fighting for his life. It's the reason why my heart is breaking from the weight of grief and regret. In my hands I hold the picture from beside my bed. The only picture I own of Adam with both of his daughters. The single photograph I own of the four of us together. Jace risked his life to save this one thing because he knew it could never be replaced and he knew how much it meant to me.

I've been so stupid.

Chapter 34
Miranda

I can't sit still. Even though I am beyond exhausted and sore everywhere, I pace back and forth wearing a hole in the linoleum floor of the ER's waiting room. I haven't been able to get any information on Jace's condition. Everyone I ask repeats the same thing over and over, 'The doctors are with him now and as soon as they have more information they will let you know.'

Katelyn and Paige are curled up together on a row of chairs against the far wall of the waiting room. Their hair is a mess and they're dirty from head to toe, but they were so tired they couldn't keep their eyes open any longer. The paramedics checked them out before we could leave to come here. Katelyn made it out without a single bump or bruise. Paige has a small bump on her head and a scrape on her arm, but nothing serious. It makes me sick to my stomach to think what could have happened.

I eye the nurse's station each time I pass, hoping to overhear a tiny piece of news about Jace, but nothing so far. My thumb nails have been bitten down to the nail bed and are beginning to sting. My legs ache, my feet throb, and my shoulders are sore. I think if I can just hear he is going to be all right I'll be able to relax.

"Oh my god, I'm so glad you're safe." Claire appears out of nowhere and throws her arms around me. "When I heard the call come in I never in a million years would've guessed it was Jace. When I saw them wheel him through the door I nearly passed out. I could barely form a full sentence until they assured me everyone else at the scene was all right. My supervisor almost pulled me off the case, but I finally convinced her I had my head together."

"I'm fine. Katelyn and Paige are fine." I nod my head and Claire looks around me, to where the girls are sleeping. "We're fine," I say again.

"Jesus, look at them." Her eyes begin to swell with tears. "If anything had happened –"

"We're fine," I repeat. "They're okay or they will be. They're just tired."

She pulls her phone from her scrubs. "Sam was up north visiting your mother. He's not back yet, but I imagine he'll make it here in record time. Let me call my sister and see if she will come get the girls. She can take them back to her place, so they can at least wash up and sleep in a bed instead of these cruddy chairs."

"I don't want to bother Lindsey. It's so early."

"She'll be happy to help, trust me."

I'm about to argue further, but I don't have the strength. "Thank you."

After calling her sister, Claire guides me over to a row of chairs and sits. I'm dying to know if she has information on Jace.

"So, how is he?"

"He's unconscious but stable," she begins. "He has first and second degree burns on his limbs. Those are being treated and bandaged. He also has third degree burns on sections of his back and neck. They're cleaning those wounds. He may need surgery to repair those areas."

I swallow hard.

"The biggest concern right now is the smoke inhalation and the damage to his throat and lungs. The lining of his airway was burned, causing fluid in his lungs. He's on a respirator."

Tears flow freely and I make no move to dry them. I don't know what I was expecting to hear. I thought I had braced myself for the worst, but hearing her describe Jace's injuries makes me feel like I have been kicked in the stomach.

"Will he make it?" I have to know.

"The next twenty four hours are critical," Claire says, taking my hands in hers and squeezing.

"Can I see him?"

"They're moving him upstairs to ICU now. Once they have him settled I will bring you up."

I take a deep breath and blow it our slowly. "Thanks, Claire."

"god, Miranda," she pauses and looks towards the Katelyn and Paige, "what was he doing in the house? Why wasn't he with you guys?"

"He was. Actually, he's the one who got Paige out of the house. I couldn't get her door open. He showed up out of nowhere and pulled her out." I push up from the chair and tiptoe across the room. I pick up the burnt frame. "He went back in for this." I hold it up for her to see.

Claire gasps, her hand covering her mouth. She stares in disbelief for a moment and then wraps her arms around me once again. We stay like this for several minutes, both of us leaning on the other for support. Finally, she takes a step back. She sniffles and wipes her face with the back of her hand. Fixing her hair, she straightens her scrubs and turns for the door. With the promise to come back to get me as soon as she can, she disappears down the hall. I collapse into a chair, close my eyes, and drift in and out of sleep.

THE SECOND VERSE

Chapter 35
Jace

My eyes spring open. The room is dimly lit with streams of evening light coming through the window. A rhythmic beeping plays in the background and there are voices in the distance. The chemical scent of cleaners and bleach is thick in the air. It takes a moment to realize where I am - a hospital. The memories replay in my mind on high speed - the fire, Miranda, Katelyn, Paige. I jerk upright needing to find them.

I'm surprised to realize I'm not in any pain. I roll my shoulders, but there's no tightness. I lift my arms above my head, stretching, but my muscles feel loose. Tilting my head from side to side I don't feel any tension. Swinging my legs over the side of the bed, I stand on the tile floor, which is pleasantly warm beneath my bare feet. Gingerly, I place my weight on my legs, but there is no soreness in my knees or feet. Even the muscles in my thigh don't throb and my scars don't itch.

"How long have I been here?" I say aloud to the empty room. I expected my voice to be hoarse and my throat sore, but neither is the case.

I look around, searching for clues. There are vases of yellow and white flowers on both small tables near the wall. There's a small trash bin by the door, overflowing with paper coffee cups. I take a few steps toward the door, but a little snore makes me stop. Turning, I see a foot hanging over the edge of the one and only arm chair. I move closer and catch a glimpse of black hair. Miranda. Miranda is here, curled up under a blanket. I look down on her for a moment, but the need to touch her, to feel that she is all right, is too great. I reach out to brush the hair from her forehead, when a voice from behind stops

213

me.

"She is beautiful, isn't she?"

Startled, I quickly swing around. A man around my age wearing jeans and a black t-shirt is leaning against the door frame. He is an inch or two shorter than me and much thinner. His light brown hair is cut short on the sides and longer on the top. Although his expression is serious, there's a twinkle of mischief in his familiar light brown eyes.

"I always loved watching her sleep," he says, pushing off the wall and coming closer. I step to the side, placing myself between him and Miranda. The hair on the back of my neck stands on end.

"Who are you?"

He smiles at me, but doesn't answer. Stopping a few feet from me, he stands on his toes to look around me and down on Miranda. The lines around his eyes soften when he sees her. His face melts into a warm smile, as if he is looking at the most precious thing in the world. Miranda snorts and murmurs in her sleep, snuggling further beneath the blanket. The man laughs.

"She would never admit she snores. Do you know how many times I was tempted to record her, just so I could prove I was right? I never did though. A part of me loved teasing her about it and I could tell she only pretended to be offended."

I listen to him talk and watch his features, but none of it makes any sense.

"Who are you?" I ask again, this time a little louder.

He looks up from Miranda. The adoration that was there is now replaced with remorse.

"I thought you would have figured that out by now. Maybe I should have waited a few more minutes. Gave you a chance to think about it." He offers me his hand. "I'm Adam, Adam Cross. I wish I could say it's a pleasure to meet you Jace Harper. Maybe it would have been under different circumstances."

I stare at him in complete disbelief. This isn't right. It can't be. This is some cruel joke. I open my mouth to speak, but I can't find my words. That's when it hits me. Looking closer, his eyes, that shimmer of amusement, I've seen them before. They're Paige's eyes.

The constant beeping in the background gets louder and faster.

"I ... uh ... I don't understand." My tongue is in knots.

"I know. It doesn't make sense because it doesn't seem possible, but it is."

"How?"

Adam tilts his head and then looks back. I follow his line of sight. This can't be happening. A few feet from where I stand, I lay in bed. There are tubes and wires stuck in me in various places. A machine beside the bed hisses as it moves up and down, pumping air in to my lungs. A monitor to the right blinks at the same rate as the beeping I hear. My face is pale and my cheeks so sunken I almost don't recognize myself.

"I … what ... how? This isn't true. This is a dream. That's all. I'm going to wake up soon and this will all go away."

"I wish that was true. Really I do." Adam looks from me, to the bed, and then to Miranda.

"She's happy with you. I could see it in her eyes. There were moments when she would look at you the same way she used to look at me. I wanted to be mad at her or hate you, but then I heard her laugh. You made her laugh." Adam looks up with admiration. "I realized I had no right to be upset. I had a good life with a woman I loved. It wouldn't be fair to not wish her the same." He pauses. "It's strange though, every memory I have has her in it. Whether it's from my childhood or as an adult, she's there. But she now has memories without me."

He looks from me back to Miranda and laughs. Dragging his hands over his face he says, "I never thought I'd say this, but I think my wife loves you."

"I love her too." The words spill out before I have a chance to stop them.

"I know. That makes this so much worse."

"I don't understand. Why are you here? What is going on?"

Suddenly buzzers and alarms begin to sound behind us. I begin to feel this odd pulling sensation in the center of my chest, like something has grabbed a hold of me and is pulling me across the floor.

"What's happening?" I ask frantically.

Miranda, awake in a flash, rushes from the chair to my side in the hospital bed. Her wild eyes scan my face and then the machines. She places her hands on my chest and shakes.

"No, no, no," she repeats over and over. "Someone! HELP," she screams.

Seconds later people spill into the room. Miranda is pushed to the side, nudged farther and farther way. She pleads with the nurses and doctors, asking what's going on, but no one answers her.

"He's in cardiac arrest," one doctor yells above the chaos. The bed is lowered and the fabric of my hospital gown torn open.

"Get her out of her," someone points at Miranda. A nurse grabs her by the arm and begins dragging her from the room.

"No, I am not leaving him." She shoves at the smaller nurse. "Jace, you can't do this to me. Please!"

"C'mon, let's go out into the hall and give them some space to work." A larger nurse moves in front of Miranda, placing her hands on Miranda.

"Jace, please! I love you. I should've told you, but I was scared," she yells as the nurse pushes her through the open door. "I'm sorry. Please. Don't leave me!" Her screams and wailing continue in the hall, but are drowned out by the noise inside the room.

A defibrillator is charged and placed on my chest. "Clear!"

I feel the jolt from feet away. My muscles squeeze as the electricity runs through my nerves.

"This can't be happening," I scream, but no one can hear me. "Miranda!"

"He's not responding. We're losing him," the doctor calls out. "Again. Clear." Another shock jolts through me, this one stronger than the first and I lose my balance. I brace myself on the small side table, trying to catch my breath. I turn, looking for Adam. He's leaning against the chair Miranda was just sleeping in. His arms are crossed over his chest and his eyes fixed on the scene behind me. The muscles in his jaw tick. Miranda's cry echoes above the rest of the noise and he cringes.

"There must be something I can do. This can't be it. Not after everything. I can't die. Not like this. Not now." I feel my throat tighten. Another jolt tears through me and I collapse on the floor. My eyes burn, but I don't bother trying to hide the tears.

"I'm sorry, Jace. Death is the only thing certain in life. Sometimes you don't have a choice when it takes you."

"And the other times?" I ask, trying to push myself up from the floor.

He smiles sadly.

Chapter 36
Miranda
Then

Spinning.

Around and around.

Shapes shift and faces blur.

I watch the doctor's lips move, but I can't hear the words he's saying. I feel like I'm under water. "Did you hear what I said Mrs. Cross?" My eye lids feel heavy. Blinking slowly, I stare at the man with the gray hair sitting in front of me.

Falling.

Down and down.

Nothing to grab and nothing to hold.

This has to be a mistake, some horrible cruel joke. "I'm sorry to have to tell you this, but your husband passed away this morning."

Words. There are words stuck on my tongue. Questions. Questions I need to ask. My mouth opens and closes like a guppy gasping for air.

"Mrs. Cross? Miranda? Do you understand what I'm telling you? Your husband is gone."

Color fades to white.

To gray.

Black.

Chapter 37
Miranda

Stepping outside, I tilt my head to the sky. After a long dreary winter I thought would never end, the warmth of the May sun feels good on my face. A light breeze lifts the ends of my hair and causes my skin to prickle with goose bumps. I wrap my pale pink shawl around my shoulders and find a quiet corner to sit. Somewhere I can be alone for a few minutes.

Just beyond the patio doors are the sounds of music and laughter. Many thought this day would never come, including me, but it did. Today my brother and Claire finally got married. Their day was perfect. The weather was just right. Everything happened right on schedule, just the way it was supposed to. At precisely four thirty Claire walked down the aisle and, hand in hand, she and Sam exchanged their vows.

To say I'm happy for them would be an understatement. Yes, during the ceremony I felt people look in my direction and I also overheard my aunts whispering *"The poor dear"* in the back of the church when I walked by, but today isn't about me. It's about Sam and Claire, and I wanted it to be perfect for them. However, now that the ceremony is over and the toasts have been made, I need a quiet moment to myself. I think I've earned five minutes of peace.

I try not to think of all of the things I need to do when I get home. The laundry and the dishes will be there and worrying about them won't help. I try not to think of all of the things I'll have to do at the shop next week, when Sam takes off on his honeymoon. I push all thoughts of karate competitions and show choir performances aside. I try not to think about the past I can't change

218

and the future that will never be the same. For just a second, I want to think about nothing.

No sooner do I slip off my shoes and lean back in my seat do I hear, "Hey, Mom."

I groan. So much for five minutes.

I take the last remaining sip from my wine glass before setting it on the table.

"Yes, love."

"It's time for their first dance. Are you going to come inside?" Katelyn asks.

"Of course," I sigh before I stand, cursing my cute shoes for pinching my feet. Looping my arm through hers, we walk back into the ballroom. I ignore the looks we get as we pass the cocktail seating area.

When we enter the ballroom, I notice most of the tables are empty and many of the guests are on their feet. The majority of them are crowded on the dance floor in a circle. In the center are Sam and Claire.

Claire looks absolutely radiant in her strapless gown with her hair pinned up in cascading curls. My brother complained for weeks over having to wear a tux, but tonight he has never looked better. Together they are adorable.

Right on cue, Ed Sheeran's "Thinking Out Loud" begins to play. Sam scoops up Claire and they begin their first dance as husband and wife. I can see the look on Sam's face as he looks down at his bride, and I have to press my hand to my heart to ease the ache. Tears prick the back of my eyes and I blink rapidly to stop them from forming. Katelyn, still at my side, rests her head on my shoulder. I hear her sniffle only once, but it's enough to cause a single tear to roll down my cheek.

"I love you," she says quietly.

"To the moon and back," I whisper, pressing a kiss to her forehead.

Soon the song ends and the crowd begins to disperse. Katelyn and I turn to make our way back to our table when I hear it. The heavy drum beat and synthetic keyboard would've been unmistakable before, but now the recognition is instant. "Billie Jean."

"Oh my god." Katelyn turns around quickly, eyes wide, looking over toward the DJ. "Mom, I thought you told them not to play this."

"I did," I choke. "Shit, where is your sister?"

I turn on my heels with a sinking feeling in my stomach and push through the crowd, back to the dance floor. I scan the sea of faces and then I see who I'm searching for. Across the room a group of people part making more space, and I can't help but roll my eyes.

Paige squeals, jumping around and bopping her head side to side. She kicks her legs out and shakes her hips in the most unusual and uncoordinated fashion. Seeing her happy makes me smile, but then I see her dance partner and I shake my head.

Arms flailing and feet sticking to the floor was he attempts to moonwalk, Jace looks like a fish out of water. To be honest he looks like a complete idiot, but he doesn't seem to mind. I think some of his antics are to amuse Paige. At least I hope they are, so I let him do his thing.

I watch has he holds her hands and swings her around. Paige giggles the whole time, her face turning red. I come closer and Jace lets go of one of Paige's hands and takes one of mine. I let him twirl me around the floor until the song finally ends and is replaced with something slower.

"Paige, would you mind if I danced with your mom for little bit?" Jace asks.

"Nope. Mommy can I have your piece of cake?"

"Sure."

"Woot woot," she calls out, throwing her hands over her head before disappearing into the crowd.

Jace gathers me in his arms and holds me close. I rest my head on his chest and follow his lead. I listen to his heartbeat, the thumping reassuring me he's alive.

I still can't believe I lost him last Thanksgiving. Even if it was only for ninety -two seconds, he was gone and I thought my world had ended for a second time.

He has tried to explain pieces of what happened, but I don't want to know all of the details. He may have a few more scars, but none of that matters. All that does is he is here now, and as long as I have a say in it, I'm never letting him go.

We sway calmly to the soft beat, relaxing into each other's arms and letting the rest of the world fade away. The weight of his embrace around my waist and the low tenor of his voice as he sings the lyrics softly in my ear is something I will never take for granted again. I love this man with every fiber of my being. If I hadn't lived it myself I would hardly believe it, but for seven years I drifted. Floating. Drowning. Until the day he came and breathed life back into me. He saved me when I didn't know I needed to be saved, and I will spend the rest of my life trying to repay him for the second chance he has given me.

THE SECOND VERSE

Just then, I feel him tense and I lift my head to see what's wrong. Jace stares over my head, across the room. I look over and smile. Behind us, Katelyn dances with her boyfriend, Matt. They hold each other at a respectable distance, and Matt's hands don't seem to be wandering.

Jace growls and I swat his chest. "Leave them alone," I warn him.

"I don't like him," he says, matter of fact, still giving the poor boy an evil glare.

"You're ridiculous. You know that right?"

"She is too young to date."

I scoff. . "She is almost fifteen. Besides, he's a nice kid."

Jace snorts. "Yeah right, Blue. I was his age once. No boy his age is nice."

I reach my arms around his neck and pull his head closer to mine.

"Leave them alone. She's happy." I kiss him quickly and then snuggle my head against his chest once again. He makes a noise in this throat, but resumes slowly turning me to the music.

"It was a nice day, wasn't it?" he asks, resting his chin on my head.

"Yes, it was."

"Is this what you would want?"

"What? A wedding?"

"Yeah, when we get married. Do you want a big wedding like this? I know you didn't get the wedding of your dreams the first time."

I lift my head, so I can see his face. I have to think about it for a moment. He's right. I didn't have the wedding I wanted when I married Adam, but I've never felt like I missed out on something.

"No, I don't think so. I think I would want something small. Just family. Katelyn and Paige, my brother and Claire, and your mother. No, I wouldn't want something big." He makes a humming noise and I stop dancing. "Why? Are you asking me to marry you?"

"Trust me Blue, when I ask you to marry me, you'll know. And I wouldn't do it at your brother's wedding. When I ask you to be my wife the moment will be all about you and me." He kisses the tip of my nose. "And the girls."

His warm chocolate eyes swim with adoration. His lips curl into that crooked smile I love so much and I smile back up at him. I never thought I would get a second chance at love. I never thought I would ever feel complete again, but with Jace everything feels right. I will never doubt what we have.

Leaning up on my tiptoes, I kiss him softly.

"I love you, Jace."

"I love you, too, Blue. Past and present. Now and forever. To the moon and back."

Janet Lee

The Wounded Warrior Project is a non-profit charity and veterans service organization that offers a variety of programs, services, and events for wounded veterans who served in the military following the events of September 11, 2001.

To learn more about the services they offer and how you can help, please visit - http://www.woundedwarriorproject.org

Playlist

Bent –Matchbox Twenty

Best I Ever Had (Grey Sky Morning) – Vertical Horizon

So Far Away – Mary Lambert

Gravity – Sara Bareilles

Dark Horse (Acoustic Cover) – Megan Davies

All I Ever Wanted – Megan Davies

Bonfire Heart – James Blunt

I Don't Dance – Lee Brice

One Hell of an Amen – Brantley Gilbert

I Do (Cherish You) – Mark Willis

Who I Am With You – Chris Young

Billie Jean – Michael Jackson

Acknowledgments

Thank you for taking the time to read Miranda and Jace's story. When I started writing *The Second Verse* I never thought anyone would see it. Knowing you have makes me giddy, because my wildest dream has come true.

To my daughters - thank you for waiting "just one second" while I spent ten more minutes finishing a paragraph and for eating chicken nuggets and Ramen more often than you should have. Payton, there's always some truth in fiction, and I hope one day you will read this and smile when you notice the little pieces of you in Paige. Kayla, thank you for the best advice I have ever been given: "When writing, you need to shut off your inner editor and just write." You are wise beyond your years.

To my husband - thank you for not thinking writing a book was a silly idea (or at least keeping your eye rolls to a minimum). You're more than my husband, you're my best friend. I couldn't imagine a more perfect person to spend my life with.

To my sister - thanks for introducing me to FSoG, without which my crazy reading obsession would never have begun and the thought to write a novel would have never seemed possible.

I need to give a huge thank you to two very amazing authors, Sara Mack and S.M. Koz. Thank you for showing me that it is possible. If it weren't for both of you, I don't know if I would have ever found the courage to sit down and put words on paper. Thank you for listening and for giving me the motivation to continue when I wasn't sure if I should.

Last, but certainly not least, thank you to Red Ribbon Editing for the amazing cover. It couldn't be more perfect. Without you, I would have pulled my hair out trying to create something that wouldn't have turned out half as good.

About the Author

Janet Lee is a wife and soccer mom, with a "real" job that keeps her trapped at a desk most days. She lives with her family in southern New England. When not in the office or at the soccer field, she can be found trying to hide from her family with her laptop or Kindle nearby.

Made in the USA
Coppell, TX
07 January 2023